IN THE SHADE OF THE CRIMSON TREE

IN THE SHADE OF THE CRIMSON TREE

MANDAR A. PATTEKAR

GYAN

Published by

Gyan Publishing House
5, Ansari Road
Daryaganj, New Delhi-110002
Phone: 011-47034999, 9811692060
E-mail: books@gyanbooks.com

Distribution Network
gyanbooks.com
India, USA, Canada, UK, Australia, France

ISBN: 978-93-7014-227-5 (PB)
First Published, 2025

Printed at: Gyan Press, Delhi.

IN THE SHADE OF THE CRIMSON TREE
Author : MANDAR A. PATTEKAR

This book is dedicated to the innumerable martyrs who sacrificed their everything to preserve my culture and its pan-humanistic philosophy.

Acknowledgment

This book would not have been possible without the support of my wife, Mugdha, who encouraged me to write and constantly motivated me to continue even through the difficult times of my life when I was recovering from a severe stroke. I would also like to thank my youngest daughter, Shreeya, whose love of fantasy novels gave me the idea of writing this book. I would also like to acknowledge Ms. Pearl Patel, a brilliant young woman who edited my manuscript. Another person who served as my beta reader was Dr. Pallav Ranjan, who critiqued the early versions of this book. The map of Shantiprastha was drawn by my daughter, Shruti. The cover idea, was conceptualized by Sri Vaishnavi Peyyalamitta, a very talented artist.

Author's Note

The soil in which a tree grows determines the taste of its fruits. Similarly, this book has a composite flavor of the history lessons I soaked up during my childhood in India and my early adult life in the United States of America.

While growing up, many of the awe-inspiring incidents from the lives of heroes from India like King Shivaji Bhonsle (popularly known as Chhatrapati Shivaji Maharaj) and King Maharana Pratap Singh Sisodia (popularly known as Maharana Pratap), have been etched on my mind. Other innumerable historical figures from around the world who have stood up to the tyranny of bigoted fanatical invaders have also shaped my worldview. These subconscious mental impressions are manifested in my real-life behavior and my writings.

Throughout the story, I have interspersed tidbits of ancient wisdom and philosophies, which apply to everyone regardless of whether they follow any or no religious tradition. In this book, I have attempted to share answers to common questions that arise in our minds when faced with difficult situations. I learned these answers from revered teachers spanning the entire spectrum of philosophies of the world. I am not trying to proselyte any religion or besmirch any historical character. If you get offended by any part of my writing, please forgive my insolence. I request you to finish reading the book before you cast it into the fire of obscurity. After enjoying my maiden attempt at writing a novel, I hope to leave you with a residual assortment of good human values, which will be helpful in each of our everyday lives.

All characters in this novel are imaginary. A few have the essence of historical people.

* * *

While the era of these happenings does not correlate with our timeline, the technological development corresponds to the 13th-14th century Europe of our times.

* * *

In this book, the major difference between the Mulkan's and the Daitya's concept of Divinity was that the Mulkan thought permitted its followers the freedom to define their personal relationship with the Divine. They could worship through a physical form (statue, crystal, tree, symbol, etc.) or pray to the Divine, conceptualized as formless. The Daitya faith only accepted a formless Divine. Anyone who did not follow its belief system or questioned its tenets was considered evil. By their dogma, non-believers were to be converted by any means or destroyed.

MAP OF SHANTIPRASTHA

Contents

Chapter–1

Dawning of the Eastern Sky

Vows are just ordinary words by ordinary people. But, when people live and die by them, both the people and their vows become extraordinary.

On a warm summer morning three hundred years following the first horde of the Daitya (*Daee-tyaa*) invasion, a group of five Mulkan (*moolkaan*) teenage boys streamed in a single file through the corridor leading to the inner sanctum of Gireshwar (*hard G-like goat; Gee-resh-war, Lord of the mountains*) shrine. Gireshwar was a very ancient shrine dedicated to Dramho (*Dram-ho*), the name given to the unmanifest Divine by the Mulkan inhabitants of Shantiprastha (*Shaantee-prstha*, *the abode of peac*e).

Shantiprastha was a massive plateau extending around fifteen hundred miles north-south and about one thousand miles east-west. On the west side, the ground dipped towards the Swamini Sea with a narrow sea-level coastal strip.

The worship of the unmanifest Divine-Dramho was facilitated by representing it with a crystal. The Mulkan people addressed the crystal itself as Dramho in the Mulki language. Every crystal Dramho was formed in the ground by crystallization of the dripped sap of the zavba tree over hundreds, if not thousands, of years.

Once a massive splendent structure constructed of intricately carved black granite stones, the Gireshwar shrine was in ruins at the time of this vow. The Dramho crystal was a silent witness to the once great splendor of the Mulkan culture and its current shameful state.

Admiring the partially damaged painted murals on the ceiling, the boys meandered through the passage. The first mural showed a large black cow with long horns defending her calf from a mountain lion. Next was a barely visualized mural with a giant olive-brown snake writhing, covered with innumerable red ants. The partially scraped third picture depicted a hefty man carrying an older woman on one shoulder and a man with no legs on the other shoulder. Last, the fourth and largest one showed a peaceful pastoral scene of houses, farms, children playing, and a Dramho shrine with a Crimson flag on its top.

The group looked strange in many aspects. Their attire and degraded from regal to ragged, from the leader to the end. The boys in front wore typical warrior-class clothes with long-sleeved shirts that flared below their waist, reaching their knees. A boy just a few months past fifteen was leading the group. He wore a red shirt with beautiful embroidery, using gold thread and pearls. The second boy had yarn embroidery on his cream shirt with colorful beads, while the third wore a plain white shirt, slightly yellowing because of repeated soiling and washing. To cover their legs, they wore loose-fitting white pants to the ankles. Following them, after a small gap, were the last two boys who wore shirts of thread bare material and mismatched pants with patches sown to cover the holes. The first three boys were well-nourished, while the following two appeared scrawnier. Their physical bearing decreased from a confident leader to the last boy, who looked like a trailing lost puppy.

The royal boy pointed at the murals, saying, "Our ancestors have left these murals to guide us. This first one tells us that if the peaceful, docile cow becomes strong, she can protect her weak and young calf. Our society is protected if all its men and women become strong. The second one shows that even though they are tiny, the ants can destroy the giant snake when united. If we are united, we can defeat even a formidable enemy. The third mural tells us to lead a virtuous life. Every powerful and wealthy person should take care of the weak and needy. If these three conditions exist, there will be peace and prosperity, as seen in the fourth mural." As the boys listened, their youthful faces beamed with respect and awe.

A small, low, heavy wooden door damaged with hatchet marks opened into the innermost sanctum at the end of the corridor. The leader pushed open the door and entered the sanctum, a windowless space illuminated by torches on the wall. His eyes scanned the walls pocked with holes. "These walls were once embedded with precious stones, plucked out by the Daityas."

In the center of the room was the shining crystal Gireshwar Dramho, a large, very rare forearm-length colorless oblong crystal with pointy ends placed vertically, with one tip set into the ground. The ancient Mulkan masons had cut the geometrical slits in the conical roof of the sanctum based on their astronomical calculations. The slits served a dual purpose, with the night rainwater gently dripping and washing the crystal (per scriptures, Dramho likes water); and letting in the sun's rays that were now causing the crystal to dazzle. The sun's rays illuminated the few dust particles floating in the air. The leader kneeled and bowed his head in front of Dramho. As if taking their cues from the leader, the other boys kneeled, forming a circle around Dramho, and reverently bowed.

After the boys took their places, a brief silence followed as all looked toward the leader, whose eyes were steady on the Dramho crystal.

Please guide me, Dramho; I carry your name; the leader prayed. His name was Kolakwa (*one who destroys falsehood*), one of the thousand and eight names of Dramho. However, only his mother called him by that name. Everyone else addressed him as Little Naresh (Little King).

"By astrology, today may not be the best day. We can do the blood oath on another day," Kolakwa lied, trying to offer his friends one last chance to cop out of completing the blood vow of embarking on this mission. He had devised this idea a moment ago to let any of his friends back out without appearing cowardly.

He paused for a few breaths, but none of the boys appeared to take the bait.

"Let us begin," Kolakwa said in the deepest voice he could muster.

"We vow to dedicate our lives to overthrow the yoke of foreign rule and establish Atmaraj for all people. In Atmaraj, no one will be oppressed. Everybody's land, body, and mind will be protected." Five youthful voices rose in unison, sounding out the phrase they had practiced hundreds of times.

As the echo subsided in the cavernous room, all eyes turned to Kolakwa's face. Kolakwa was a beautiful boy, but he hated that adjective when his mother used it. It was an anathema for a future warrior. His well-proportionate face,with alert, wide-set, kind eyes, full cheeks, and straight nose, set him apart from his fellow boys. The rest of his body resulted from years of early morning training for strength, agility, and weaponry. Kolakwa stood up and unsheathed his sword with his right hand. He held his left hand straight with the thumb sticking out and ran the sword's sharp edge on the pulp of the thumb. A stream of bright crimson blood dripped over the Dramho crystal. He had practiced this act before and knew how much pressure was needed to get a steady stream of blood.

"Here is my blood to sanctify my vow," he declared in his firmest teenage voice, wiping the bloodstain from the sharp blade with his sleeve as he kneeled again. Afterward, he touched the sword on his forehead in reverence. The steel felt pleasantly cool in the sweltering heat. His every action was slow and deliberate, giving his friends time to summon their courage to proceed or back out. He avoided looking at them, keeping his gaze on the Dramho crystal.

Dramhodas, kneeling on Kolakwa's right side, stood up next. On more than one occasion, Kolakwa had declared, "Dramhodas (*servant of Dramho*), you are my right hand." Two years older than Kolakwa, Dramhodas was the oldest in the group. His long,matted, unkempt black hair topped his stocky physique. His deformed bulbous nose was a deterrent to would-be fighting opponents, attesting to many bloody fist brawls with older boys.

"Here is my blood!" he declared as he sliced the skin of his thumb on his only prized possession, his father's discarded sword. Everybody had heard Dramhodas go on and on about his father's sword and how many enemies his father had killed. As Dramhodas sat, he looked around the circle. While their eyes locked briefly, Kolakwa remembered when Dramhodas first got his father's sword. After showing it off to his friends, Dramhodas had confided to Kolakwa, "My Little Naresh, my father, his father, and many before him were great warriors, but they were all someone's servants. They fought for salary and rewards. They fought somebody else's war. Every day, I pray to Dramho to grant my wish that I will not die as somebody else's servant."

The next boy was Rokba (*a red-colored precious stone*). Nothing wasvisible on his body from the outside, which could be called 'precious' except his intense, penetrating eyes. His daily encounters with thorny shrubs, jagged rock edges, and ferocious beasts did not leave even a palm-sized area of unscratched, unblemished skin on his body.Childhood malnourishment had stunted his height.

Rokba looked as though he was about to rise but hesitantly glanced at Krikaneel. After waiting for three long breaths, he stood with remarkable agility. Rokba tucked the torn cloth flap off his left sleeve and raised his long, stout knife. "Here is my blood!"

"*My precious Rokba.*" Kolakwa restrained his urge to glance at his friend. Kolakwa sadly remembered that Rokba had asked him a few days ago, "I am of low birth. Is my blood too dirty as an offering to Dramho? Will he get offended by my offering?" Kolakwa had rested his hand on Rokba's shoulder andassured him, "Dramho loves everyone; he gave you your friends, your strength, and your goats. He blessed you with a desire for freedom." Kolakwa always made it a point to stand near Rokba preferentially when in a group, especially when people watched. He knew ordinary villagers considered Rokba too dirty to come close to him.

"My little Naresh, I was born a nobody. I do not have a past. No family, no inheritance. All I have is the present and future. Every morning, I pray to Dramho, 'Please make me somebody before I die.'." Rokba's eyes had teared as he confided to Kolakwa.

"Here is my blood!" a high-pitched voice was the loudest. Even the small knife looked massive in Mahadoo's hand. His face unsuccessfully tried to suppress an expression of obvious pain. A single tear escaped from his left eye, rolling over a scar on his cheek where a village boy had hit him with a rock. He glanced at Rokba and then tightly closed his eyes, half-smiling through his pain. Mahadoo looked younger than his twelve long years. Considering his age, Kolakwa almost did not want Mahadoo to join them for today's ritual. But Mahadoo arrived at dawn looking extra-fresh from scrubbing himself during a long bath, wearing freshly washed clothes darned at many places, and his ever-present disarming smile. Kolakwa could not bring himself to stop him.

Breathing deliberately as he waited, Kolakwa felt that the aroma of the few fresh flowers and the incense sticks had become more pronounced, as if even the air had stood still, waiting for Krikaneel. Krikaneel rose carefully, dodging the dangling oil lamps hanging from the ceiling, forming a circle above Dramho. A recent growth spurt had made him the tallest boy in the group. His aquiline nose garnered everyone's attention. The high cheekbones and a large mouth with thin lips complemented the elongated face. Kolakwa had seen him sharpen his sword again this morning. He awkwardly held the sword in his left hand. He raised the weapon and thrust forward his right hand with the thumb sticking out. Kolakwa was perplexed at this unusual handling of the sword by the right-handed Krikaneel. Before Kolakwa could react, Krikaneel calmly said, "Hail Dramho," and brought down the blade on his right thumb. His severed thumb bounced on Dramho as everyone's gaze followed the gush of blood erupting from the gaping wound.

"What have you done, Krikaneel!" Kolakwa cried as a collective gasp erupted.

Krikaneel was unflustered. He looked at Kolakwa. "My Naresh, I can never hold a sword without my thumb. I cannot fight. There will be no doubt of me usurping your rightful place. I will always be your servant. My body, mind, and heart will always serve you." Krikaneel bowed respectfully, calmly looking at Kolakwa. The flickering flames of the large oil lamps reflected in his determined eyes.

Kolakwa's eyes teared as he uttered, "I never doubted you." He spoke the truth, but the story of their births always cast a lingering uneasiness about their relationship in Kolakwa.

"Now, no one ever will," whispered Krikaneel.

* * *

All the boys lowered their heads and closed their eyes. Kolakwa prayed silently, "*O, Dramho, please grant us wisdom, bravery, and strength for our quest of Atmaraj to succeed.*" The word Atmaraj (*self-rule*) was imprinted deeply on all their minds. Stories of historic heroes ended with lamenting the loss of Atmaraj. Self-governance. Just governance. Freedom from oppression. The marauding Daitya invaders had trampled the ancient concept of Atmaraj into the dust.

Kolakwa opened his eyes, concentrating on Dramho. As he waited for his friends to finish, his mind drifted as he remembered the unease he felt while riding to Gireshwar. The thought of leading his friends along a path that would cross the most powerful empires in the world had gnawed at his insides. *Our quest would most likely end with our deaths and destruction, with little chance of victory. I was born for this mission. But do my friends realize the gravity of their vow? Would our efforts be too little, too late*?

Kolakwa had heard that the Mulkan Zigador[1] (warlord) of Fort Devagiri had recently converted to the Daityafaith. The Zigador had a reputation for committing atrocities on his subjects. On the pretext of the complaints from his Mormos[2], the Ruler threatened to remove him from the post of Zigador unless he converted to the Daityafaith. He converted to preserve his power.

After his conversion, the Daitya preachers, with their enforcers, rushed to his lands in vast numbers, forcefully converting his subjects from their ancestral Mulkan to the Daitya faith. They severely tortured those whore fused to convert. If they persisted in refusing,the enforcers put them to harrowing deaths[3]. After conversion, the Zigador continued his vile ways without interference from the Ruler's men.

1. A Zigador was a warlord who had a thousand to five thousand horsemen under his command. Few had more than ten thousand. They administered large swaths of land in the empire, paid annual taxes to the Ruler, and swore allegiance to him. They supplied men and resources to the Ruler, in case of war.
2. A Mormo was a warrior who had twenty-five to one hundred men under his command. Some or all may be horsemen. A Mormo administered two to five villages of his Zigador's realm. All Mormos swore allegiance to a particular Zigador, and through him to the Ruler.
3. Equivalent happenings in our dimension are the Spanish Inquisitions in Southern Europe, South America, and Goa – India. Also, during the Islamic invasions in the Indian sub-continent.

By the time we grow up and have enough strength to resist, will there be any Mulkans and left? Kolakwa sighed.

* * *

Kolakwa's reverie was broken by the neighing of their horses and the ringing of the outside bell. Someone had arrived at the shrine's entrance. He looked around the sanctum. The boys had finished praying and were gazing at him. Kolakwa stood up and walked towards the door. Others followed him silently. Mahadoo was the last to approach the door. He forgot to bow down and banged his head on the top of the door frame. His howl alerted others of his predicament. Everybody tried hard to suppress their laughter. "The low door ensured the visitors bowed their heads as they entered the holy room," Kolakwa tried to bring back the solemn mood. "And pay attention when they exit," added Mahadoo, rubbing his forehead.

They filed out of the sanctum and walked toward the small lake next to the temple. They sat on the crumbling parapet, circling the water. Through the clear water, they saw pieces of the broken statues at the bottom of the lake, thrown in by the destructive Daitya invaders.

"After we defeat the Daityas, we should make them rebuild every shrine they have broken," Mahadoo said to no one in particular as he reverently touched a piece of broken statue on the wall.

As the clouds shifted, Kolakwa could see his reflection in the lake's water. His first point of attention was on his forehead. Every morning after bathing, he drew a solid crimson circle superimposed on a golden rising sun on his forehead. He remembered his mother explaining, "The crimson circle is the symbolic third eye of wisdom. The wisdom to discriminate between the truth and the falsehood in the world. Many times, the two physical eyes get fooled by illusions." The golden rising sun and rays under the circle were Kolakwa's fanciful addition.

He vainly admired his sparse teenage mustache, which he had fashioned to copy the grown men in his region. Most men would proclaim their virility by maintaining long mustaches, stiffening the ends with clarified butter, rolling them, and pointing them upward. They would balance a ripe lemon on each side to show off to friends before slicing and squeezing the lemons into their alcoholic drinks. His weedy beard was made pointy by similarly applying butter, making him look older. Kolakwa tilted his neck to look at his long hair and long sideburns, inadvertently flexing his arm and puffing his chest.

As he noticed his hand and fingers, the thought of Krikaneel's sacrifice of his right thumb dampened his self-admiration.

Kolakwa could see another reflection appear to his right. Krikaneel had come and stood next to him. *My wise brother. Only the absence of his parents' wedding ceremony snatched everything from him that was rightfully his. Everyone loves him more than me, even myself. By sacrificing his right-hand thumb and unequivocally accepting his deferential position, Krikaneel has been enthroned in the hearts of all who matter, a status superior to any throne in this world or beyond.*

The memory of his absent father, Shamonda, flashed through Kolakwa's mind. A life-size portrait of Shamonda hung in the meeting room of his home, Fort Vitora. His father, Shamonda (*point of the arrow*), was a powerful Zigador. Since birth, everybody expected Kolakwa to be a warrior, ultimately a Zigador, like his father after growing up. All Zigadors were in the service of the Daitya Monarch, who me very body called 'the Ruler.' The current Ruler was named Dingir (*one who causes enemies to tremor*). All Mulkans with warrior skills worked for the Ruler, either in his army or working for a Zigador who worked for the Ruler. There were no independent Mulkan kings. All were killed by the Ruler or accepted becoming a Zigador under the Ruler's over lordship.

Shamonda was respected and feared by other Zigadors. He had an esteemed status in the Ruler's Court, unheard of for a Mulkan. Dingir's father, the then Ruler, had promoted Shamonda from a Mormo to Zigador to appreciate his valor in the Great War. Although Dingir was now the Ruler and the head of the Daitya empire, the actual power was in the hands of a person named Gangwo (*kindhearted*), the paradoxically named giant of a man who was incredibly strong, cruel, and devious. Gangwo, the brain and muscle behind the puppet Daitya emperor, had no official job title. Everyone called him by his name, and he called himself a'mere servant' of the Ruler.

* * *

Kolakwa did not see his friend Dramhodas anywhere. He called out sharply, "Dramhodas!" Dramhodas came hurrying from the back of the temple. He scowled as he tried to control himself. "I was chatting with a devotee. Daitya soldiers raided his village last week. The Zigador of their lands told them he could not help against the Daityas. The villagers are angry but cannot defend themselves alone." As the blood rose on his face, Kolakwa declared, "If Dramho desires, soon we will end these atrocities."

Kolakwa remembered the stories of how in the areas they conquered, Daityas broke the statues in the Mulkan shrines, calling them false gods. The Daityas did not care to understand that the Mulkans used these statues as icons representing their preferred attributes of the Divine. The beauty of the Mulkan place of worship was to attract the devotees' attention and prevent distraction from the world outside the shrine.

After destroying and defiling the Mulkan place of worship, the Daityas shifted the broken but recognizable pieces of the statues to the nearby Daitya place of worship, where they put them together topsy-turvy to construct stairs. The local Daityas daily stepped upon these stairs to humiliate the Mulkan sensibilities.

Kolakwa felt anger rising in him.

O Dramho, help me control my anger.

Anger is like fire. When kept under control, it can be useful. Just as a controlled fire can cook food and provide warmth, a controlled anger can motivate you. Uncontrolled fire burns down the house, while unbridled rage will destroy your mind. Kolakwa remembered his mother's words.

As the boys gathered around him, Kolakwa picked up a stick and started drawing on the dirt. First, he drew a tiny flag with a circle around it. Next, he drew smaller circles at various distances around the first mark. He pointed to the flag and said, "This is Fort Vitora." Then, pointing to the surrounding circles, he said, "In the next five years, we should capture these forts," before rattling off the names of forts of the surrounding Zigadors.

"Once these forts are ours, they will form a circle of strength to protect our capital, Vitora. Then we can expand south and then to the east. We will have to wait to become much stronger before we can fight the Ruler in the north." Kolakwa spoke with genuine confidence.

Mahadoo crouched down as if studying the rough drawing carefully."That is a splendid plan, my Little Naresh. But where will we find soldiers to form our army? Five of us are not enough."

Everybody laughed half-heartedly.

After scrubbing his drawing in the dust, Kolakwa ordered, "Let's go back to Fort Vitora." Everybody mounted their horses. A few steps outside the gate, Kolakwa pulled the reins of his horse and turned it toward the shrine. Others followed his action. They looked up to the apex of the conical dome-shaped roof of the temple toward the fluttering Crimson flag, straightened their backs, and bowed their heads to salute.

The crimson-colored flag, shaped like an axe, was the ancient symbol of the Mulkan spiritual philosophy. It flew over the Dramho shrines and other holy places. Before the subjugation by Daityas, the flag also flew over many forts. Spiritual teachers, over many generations, attributed various meanings to the color and the unique shape of the flag. The Mulkan people accepted all these explanations. Crimson was the color of dried blood, symbolizing sacrifice. Teachers of one school of philosophy explained that the shape of the flag represented the holy zavba tree on its side, demonstrating humility. Other teachers taught that the form of the flag meant the shape of an axe, which symbolizes cleaving your false ego by self-control. The crimson color and the holy zavba tree were further linked because the leaves of the zavba tree turned crimson during the winter when many Mulkan festivals took place.

As Kolakwa looked around at his friends, he sensed a gentle gust of wind. *This breeze feels like Dramhois showering his blessing on us. But is this a blessing for success while alive or martyrdom for a noble cause? Will we realize our dream of Atmaraj? Who among us will be alive to witness it?*

Somberly, he heeled his horse.

Chapter–2

Early years

Nine years before the Gireshwar vow, on a crisp winter morning, eight-year-old Kolakwa was being dressed by his servant to go on the weekly excursion. As the servant tied the little sword to his waist belt, Kolakwa remarked, "One day, I will carry a full-sized sword like our Mormos."

"Yours will be bigger and heavier, my Little Naresh," the servant commented. "You will grow up to be a powerful man, just like your father," the servant commented.

Kolakwa's eyes moistened. His father had left when he was four, and Kolakwa had only seen his father's portrait. After checking his reflection in the mirror, Kolakwa briskly walked to his mother's chamber. The child's posture was very erect, unusual for such a young boy.

He respectfully waited at the door, watching his mother, Mamalu, talk to a Mormo. "Are all the arrangements for the excursion in perfect order?" Mamalu asked the Mormo.

"Yes, Mother, I am sending twelve of our best soldiers. We have packed enough food and camping materials. I have asked the clerks to take enough coins if Little Naresh wants to donate at a shrine. You need not worry. This trip is well within our realm, so any danger from Daitya raiders is minimal," the Mormo replied.

"Send ten more soldiers with the party," she ordered.

The Mormo's face barely hid his annoyance.

"As you wish, Mother," he said, leaving Mamalu's chamber. The man fumed that Mamalu questioned his judgment. Defying her order, he did not add the soldiers.

After the Mormo left the chamber, Mamalu looked wistfully at the portrait of her husband, Shamonda. Four years had passed since Kolakwa's father had left for the campaign against the Northwestern Kingdom. News came two years ago that he had defeated the king of the North western

Kingdom and was now administering the lands on the Ruler's behalf. There were rumors that Shamonda had remarried a local princess and had a separate family with two sons.

Kolakwa knocked on the door. "Mother, we are ready to leave."

He entered the room, touched the ground before his mother's feet, and sought her blessings. Mamalu placed her hand on his head and blessed him, "May Shreeti protect you." She fed him a small piece of sweet cake from the offerings she had placed at the altar of Shreeti, her preferred feminine form of the Divine. Mamalu affectionately adjusted Kolakwa's necklace and patted his back before sending him on his way.

After Kolakwa left to join the traveling party, Mamalu lit a silver oil lamp before the Shreeti altar in her chamber and sat down to pray. As she closed her eyes, instead of concentrating on the prayer, her mind wandered to her childhood. The youngest child and the only daughter of the Mulkan Zigador of this Bunei region, she was born in Fort Vitora. While growing up, she heard adults complain to her father about Daitya soldiers taking crops, damaging shrines, and abducting women who worked in the fields. There were stories of young boys being kidnapped and castrated to be made into eunuch slaves. At that age, she did not know many of these thingsbut guessed that they were terrible based on the wailing of the distraught families. Her father, a mid-level Mulkan Zigador, could not punish the marauding Daitya soldiers due to fear of invoking the Ruler's wrath. The helplessness of the Mulkan warriors in rising against the Daitya Ruler saddened her. She often felt unfortunate that she was born a girl and could never lead armies against these foreign oppressors.

Mamalu did not realize the passage of an hour when her servant knocked on the door announcing lunch, pulling her from her memories. Mamalu moved over to the table, and as she started eating, she conversed with the miniature painting of her mother on her desk, "I am a mother now, too. My little boy, Kolakwa. How much should I expect from him? My life's purpose, obtaining freedom for my people, is intricately interwoven with the results of my son's upbringing. If he grew up either a tyrant, a coward, or a lazy person, my dreams would be dashed to bits."Her attendant servant, who had entered the room to replenish her glass of water, saw her talking to the picture and retraced her steps out of the room.

Mamalu spentthe afternoon working at her desk. She examined the communications from headmen of various villages of her realm. There were always reports of minor skirmishes between her soldiers and the men of the neighboring Zigadors. However, because of the fear of reprisal from Shamonda, nobody dared to attack her openly. But the ever-present danger of open warfare still hung in the air. The training by her father while growing up made administering, in the absence of Shamonda, less effortful to Mamalu. For the fifth time in the last three years, she denied the request of a fanatic Daitya preacher from the north to visit Bunei under the pretext of checking on the Daityas living there. She gave a false excuse of increased incidents of highway robbery at the borders with the Daitya neighbor.

Early in the evening, Mamalu went anxiously to the window, glancing at the courtyard of the fort.

She returned to her desk and started writing a letter to her brother, consoling him about his wayward son. Her older brother's son had converted to the Daitya faith after falling in love with a Daitya girl. The girl's parents wouldlet them marry only if he would convert to the Daitya belief. After initially resisting, the boy relented. Over the years, the constant campaigning by the preachers and the girl's family drew the boy away from his family. Now, he had become foremost among the Mulkan haters.

In his letters to her, Mamalu's brother blamed himself for his son's giving up his culture, way of worship, and family for a pretty girl. Mamalu's brother had tried to convince his son that even after he converted, he could still do his Mulkan rituals in the privacy of his home, but to no avail. His father warned him thatalthough he had converted, he would always be held at a lower station than the Daityas, originally from the Daitya homeland.

It wasn't till two hours later that Mamalu heard the horses return. Rushing to the window, she could see Kolakwa. She silently thanked Shreeti and Dramho and returned to her chamber. She failed to notice the obvious addition to the party.

After a few minutes, the guard outside her chamber announced Kolakwa's request for an audience. Kolakwa ran towards Mamalu, over flowing with excitement, and hugged her. Only after this did she notice that the head administrator was with him.

"Mother, we had a grand adventure. Daitya raiders attacked us. But a holy man saved us. He has agreed to be my teacher," Kolakwa blurted effusively.

"What happened?" Mamalu's voice trembled as she questioned the head administrator.

"After finishing the collection of taxes in one village, we saw a crimson-clad monk resting under a tree on the outskirts of the village. He was unusual in that a mule with a large bundle accompanied him. Our little Naresh introduced himself and appropriately paid his respects. We inquired about the monk's name and his destination. The monk's name was Saumitra, and he was traveling to find a place to start school to make young boys into warriors."

Shifting uncomfortably, avoiding Mamalu's gaze, the administrator continued, "Little Naresh requested him to come with us to Fort Vitora and meet you before I could make further inquiries."

As Mamalu continued to glare at him, the man replied, "On our return journey, the pathway to the next village climbed over a hillock. We noticed a large party of Daitya soldiers cresting the hillock. There were six horsemen, and twenty to thirty soldiers were on foot. They vastly outnumbered our twelve bodyguards and three lightly armed administrators. When the head of bodyguards announced our party and questioned the Daityas, one of them threw his spear and impaled our man. We at once formed a tight circle around little Naresh."

After taking a deep breath, the administrator continued, "Suddenly, the holy man, Saumitra, jumped from his mule and yelled, 'Hail Dramho!'. He pulled out a strange weapon from the bundle in the back of his mule. It looked like a whip, but instead of one leather tail, it had five long floppy, flexible metal blades, each a three-finger breath in width and almost six forearm lengths long. With that weapon in his right hand and a round shield in the other, he rushed toward the Daityas. He swung the blade around, slashing the Daityas to pieces. Their swords could not block his flexible blade. He deterred the spears thrown at him with his shield. The Daityas panicked at this sudden change of scenario. Our bodyguards attacked the remaining Daityas with renewed vigor, finishing them in no time. Saumitra also saved little Naresh by warning him of a spear thrown at him by the head Daitya, whom Saumitra impaled with the same spear."

Mamalu barely stood upright, holding on to the chains of her swing. The blood had drained from her face, thinking of the averted calamity. She composed herself after drinking a glass of cold water from the earthen pot.

"Present this holy man," she ordered.

After a few minutes, a crimson-clad, tall, sinewy man with a top knot, a long, flowy black beard, and a mustache tinged with a few gray strands stood upright before her. He saluted her by touching his forehead with his right hand, and she, too, paid her respects. She sensed the aura of someone who had spent a considerable time contemplating the Divine.

"My name is Saumitra. I am from the northern mountains. My teacher ordered me to spread knowledge to young ones who will grow up to better the society," Saumitra volunteered.

Without further inquiries, Mamalu requested, "Please stay at Fort Vitora and become Kolakwa's teacher." Saumitra readily agreed and was allotted living quarters.

The following day, Mamalu requested Saumitra's audience in the meeting room.

"Before you teach Kolakwa, you must know about our history." Mamalu pointed to a chair. Taking a seat, Saumitra listened attentively and respectfully, glancing at the multiple portraits on the wall.

Pointingat the portrait of her grandfather, Mamalu stated, "Bunei has been my ancestral land for at least five generations."

She continued to the next portrait, "A decade ago, during the Great War in the north, my Zigador father and three elder brothers died fighting for the Ruler's army. Secret sources told me Gangwo treacherously ordered their murder because they were gaining too much power in the Court. Saumitra shook his head, acknowledging that he knew about Gangwo."

The next painting was of a kind-looking woman. "Growing up, my mother had taught me the glorious history of the Mulkans and how we ended up being enslaved by the savage Daityas."

"The murder of my father and brothers added the quest for vengeance to an already fiery desire to free my people," Mamalu said as she pulled out a sword from the display on the wall. Mamalu's voice quavered as she reverently touched its blade to her forehead," My father gave me this sword."

After replacing the weapon, she continued, "Although my father had taught me the basics of sword fighting, I am not a warrior. I cannot lead a fight against the Daityas. The only way for me to free my people was to marry a warrior and give birth to warriors who would throw off this yoke of slavery and establish Atmaraj."

Mamalu glanced at her reflection in the decorative mirror on the wall. She realized that the similarity of the facial features of the mother and son would be evident to Saumitra. Both Kolakwa and Mamalu shared a straight noseand wide-set, kind eyes. They had symmetrical, well-proportionate faces seen only in the fortunate people who are called beautiful by society. The crimson circle in the center of the forehead, which every Mulkan male or female drew, added to her beauty.

Before her wedding, her aunt had explained to Mamalu, "After marriage, the wife and the husband became providers for their families and the non-earning sections of society, including the students, the elders, and the monks. Your house will be a refuge for your family, aged relatives, and traveling holy people."

"In the Great War, my future husband, Shamonda, fought for the Ruler and showed incredible bravery. As a reward, the Ruler appointed him a Zigador and presented him with my family's lands,which no longer had a master. The Ruler also suggested he marry me. A suggestion from the throne is an order for everyone. For me, the wedding was primarily political to get a powerful person to protect me and my people of Brunei. But also, being the Zigador's wife would give me a voice in the administration of Bunei."

"You are a wise mother of your people," Saumitra said with intense admiration for her political acumen.

"By Dramho's grace, Shamonda was a good husband. Our relationship matured over the months after the wedding, and I genuinely developed an affection for him. On multiple occasions, he realized that I had been well-trained by my father to administer the lands. So, in time, he gave me increased responsibility in the administration."

Mamalu absent-mindedly picked up her seal of authority from the desk and briefly glanced at it.

"Time flew by fast, and as cold winters started blowing from the north, I discovered I was pregnant. I intensified my worshiping rituals to protect my unborn baby. I had priests visit me daily, reciting scriptures of Dramho and my mother's native deity Shreeti. Every morning after my bath, I read epics of past heroes and sang odes of our glorious history to the unborn fetus. I meditated on my ancestors' moral characters so that the baby's developing mind bathed in an auspicious environment."

Mamalu took in a deep breath. Then, as if deciding something, she continued, "Since you will be the teacher for all the boys, you should know the history of Krikaneel."

Saumitra nodded.

Mamalu continued, "A year before the discovery of my pregnancy, a widow and her daughter had come to Fort Vitora, seeking protection from the marauding Daityas. Unfortunately, the refugee daughter became pregnant less than three months after their arrival. My handmaiden informed me of the secret news. I summoned the widow and her daughter to my chambers to find out if a soldier had given false marriage promises and impregnated the girl. As I questioned her, Shamonda walked into the chamber, and on seeing the girl talking with me, he hurried out. The expression on the girl's face, as she looked in Shamonda's direction, explained who the father was."

Mamalu became silent, her face turning stern as she looked at Shamonda's portrait. She took a deep breath, and her face softened as if the inhaled air was a soothing salve over the still raw emotional wound of discovering her husband's infidelity.

After pulling herself together, Mamalu went on, "That night, I informed Shamonda of the girl's condition, staring directly into his eyes. He averted his gaze and left the room without replying. With that, I received confirmation of his indiscretion. Like any other scorned wife, I was distraught and cried. My mother left this world when I was still a child. I sought solace with Goddess Shreeti, seeking her guidance. In her calm, comforting presence, I realized that although I was furious at the situation, I could not blame the girl for her pregnancy. My husband was the master of the fort, and the girl was under his guardianship. He betrayed everybody by dereliction of his duty and abusing his position. Although illegitimate, the girl's fetus was still the child of the master of the fort. The unborn child was innocent of his father's misdeeds."

Saumitra looked surprised by Mamalu's magnanimity.

Mamalu continued, "I arranged for the girl's care. Over time, she gave birth to a healthy boy named Krikaneel (*Kreekaneel, thunder, because of his loud cry at birth*). In a short time, the senior members of the administration realized his paternity. They could not determine which station in life to allocate the boy. Over time, he became so well-loved that everyone treated him with respect, earned by behavior, not birth. He even won me over, despite the circumstances of his birth."

Mamalu took a break from her narrative. She gazed out of the window and saw Kolakwa instructing a guard. She smiled. "On the day of the festival of Dramho, a healthy boy was born to me in the middle of a stormy night. We named him Kolakwa."

Then taking a deep breath, she concluded, "Please, come to me whenever you need insight into the local people or our lands. Otherwise, you are free to instruct the boys of the fort at your discretion." Then, bidding farewell, Saumitra saluted her and left to check the classroom preparation.

Mamalu sat on the massive carved wooden swing suspended in the room, reminiscing about Kolakwa's birth, the best day of her life. That day, the heavens applauded as thunder. The heavy rains transformed every tiny rivulet into a giant frothing, galloping torrent of water. Dead branches and loose soil washed away, exposing the underlying solid rock in the riverbeds and the riverbanks. The lusty cries of the healthy baby boy heralded his excellent health. The proud Shamonda came to visit after delivery.

"Just a small token," Shamonda presented her with a lovely necklace made in the theme of lotus flowers[1] crafted in gold and rubies.

He gingerly picked up the smiling baby and slowly glanced at the left side of his face. He completely ignored the head full of curly black hair, deep black eyes, cute dimples, and a straight nose. What he saw on the left side of the baby's face pleased Shamonda. He grinned and roared, "Just like his father. The next Zigador of the Braznee clan." The boy had a cluster of nodules just in the front of his left ear, like his father Shamonda and grandfather Raiba before him. While this anomaly is commonly seen, the nodules in Raiba's family uniquely resembled their village hills. Grown men in his family had hidden this deformity by growing thick sideburns and beards. Shamonda tied an amulet around the neck of the baby containing a tiny Dramho crystal to ward off evil and bring Dramho's blessing. As Shamonda was engaged with the baby, Mamalu couldn't help but stare at the rather plain earrings that always hung from Shamonda's ear lobes. They were simple copper wires wrapped around a small Dramho crystal. Given the other exquisite jewelry Shamonda wore, those looked out of place. Once, she had asked about them, but Shamonda had avoided answering.

After Shamonda left, Mamalu looked into her son's twinkling eyes. Gently, she whispered in the baby's ear, "Will you make my dreams come true?"

* * *

As Kolakwa turned four, Mamalu scoured the lands for excellent teachers. Although she primarily hired the teachers for Kolakwa, others likeKrikaneel, Dramhodas, and the children of other officials livingin Fort Vitora also attended the classes whenever they could. While most of the students were boys, a few girls were also in attendance. His earlier teachers taught Kolakwa essential skills like reading, writing, and basic sword-fighting techniques practiced with wooden swords. As he matured, teachers inculcated warrior skills like horseriding along with history, political geography, and basic administration to be an effective leader of his people. Both Kolakwa and Krikaneel were natural learners and absorbed knowledge instinctively.

While Kolakwa was training to be the future warrior and administrator, Krikaneel was also struggling to understand something more fundamental: his identity and station in life.

---

1. Lotus stands for regeneration. This hints at an apology gift to Mamalu towards the regeneration of their relationship.

Although officially a fatherless child of a servant girl, he was treated differently than the children of other servants. The uncertainty of his station in life became confusing to the little boy. Sometimes, the other boys made snide comments about his fatherlessness. When any adult saw a child tease Krikaneel, the adult quickly chastised the offender. One day, while his mother was putting Krikaneel to sleep, she saw tears in his eyes.

"Why are you crying, my baby? Are the other boys bothering you again?" his mother an her fingers through his hair.

Trying to hold back his tears, Krikaneel asked, "Who is my father? Why is he not with us? Did he die fighting our enemies? What was his name? Do I have any uncles or cousins?" Krikaneel's mother's eyes filled with tears. She turned her head away from Krikaneel and dabbed her eyes with the loose end of her dress. In a firm voice, she declared, "You are the child of Dramho. All of us are children of Dramho." She got up from the bed and got water for Krikaneel in an earthen cup.

After Krikaneel drank the water, his mother asked, "From where did the water come?"

"From the cup," Krikaneel answered.

"Before the cup?" his mother continued.

"The pitcher," Krikaneel said.

"Before the pitcher?" his mother was persistent.

"The well." Krikaneel liked this game.

"Before the well?" His mother put one arm on his shoulder.

"Rain."

"Before the rain?" Mother put her other arm on his shoulder.

"Dramho," Krikaneel concluded.

"Correct." His mother pulled him towards herself and tightly hugged him.

"Everybody's father, mother, grandfather, and grandmother are like cups, pitchers, and wells. We all are like water and come ultimately from Dramho," she whispered in his ears.

Krikaneel wiped his teary face with his mother's dress. From then onward, he ignored any insults from the other children. He prayed to Dramho with more dedication and shared his innermost thoughts before the Dramho crystal. Krikaneel never asked about his father again. One day during his early teenage years, he overheard two old ladies gossiping about the perceived special treatment allotted to him and his mother, along with the circumstances of his birth. The news shocked him, but he never shared it with anyone, not even his mother.

As Krikaneel got older, Saumitra took him on long walks and gave him discourses in private."Remember, each word I say," the teacher urged. "You were born to uphold. You are a stone in the foundation. You will always be buried under the fancy artwork, never seen or appreciated. If you are seen and known, you have failed. That means the building you are upholding has collapsed. Become strong, become wise, but only to support. Everyone will look at the golden spire on top of the building and talk about its beauty and height. This spire may change. Your existence is to make sure that there is an intact place to keep the golden spire."

Year after year, Saumitra repeated those lessons. As he peered into Krikaneel's eyes, Saumitra prayed to Dramho that those eyes foretold a burning desire for Atmaraj, not an inferno of envy of Kolakwa.

Chapter–3

Laying the Foundation

Everyone dreams, but the dreams of most ordinary people remain fantasies. Only true visionaries lay the foundation of sweat and blood on which their dreams can become a reality.

Soon after Kolakwa's birth, Mamalu started laying the foundations for Atmaraj, one person at a time. For this child to build an independent Atmaraj, he had to have a large, powerful army of dedicated, trained fighting men. These men would be with him not for employment, power, or blood ally ship but because they shared the same goal of Atmaraj—self-rule.

Not a month had passed after Kolakwa was born, and Mamalu called Ordora, Fort Vitora's Brago, the chief of the guards. "Spread the word in villages that I am looking for orphan boys and girls. We will place them with our spies in the realms of the neighboring Zigadors and also in the Ruler's lands."

Mamalu knew her Zigador father maintained a group of traveling merchants who spied on the neighboring Zigadors.

Mamalu gave each merchant one orphan to raise as their family member, calling them nephews or nieces.She instructed the adoptive parents to in grain in the child a desire to fight for freedom from the Daitya tyranny.

Besides these loyal children, Mamalu implemented a plan to make sure that when Kolakwa became an adult, there would be many well-trained fighters in the Bunei region, with adequate training and a thirst for freedom. On the first day of every Mulkan new year, Mamalu assembled her administrators and instructed them, "Send priests to various parts of our lands to rejuvenate the old Dramho shrines destroyed by the Daityas. Only recruit young priests willing to learn the art of fighting. Before going to their assigned shrine, each new priest must spend six months at Fort Vitora. Have our weapons teachers teach the priests physical exercises and fighting basics during this time. The teachers should also instruct them on how to teach these skills to the village children."

Mamalu's foresight to plan for these children ensured that as the children grew up, successive crops of strong, skilled patriotic soldiers would be ready for harvesting.

Shamonda had an inkling of what his wife was doing. However, he never interfered. She was unique, and he respected that. Sometimes, he silently prayed to Dramho to protect her and his infant son.

The first four years after Kolakwa's birth were uneventful. During this period, Shamonda would go for a month or less for local expeditions and return home.

However, one day, a messenger arrived from the Ruler with a summons for Shamonda. Later, Shamonda sat beside Mamalu in their private chamber and lightly put his massive arm around her shoulder. He gently said, "I need to take leave for a while. After completing my mission, I will be back as soon as possible. Take care of yourself and our little Zigador." Shamonda left for the expedition to the Northwestern Kingdom, leading a large army allotted to him by Gangwo. Shamonda left behind a small but potent group of trusted fighters and administrators to protect and manage Fort Vitora in his absence. Months passed into years. Initially, letters from Shamonda were heartfelt and accompanied by elaborate gifts. But gradually, the letters and gifts became less frequent and eventually stopped.

She kept getting news that Shamonda was well and that no harm had occurred to him. At times, Mamalu felt resentful. She reflected, *Was I just the means for Shamonda to gain this land and get a son?* In anger, she used to look at the necklace he gave her after delivery and wanted to throw it away. But after a prayer to Shreeti, she realized the Divine worked in strange ways. *"The Ruler could have been awarded land to my husband anywhere in his realm. Without Shamonda as my guardian, some cruel Zigador would have overrun Bunei. Hopefully, the child we have begotten will be an illustrious son for me and all our people's future,"* she mused.

Sometimes, Mamalu would be sad that she had only one son. But her wise old nurse told her, "It is preferable to have one exceptional son than a hundred ordinary ones. One moon is enough to eradicate darkness, which the millions of stars cannot do."

* * *

"Today we are going to learn to throw a chakram," Saumitra announced one morning during the weapons training class, as he produced a metal ring about forearm length in diameter with sharp edges.

Over the last few years, the boys had progressed from wooden swords to blunt metal ones. Everyday, as the first class in the morning, Kolakwa and the boys performed a sequence of stretching and postures, with which they maintained their flexibility, quick reflexes, and concentration. These exercises were followed by weight training with wooden and iron weights. After the exercise and morning ablutions, Saumitra assigned three hours to weapons training, when they learned how to spar with swords, shoot arrows, throw a spear, and wield other weapons like punch daggers, tiger claws, and darts. They also learned to fight asymmetric battles with opponents on the ground and on horse back.

"Hold this," Saumitra handed the heavy Chakram to Kolakwa. Looking at his friends, Kolakwa tried to act casual as he strained to lift the ring. Servants placed a large wooden block fifteen steps away on which Saumitra drew an outline of a man with an X on the forehead. Saumitra walked back to Kolakwa and took the chakram. In slow motion, he postured his body, describing each step as he cocked his arm. Then, in one smooth motion, he threw the ring, which hit the 'X' with its sharp edge and lodged into the wood. Afterward, the boys tried a smaller, lighter chakram with little success.

During the weapon training, another unlikely person always joined the group. Every day, a small girl, Manu (*short form for Manikarnika—an earring containing a jewel*), used to come and sit on the floor in the corner of the practice area. She was the daughter of a senior administrator. After many failed attempts to confine her to her living quarters by offering treats and threats, Saumitra allowed her to watch from a safe distance. The child found a small stick during her wanderings and copied the boys as they practiced. Although Manu was five years younger than Kolakwa, she learned the same skills as the older boys as she grew. Sadly, when Manu was ten, her father died. Her mother moved the family to her maternal household in the lands south of Bunei. Everybody was very sad. Together, the boys carved a wooden sword inscribed with a hymn to Shreeti and gave it to Manu as a parting gift.

* * *

During history lessons, the boys learned about the proud history of the Mulkans. They learned of the great Kings of the past, their civilization, and the Mulkan philosophy. Saumitra's tone was always calm but carried intense energy.

Gazing toward the Dramho shrine, he said, "Our philosophy emphasizes the four principles: peacefulness, austerity, honesty, and respect of ideas that are not akin to yours. Peacefulness is the primary principle but should be temporarily suspended to protect the other three." The boys recited the four principles to memorize them, expecting them in the examinations.

"Battles are to be fought always as a duty, without passion or hatred for the enemies. Always consider yourself the instrument of Dramho, doing your duty."

"What about the booty collected by the winning army?" One student asked. His prized copper bracelet was given to him by his father, which was taken from a killed enemy soldier.

Saumitra raised his voice."Stealing should never be the aim of any war. Only take enough resources from the enemy to prevent them from using them against you and to support the moral cause. Do not harm non-combatants. Women and children are not resources. They should never be taken by force."

The boy felt the bracelet burn his wrist. He shyly removed it and kept it on the ground, later slipping it into his pocket. As the boys got older, with Kolakwa turning thirteen, Saumitra taught the Daitya history and their worship dogma. He narrated, "The original Daitya people were from a faraway, frigid, arid land. It lacked food and other resources needed to sustain a comfortable life. Violentinteraction with each other for meager resources was the way of life for the Daityas tribes. A few hundred years ago, a leader of a Daitya tribe started a new way of worship and social order to organize and civilize the Daitya savage barbarian society. In this new worship dogma, the divine power was called Ghumu. The leader ordered his people to worship the divine only as the formless Ghumu. Any other form of worship was prohibited and punishable by death."

"What is that marking on the face of every Daitya man?" one boy asked Saumitra.

"Every Daitya male has a scar of three parallel lines on the left cheek extending from the left ear to the corner of the mouth. On the fifth birthday of every Daitya boy, the family holds a special ceremony. The preacher makes cuts on the face with a three-pronged knife. He then fills the cuts with a powder to cause thick scarring. Similar marking is also performed for every new male convert."

The boys grimaced at the thought of such a painful ritual. "What if someone wants to leave the Daitya fold?" Dramhodas asked.

"They kill anyone who even mentions such a possibility. If such a person escapes, he must hide his whole life," replied Saumitra.

"Or grow a thick beard," quipped Krikaneel.

Everyone looked at Saumitra's long beard and laughed.

Saumitra continued, "As a child, a wild animal had mauled the founder, who miraculously survived but with a facial scar. The survival and its reminder, the scar he received, were advertised as a sign that he had the protection of Ghumu. In the early days of the Daitya religion, only the most fanatical adherents to the Daitya religion made this scar on their children's faces to show the degree of their devotion. Later, the scar became a requirement for all Daitya males."

"I wish the wild animal who mauled the founder of the Daitya religion had killed him," Dramhodas murmured to a boy beside him.

Saumitra overheard the comment and glared at Dramhodas. He continued, "Over a hundred years, the individual tribes of Daityas united as worshipers of Ghumu under a single leader. The act of community worship led by fanatic preachers transformed the unorganized tribes into a single, unified force. They invaded Shantiprastha as a ravenous and vicious force. Using their deceit, inhuman cruelty, and divisions among local Mulkan kings, the Daityas overran the whole plateau."

* * *

One day, Saumitra and the boys visited a destroyed crumbling shrine overgrown with thicket. The shrine was next to the remains of a razed village, whose only remains were the outlines of the building foundations.

As they walked around, Kolakwa examined the residue of the shrine, gently touching the damaged statues as if they were injured living beings.

Krikaneel asked, "Why do the Daityas break our shrines?"

Saumitra explained, "The Daityas are intolerant of other ways of worship. They dislike that the Mulkan belief system allows people to worship a physical representation of the Divine and lets them choose the form. The Mulkan way of worship encouraged questioning the teachers, and self-exploration. The Daityas do not allow questioning of their dogma. Their religious leaders punished anyone who questioned their writ, with death or cutting of the tongue being the commonest punishment.All worshipers of Ghumu must pray precisely in the same pattern, using the same prayer, at the same time of the day."

They stopped under a tree outside the ruined shrine. At a driedwell partly filled with soil, Saumitra narrated, "In the village whose remains we just crossed, the Mulkan villagers, under the leadership of a local monk, refused to renounce their faith when ordered by the invading Daitya Zigador and his accompanying preachers. The Daitya soldiers destroyed the village. Theydragged the monk and all the villagers to this shrine. 'Pray to your Dramho to save you and his shrine,' the Daitya Zigador is said to have challenged the monk. The monk tried unsuccessfully to educate the Daitya Zigador that Dramho and Ghumu are the names of the same Divinity, worshipped differently. Failing to convince the monk to accept conversion, Zigador tortured the monk and mutilated his body. The monk endured the inhumane torture, praying silently and refusing until the end. After finally beheading the monk, the Zigador ordered his soldiers to destroy the shrine in front of the villagers."

The boys stood still, listening with boiling rage. They glanced worriedly at each other, hearing Saumitra's otherwise stoic and sturdy voice quaver as he continued, "Even after that, when the villagers refused to convert, the Zigador ordered his soldiers to push the villagers into this well. Some of them drowned, but many were buried alive when Daityas poured soil over them and filled the well."

The group prayed silently, each in their own way, asking Dramho's blessings to help them prevent such atrocities in the future.

On another trip towards the northern part of Bunei, they had stopped at a rundown building where an ancient massive library had stood before being demolished and burned by the invaders. Kolakwa asked Saumitra, "Why did the Daityas win over us? Were they better fighters, were they more in number, or did they have better weapons?"

Saumitra looked at Kolakwa with sad eyes and said, "No, Little Naresh. There are two reasons. The main reason was that the Mulkans lost because they were not united. Our way of worshiping the Divine allowed people to choose and practice devotion based on their aptitude. People represented the Divine in many physical forms, widespread in our area being the Dramho crystal and Shreetistatue. This diversity resulted in many divisions among our people based on minor differences in their worship. They did not come together in time to fight against the common enemy."

"How did the Daityas stay together?" Kolakwa asked earnestly.

After a long pause, Saumitra answered, "Hate and fear of a common enemy are the great unifiers."

"Hate against us?" Krikaneel interjected. "What is there to hate about us?"

"Their preachers preach hatred against everyone who is not Daitya. If you hear a false message repeatedly, over time, you start believing it. They also spread fearful lies about the culture and rituals of people who do not follow the Daitya faith.Fear and hatred unite the Daityas against everybody else." After a pause, Saumitra said wistfully. "Even the kind and loving ones among them become hateful and cruel because of the influence of others."

*Kind and loving Daitya!*Krikaneel was baffled but said nothing, noting Saumitra's sad face. As the group was busy discussing, they overheard boisterous yelling from the other side of the building, interspersed with voices pleading and crying. The boys pulled out their weapons and rushed towards the noise. In the back courtyard was a familycomprising a couple, their teenage daughter, and an older man, surrounded by four Daitya soldiers. Two soldiers held the man while an older man pleaded with them, offering a bundle he was carrying. Two other soldiers were eyeing the women in a lecherous manner, making indecent gestures.

"Let them go," Kolakwa yelled in a loud voice. The soldiers were caught off-guard and looked toward the voice. They laughed since they only saw Kolakwa, the first to reach the courtyard. By this time, the entire class of seven boys had reached the area. The soldiers released the man and grabbed their weapons. They started assessing their situation. Long used to committing atrocities on the helpless Mulkan villagers, they became perturbed being outnumbered by these teenagers who looked young but had the attitude, physique, and sword-wielding stance of mature warriors.After looking at each other, the soldiers ran away.

This unexpected rescue overjoyed the family.Tears of relief and joy inundated their faces. The boys stopped them as they attempted to touch the ground before the boy's feet.

"We were on our way to visit my wife's sick father in the neighboring village. As we stopped here for a quick break, disaster struck. Fortunately, Dramho sent you. Hail Dramho."

Saumitra stood observing from the shadows. He re-sheathed his drawn sword and emerged, declaring, "If Dramho wishes, we will soon have Atmaraj, under the leadership of our Naresh Kolakwa, where such injustice will not take place."

Dramhodas went around the complex to ascertain that the soldiers had left. Bidding farewell, Saumitra and the boys departed amidst the family chanting, "Hail Atmaraj, Hail Dramho."

As they continued their excursion, the boys were elated by their adventure. They laughed about the change in the soldiers' facial expressions after the boys advanced towards them. Saumitra grimly said, "Fortunately, those soldiers were cowards. Regular soldiers would have attacked you, and the fight may not have been favorable. Keep on practicing every day. Soon, you will enter battles against adult, highly skilled, and disciplined enemy soldiers." The boys became serious and silently continued the journey.

Saumitra continued his interrupted lesson at the next stop. "Now, for three generations, vast numbers of Mulkans have converted to the Daitya faith. Almost all Mulkans were converted under threat of torture and death in the areas under the direct rule of the Ruler or through the Daitya Zigadors. Few found it convenient to willingly follow the Daitya faith to maintain their power and position in the society."

"Is anyone resisting the Daityas?" asked Dramhodas.

"Initially, many Mulkan warriors resisted the Daityas. But they were neither organized nor united. The Daityas defeated them and severely punished them and their families. Now, the Mulkan self-respect has been broken. The once-proud Mulkan warriors are competing against each other to be better servants of the Daitya Ruler. When any Mulkan rises against the Rulers, the Mulkans themselves defeat their brethren to prove their loyalty to the Ruler."

Dramhodas became visibly agitated, thundering, "We should first eliminate the traitor Mulkans among us. Then, our people will think twice before siding with the Daityas. It is easier for people to do the right thing if they fear punishment rather than by relying on their good nature."

As they stopped for lunch, one boy asked, "How did Mother Mamalu get Fort Vitora?"

Saumitra replied, "As Daityas consolidated their hold over Shantiprastha, many Mulkan warriors of the defeated Kings accepted employment and over lordship of the Daityas. Many proved useful to the Ruler in the wars against the Mulkan kings and rebel Daitya chiefs. The Ruler rewarded them with land and power. After the Daitya Zigador in charge of this area died without an heir, the Ruler awarded this area to the great-grandfather of our mother, Mamalu, for his services to the Ruler. Under his administration, the Mulkans who had fled came back."

Dramhodas commented, "Luckily, Mother Mamalu is kind to all of us. But, sadly, other Mulkan Zigadors are just like the Daityas exploiting their subjects."

"Have the Daityas tried to harm you, teacher?" Krikaneel asked.

Saumitra smiled, "They tried, but I am here, am I not!"

"Are you not afraid of death, teacher? Krikaneel continued.

"When you accept the life of a monk and wear these Crimson clothes, you fear nothing. You have wholly offered yourself to the Divine. Your body and mind belong to Dramho," Saumitra closed his eyes in silent prayer.

Kolakwa sat through most of these discussions, deeply brooding. His facial expressions showcased the volcano rumbling in his mind. This volcano was different. It would not erupt in a haphazard manner. *I will unite all Mulkans. I will get together the bravest of Mulkan warriors. Together, we will drive away the invaders. Then, the abode of peace will truly be peaceful.*

Chapter–4

Childhood Years

As Kolakwa grew older, the village folks recognized his authority. They presented their issues to him during the monthly trips to the Bunei villages. Under Saumitra's guidance, Kolakwa administered justice to the farmers and traders, meting out punishment to offenders.

During one tour, a group dragged a young boy before him, who looked slightly more youthful than his age. The boy's face had an expression that reminded him of a cornered wildcat. A general look of neglect characterized his appearance, with tattered clothes, lack of footwear, and unwashed hair. After the villagers saluted Kolakwa, they pushed the boy to the ground, but he promptly got up, adjusted his clothes, and stood proudly. He awkwardly saluted Kolakwa, trying to copy the gesture of the other villagers. As he looked at Kolakwa, the confidence of being in the right shone in his defiant black eyes.

"Little Naresh, please punish this boy. He killed a man," the village headman said.

Kolakwa felt the eyes of villagers examining him. Never was a person brought in front of him whose crime deserved the death penalty.

Kolakwa tried not to look at Saumitra for guidance; instead he gazed at the boy, gently but firmly asked, "What is your name? Tell us honestly, what happened?" The boy's face softened. "My name is Rokba. I am a goat herder. The dead man was stealing my goats, as healways did. Today, I resisted, and he choked me. I stabbed him to stop him from strangling me." The boy rattled a steady stream of sentences as if he may not get to speak again.

Kolakwa stepped forward and examined the boy's neck. He could see the nail marks that tore through the boy's skin. He ordered, "Free the boy."

The boy requested that the headman return his knives, which the village headman did. Observing the young man, Kolakwa felt an uncommon bond with him. In an unspoken manner, he sensed a deep-seated strength of character in the boy.

"Will you work with us?" Kolakwa asked him after the crowd dispersed.

"I would be honored," replied Rokba.

"As you herd your goats around this and neighboring regions, keep your eyes and ears open for information. Come with us to Fort Vitora. Our people will teach you what information to look for."

"My Naresh, I can also climb steep rocks and will climb wherever you direct me," Rokba enthusiastically offered.

Kolakwa provided Rokba with a spare horse for the journey and was surprised at how well Rokba rode. On the way back to Fort Vitora, Kolakwa narrated to Rokba his vision of establishing Atmaraj in the most straightforward words.

* * *

On their way to the next village, Kolakwa's party noticed a caravan camp with cages of small exotic animals and injured birds. There were also strange wooden machines. Kolakwa dismounted and walked closer to examine the devices. "What are these machines, and who made them?" Kolakwa asked, peering around the structures.

A fire was burning in the corner with an aroma of cooking. From behind one cage came a boy who looked a few years younger than Kolakwa. "I am Mahadoo. I made these machines." His easy smile and the twinkle in his eyes caught Kolakwa's attention. He wore colorful clothes decorated with shiny pieces of metal and glass.

In a flash of an eye, the boy vanished before Kolakwa's eyes and reappeared on his left side. Kolakwa clapped. "That was a neat trick."

"I know many such tricks, some of which my master taught me, and a few invented myself. I travel all over Shantiprastha doing shows."

"Why did you build these machines?" Kolakwa asked, admiring the mechanism.

"I make devices whenever something strikes my interest. Some times, I make machines that make labor easier. I use these myself or sell them to villagers. Other machines provide entertainment."

"Give our Little Naresh a demonstration," an administrator arrogantly ordered. Kolakwa glared at the man. Then, turning to Mahadoo, he politely requested, "Please continue." Mahadoo gazedat Kolakwa with admiration, bowing deeply. He turned to the largest machine. "This is a catapult," Mahadoo said as he rotated the crank handle, pulling back the throwing arm, which built up great tension in a twisted rope. He then locked the arm in the cocked position. Next, he loaded a good-sized rock into the catapult basket. Then, aiming the catapult for a safe open place, he pulled back the locking bar, releasing the arm, which swung forward at a considerable momentum, flinging the rock to a great distance.

"These could be splendid weapons for tossing projectiles over walls," Kolakwa said. "Can you make them larger?"

"Yes, if I get help," Mahadoo exclaimed.

Kolakwa patted the back of the boy and looked at Saumitra, who stepped forward and ordered the clerk traveling with them to give the young boy money for sustenance.

"Move your camp near Fort Vitora,"said Kolakwa. "Start building larger catapults we can dismantle, transport, and reassemble where needed. We will award you suitable land and provide you some men and money for materials."

As Kolakwa and his party were about to leave, Mahadoo stopped them. "I have a small request for you. My late master left me a box and instructed me that whoever can open it can have what it contains."

In a hesitant tone, he continued, "Many wise men have tried their hand. I only show the box to someone I trust will not take it by force or destroy it."

Kolakwa swore, "I promise I will not get angry if I fail. I will not steal or destroy the box you will present to me. I will only accept whatever you give if you offer it most willingly."

Mahadoo sprinted to his tent and produced a beautiful polished wooden box about one adult palm length on all sides. Kolakwa scrutinized the item. One side had an embedded pattern of tiny shiny stones, which looked like the top. In the corner was a figure of Dramho drawn to disguise a wood knot. There were no hinges or an external lock. The top did not come off by twisting or prying. Kolakwa gently shook the box. Whatever sat inside seemed solid. After failing to open it, Kolakwa gave the box to Krikaneel, who stared at the dots for a few minutes. Then, he applied pressure on them, but the dots did not bulge.

Krikaneel wanted to give the box to Saumitra, who stepped back, shaking his head. Krikaneel looked at the other party members and asked, "Is anybody else interested in trying his wits?" Other members passed the box around, but nobody had any ideas. Krikaneel saw Rokba gazing at the box but not stepping forward.

After looking at Kolakwa as if seeking permission, Krikaneel said, "Rokba, why don't you try to match your wit with the box?" He handed it to the boy.

Some of the other soldiers smiled derisively. Rokba examined the box for a few moments. Then he looked at Mahadoo and smiled. He turned the box upside down and held it over his head. He turned around while examining the overhead box until satisfied, aligning it in a particular direction. All the soldiers started laughing at him, thinking Rokba was doing a comical dance. But suddenly, there was a clicking sound, and a drawer popped out from the side. The soldiers grew silent and humbly admired Rokba.

Rokba handed over the box to Kolakwa, who opened a drawer. Inside was a shining, colorless, precious stone.

"Rokba, this is your reward for opening the box," Kolakwa said, handing the box and the jewel back to him.

"How did you solve the puzzle, Rokba?" Krikaneel's voice was heavy with admiration.

"On many nights as I laid on the ground, wondering at the starry skies, I saw many patterns of stars which move as the night passed. This dance of the stars continued as one season changed into another. But there is one star that never moves. I do not know its name, so I call it 'the Dramho star.' All the stars circle the Dramho star, paying their respect. The pattern of dots on the box is the same as the Dramho star and the surrounding stars in the sky. I aligned the Dramho star on the box in the same direction as the Dramhostar in the sky. The lid, I assume, is a fake-out."

Mahadoo was staring at Rokba with great admiration.

"Please keep the precious jewel. My master found his jewel on a faraway mountain, next to the skeleton of a wild beast. The beast must have devoured the previous owner of this stone. I only wish to have the box back as a memory of my master." Mahadoo humbly requested to Rokba.

Rokba briefly looked at the jewel and handed it over to Kolakwa.

"My Naresh, I move everywhere and will lose this beautiful jewel. Further, if somebody comes to know that I possess this jewel, they will try to harm me to steal it. So please accept this jewel as my humble contribution to your mission."

"Rokba, you can sell this jewel and get lots of gold, which you can use to buy land, goats, a house, and then settle down to have a family," Kolakwa tried to explain to Rokba.

"My Naresh, Dramho has given me this life as a goat-herder. I am happy and satisfied with my life. I do not want the jewel to steal my happiness and satisfaction. Please keep to this jewel and use it as needed. It would look better in a palace," Rokba pleaded.

"Mahadoo, can you explain how the box works?"Krikaneel requested.

"The box contains a suspended lodestone that always aligns north-south. The locking mechanism needs the lode stone correctly aligned within it. If someone holds the box and its locking mechanism in the north-south direction by aligning the pole star on the box with the pole star in the sky, then the lodestone aligns correctly with the lock mechanism and opens the pin, popping the drawer out." Mahadoo explained. Everybody grinned.

After carefully storing the precious stone in his inner pocket, Kolakwa gave the empty box to Rokba to hand to Mahadoo. As the group mounted their horses, Rokba exclaimed, "Why is there a carving of Dramho on the box? Nodevotee of Dramho will use it just for decoration."He examined the carving of the Dramho. In the center of the Dramho carving was a knot in the wood with a slight depression.

"Dramho likes water. Mahadoo, can you get me a small amount of water, please?"

Noticing the concerned look on Mahadoo's face, Rokba assured him, "Don't worry. I will not damage the box."

Mahadoo returned with a small cup of water. Rokba dipped his finger into the water and dripped a drop onto the wooden knot in the Dramho image. The water droplet slowly got absorbed in the wooden knot. A moment later, a second drawer popped out, filled with cotton, and lying on the cotton was a Crimson-colored Dramho. No one had ever seen a crimson Dramho crystal.

With a gaping mouth, Mahadoo alternately stared at the Dramho and Rokba's face.

He managed to mumble, "I did not know there was a second drawer. My master told me that only a true devotee of Dramho would get happiness from this box."

Saumitra stepped forward. "A person attached to material wealth will be satisfied after discovering the jewel. Only true devotees will think about the Dramho carving," Saumitra caressed Rokba's head.

Rokba took the Crimson Dramho and touched it to his forehead. "My Naresh, you will be crowned one day when our Atmaraj is secure. At that time, please mount this Dramho in your crown so that you and, after you, the next Naresh will have the blessing of Dramho over them and our entire Atmaraj."

* * *

Over the next several years, as Kolakwa and Rokba grew older, Kolakwa asked him to teach other fighters to climb distinct rock formations and walls under various climate conditions. He ordered these climbers to train together under Rokba's leadership. During the initial training days, the men did not take Rokba seriously and made fun of him behind his back.

"Little Naresh has assigned us a monkey as our teacher who can jump from rock to rock but cannot even hold a shaving razor, let alone a sword," commented the man, who was the mischief instigator. The man was unaware that the wind was blowing from his direction towards Rokba, so Rokba and Krikaneel could hear him. When Krikaneel tried to intervene, Rokba said, "I do not feel offended by his lack of respect. But if I have to lead these men into a battle, they must respect my skills and judgment; otherwise, they would not correctly carry out my instructions."

One day, during a break in the climbing lessons, Rokba asked the ringleader if he would teach him how to use the sword. The man proudly picked up two sticks, giving one to Rokba and keeping one himself. He twirled the stick, trying to show off before his friends. When they started paring, Rokba disarmed him quickly. The man became furious, feeling humiliated. He picked up a real sword and challenged Rokba to fight. Rokba picked up his short sword. All the watching people became tense and yelled at the man to stop fighting. Although the instigator was much larger and more robust than Rokba, using superior skills and agility, Rokba easily defeated the man.

"Please forgive me for my arrogance," the man begged.

"Where did you learn to fight like that?" asked Krikaneel.

"I have spent two years with a gang of robbers who had kidnapped me and forced me to climb the walls of mansions to get inside and open the doors for them. The only good outcome of that time was that they taught me to fight with knives and swords. They also taught me how to ride a horse. Luckily, I escaped from the gang shortly before the soldiers caught them."

From that day onward, the group respected Rokba and listened to his every word.

* * *

On Kolakwa's tour of a remote village, the village chief gifted hima falcon. "This bird will hunt for you. His name is Damru."

"*We need all the creatures to support our cause. Animals never betray you for material rewards*," Kolakwa thought as he thanked the man. He hired a falconer to care for Damru and added more falcons to the cast.

During a visit to a country fair in a border village, there was a competition for horse riding skills. Most of the riders were from the Bunei region, while the rest were visiting from the neighboring lands. One event involved a timed horse ride between two flags separated by some distance. While mid-course, the rider had to shoot at a target board that faced the far end. To hit this target, all the participants passed the target, turned around, and stopped to steady themselves. Then they fired their arrows and turned back before starting again.

After the last competitor, Saumitra asked Kolakwa to ride the course. As Kolakwa got on his horse, there was a commotion in the audience. He noticed that twenty Daitya horse men had come and stopped on the side. Their leader appeared to be a Daitya of importance based on his elaborate attire, the decorated horse, and the herald carried by his accompanying horseman. Kolakwa's hand automatically reached the hilt of his sword, expecting hostility. He had heard stories of the Daityas soldiers insulting the Mulkans during religious festivals. The Mulkans would show restraint and swallow their pride due to fear that if a few of them opposed the Daitya soldiers, other Mulkans would not support them. However, today Kolakwa felt that the atmosphere seemed different. Everyone was looking at him. He straightened his posture and raised his chin, looking straight toward the Daitya chief. From the corners of his eyes, he saw that the Mulkan men did not stand facing the ground but stared back at the Daityas. The bows and the arrows in the hands of the contest competitors looked clutched as if they were ready to get into position to launch.

After a moment of tense silence, the Daitya chief raised his right arm. "Greetings, you are Shamonda's son, right? I am the Zigador of Vishal. We were passing through this area and noticed this fair. Continue whatever you are doing."

After saluting Saumitra, Kolakwa trotted to the starting point. Then, turning his horse towards the ending point, he heeled the animal and started galloping, attaining full speed. As he passed the target, Kolakwa shifted in the saddle, turned back on one side, and fired the arrow, hitting the bull's eye. Since he did not have to slow the horse, he finished the distance in a much shorter time than the other participants.

Everybody cheered for their Little Naresh. The visiting Zigador clapped without smiling. "That was great horsemanship. One day, when you grow up, I hope to see you in battle, either on the same or opposite side," he declared. Kolakwa could sense the raw hatred in the Zigador's voice.

As he turned his horse to leave, he overheard the Zigador of Vishal say to his lieutenant, "I am uneasy about this Mulkan boy. Mark my words. This tiny spark of a boy could one day become a forest fire. We need to snuff him before that." The Zigador turned back for a last glance at Kolakwa before riding away.

After the event, Kolakwa handed the reward purse to the overall best participant and told the crowd to continue learning and practicing various forms of fighting, as they may have to use them in an actual battle soon.

On many other occasions, Saumitra made sure the people got to witness that even at his early age, their Little Naresh was a highly skilled warrior.

On Kolakwa's fifteenth birthday, the boys from the fort visited a Dramho shrine on the outskirts of Bunei lands, where he had under gone a ceremony celebrating his entry into adulthood. After the evening meal, Saumitra and Kolakwa sat on boulders near the campfire. Saumitra was engrossed in his thoughts, staring into the fire. He then turned to Kolakwa and pointed at the Crimson flag on the shrine, fluttering in the evening breeze. In a calm voice, he asked, "Kolakwa, you have now crossed the threshold into adulthood. Are you willing to live your life as a living Crimson flag?"

Kolakwa sat motionless. Saumitra looked deeply into Kolakwa's eyes as if trying to read his mind. He explained, "All the attributes of the flag must shine through your conduct." He paused as if waiting for the words to sink in. "I know this is too much to ask from any human, but I believe you were born with this purpose. No other human being will want your life. If you are successful, people will remember you throughout the ages. If you fail, it will be a glorious end."

Kolakwa felt that the universe had stood still. Only Saumitra's voice continued, "Decide whether you want to choose a purposeful, difficult life or a regular, easier one. You can think till the next full moon night. I will never raise this subject with you again."

Saumitra rose and walked away. Kolakwa stared at the Crimson flag, which looked radiant, bathing in the light of the setting sun.

Krikaneel had walked towards the campfire, approaching from the back, unnoticed by Kolakwa or Saumitra. He had heard most of the discussion from afar and quietly sat on the boulder vacated by Saumitra.

After a few minutes, Kolakwa got up and walked toward the shrine's sanctum. Krikaneel did not follow him but started mulling over his own goal in life. "*I have already completely offered myself to the cause of Atmaraj. If, in an unlikely situation, Kolakwa decides not to pursue the life mission of Atmaraj, am I willing to lead it, separate from him? Am I capable? Would anyone join me? Will Kolakwa think of me as a traitor?*" Krikaneel looked at his own long shadow.

He prayed, "Dramho, please guide Kolakwa to take on this heavy mantle of leadership."

As he anxiously waited, Kolakwa emerged from the shrine. Gone was the easy smiling face. The playful eyes had turned steely. He looked aged by a few years in the last few minutes.

"Krikaneel, do you remember Mamalu teaching us the difference between right and easy paths? Today, I am choosing the right path. Will you come with me, knowing it will be difficult and may end too early?"

"Yes, my Naresh. I will be with you. I will follow you anywhere you lead, my br—" Krikaneel left the word hanging and restrained himself with difficulty.

"Krikaneel, my brother," Kolakwa hugged him. Krikaneel could not stop his tears.

As they prepared to return to Fort Vitora, Kolakwa declared to Saumitra, "I am ready to give my everything for Atmaraj."

"May the radiance of Dramho always glow through you," Saumitra blessed him. He wanted to bless Kolakwa with a long life, but living a long life was rare for people on Kolakwa's chosen path.

Chapter–5

The Crimson Flag Unfurls

One day, when Kolakwa was about sixteen, a group from the village came to Fort Vitora. They were wailing and crying for justice.

The guards presented these people before Mamalu, and Mamalu summoned Kolakwa, Krikaneel and invited Saumitra.

The oldest person in the group dabbed his tears and said, "The Zigador of Fort Javli raided our village and carried off four of our daughters. When our men resisted the Zigador's men, they set fire to the entire village and killed many of our people. Protect us, my Naresh. We have no one."

Their village was on the border of Kolakwa's lands. The Zigador of Fort Javli had become bold since Shamonda was not around. He perceived Kolakwa as a mere child, incapable of fighting back.

After Kolakwa sent the villagers back to their homes with aid and a promise to retrieve the kidnapped girls, he summoned Ordora, the Brago of Vitora. Ordora had been around for a long time. Knowing he would have great insight into the local situation, Kolakwa ordered him to gather information about Fort Javli and its Zigador.

The following day, Ordora arrived with two young Mormos. Saumitra led the group to the Dramho shrine. Saumitra chose the shrine as the place for many critical discussions to give sanctity to their decisions. "Speak freely," Kolakwa acknowledged the two young Mormos. One of them stood up. "Regardless of consequences, we need to avenge this atrocity." The others murmured their assent.

Kolakwa looked at Saumitra, who said, "The time has arrived to assert your authority. We are building Atmaraj on the foundation of justice. The faith that justice and truth shall always prevail will strengthen the oppressed. They will rise and fight for their self-respect. Administration of justice will instill fear in the oppressors, who will tremble knowing the severe retribution for their evil actions."

Krikaneel stood. "My Naresh, if we teach the Zigador a lesson, we will establish your authority and attract more supporters."

"And also, more enemies," interjected Saumitra. "But if there are no detractors, then a righteous act is not making a difference."

Sensing that everyone who wanted to speak had finished, Kolakwa said, "The time has come to suspend peacefulness to protect the innocent." He turned his head and nodded at Ordora.

"One of the kidnapped girl's cousins is a guard in the garrison at Fort Javli. If we launch a rescue mission, he will lead us through the forest and open the guard door on the side. Most soldiers in Fort Javli are sick of the atrocities of the Zigador. They are waiting for a chance to rise in revolt. They will switch sides once the Zigador is no longer around," Ordora shared.

"Have we promised any reward for his help?" Kolakwa asked. "If someone betrays his master for money, he will betray us for the same at the next opportune moment."

Ordora shook his head. "The hope of having a just master is all the reward he wants. There was no offer or demand of money."

Everyone looked at Kolakwa. After thinking for a moment, Kolakwa took a deep breath and said in a firm, clear voice. "This is what I propose. There would be three groups of soldiers going separately with individual guides. The first two will enter the fort. To avoid getting trapped together in case of betrayal, we need two separate assault groups.If we need to retreat, the third group will wait outside and fight any pursuers."

As Kolakwa announced the plan, he could see the amazement on Ordora's face. He mused, "Ordora still cannot get over my image as a baby toddling around the fort just a few years ago, playing with his mustache when he picked me up in his arms." He glanced around the room as he pondered. *They will never know how many battles I have planned and enacted in my mind. I have always wondered what I would do if an enemy came up here, there, or behind that hill. How would I capture this or that fort if it were an enemy stronghold?*

The night before the raid, Kolakwa went to see Mamalu in her chambers.

"Greetings, Mother. I seek your blessings."

Mamalu was offering evening worship at her Shreeti shrine in the corner. Without turning, she replied, "I am praying to Shreeti for your successful expedition tomorrow. I am thanking her for granting you wisdom to make good decisions."

After lighting an oil lamp on the altar, she turned, smiling. "At every critical juncture of our lives, we must all decide whether we will take the right or easy path. Often, the right path is difficult and has no immediate reward. The easier path may give immediate rewards. Fortunately for this land and its people, you have accepted the right path. May Dramho grant you wisdom to choose the right path at every fork in your life."

Mamalu had seen many capable individuals frittering away their Dramho-given gifts by choosing the easy way of servitude and comfort rather than the arduous right path of freedom and honor.

Kolakwa's shoulders subtly sank as he perceived the burden of expectations of his mother and everyone who knew him. He saluted his mother by bending at his waist and touching the ground before her feet.

"May Shreeti grant you a resounding victory," Mamalu murmured as she touched his head.

Kolakwa also saluted the Shreeti shrine. For him, his mother was the Divine incarnate. He saluted her in a manner reserved for deities and the holiest people.

As Kolakwa walked to his sleeping chamber through the corridor connected to his mother's room, a guard informed him that Saumitra and Ordora were waiting outside the front door.

"My Naresh, you should not lead the expedition tomorrow," began Saumitra. Saumitra had stopped calling Kolakwa 'Little' Naresh. It was just Naresh now. Kolakwa's temper flared. But given his great reverence for his teacher, he kept a calm voice. "But why? Don't you trust my fighting skills?"

"No, Kolakwa. When the fighting starts, you will not be able to hold back and will jump into the fray. If there is betrayal or miscalculation, the enemy will aim for you. We cannot risk putting you in danger at this stage of our struggle. If anything happens to you, everything will be lost," Saumitra said gravely.

Kolakwa tried hard to maintain his composure. He clenched his palms together. He looked at Ordora, knowing that Ordora had no authority or inclination to contradict Saumitra. "What do you suggest, Ordora?"

"My Naresh, please forgive me, but I pray you accept Saumitra's suggestion," pleaded Ordora.

"I will go on the expedition. I am sixteen years old. If you desire, I will not lead it. But I must go. If something happens to me, make Krikaneel, my brother, the Naresh, and keep fighting for Atmaraj." In one sentence, Kolakwa cleared the heavy mist on Fort Vitora since Krikaneel's birth.

Everybody walked out without further discussion. Soon, a message came from the kidnapped girl's uncle that everything was okay if the person opening the guard door bowed only once to the forward party. If he bowed three times, he was compromised.

The Zigador of Javli was a powerful man known to be an accomplished fighter. However, since he usually slept after ingesting intoxicants, Kolakwa did not expect him to put up much of a fight.

In the early evening, the raiding parties started towards Fort Javli. As he watched Ordora lead the forward party out of Fort Vitora, Kolakwa was surprised that he did not feel anxious. This mission was his first foray into an actual skirmish with an enemy. Today, he would kill people. The warriors whom he was leading could die. He may die himself. *This is what I was born for. This is my duty.* Kolakwa looked at Dramhodas, who had ridden next to him. They exchanged glances. Then Kolakwa ordered his party to start.

They met the guide at the designated place in the forest and arrived at the fort just before midnight. The cousin bowed once, indicating everything was in order. As planned, the members of the forward group had taken up position sat various strategic locations in the fort. After his entire party was in the fort, Kolakwa yelled a slogan, "Hail Dramho, long live Atmaraj. Anyone wanting to join Atmaraj drop their weapons." More of the Zigador's soldiers hated the cruel Zigador than was initially believed. Almost all dropped their weapons. Unbeknownst to Kolakwa, the news of the imminent attack had leaked to the Brago of Javli. Fortunately, the Bragohated his Zigador. He instructed his trustworthy soldiers that an attack was imminent and to surrender without fighting. The Zigador had heard the rumors of the attack but was too arrogant to believe them. As Kolakwa reached the main area of the fort, a few in the group of Zigador's loyal men rushed towards him, but both Kolakwa and Dramhodas disposed of them with relative ease.

Since the fighting was mostly over, Kolakwa told Ordora, "I will arrest the Zigador." Taking a group of five soldiers, along with Dramhodas and a surrendered soldier as a guide, they headed to the sleeping chamber of the Zigador.

When the party reached the chamber, Kolakwa was surprised to find Zigador awake and waiting to pounce on them. The senior soldiers pushed Kolakwa to the rear and faced the Zigador. Today was a minor festival of Dramho. The Zigador, a devotee of Dramho, had abstained from indulging in the intoxicants on that holy day. With a large sword in each hand, the Zigador fought with the five soldiers, and within a few minutes, he grievously injured them. Dramhodas jumped between Kolakwa and the Zigador but was dispatched with one kick.

The Zigador cornered Kolakwa. He screamed, "You little upstart. I will cut you into pieces and hang them on the entrance of Javli." Kolakwa knew he was no match in a sword fight with this man. Years of early morning practice throwing his *chakram,* which he wore around his headgear, paid off that day. He grabbed his chakram and whispered a prayer to Dramho. Kolakwa threw the chakram with all his might toward the Zigador's head. The Zigador tried to block the chakram with his sword, but it was too fast and hit him vertically on the center of his forehead. He fell backward and was knocked senseless. Dramhodas and other soldiers hog-tied the unconscious Zigador.

Kolakwa's soldiers found the location of the four kidnapped girls and freed them. Kolakwa, the released prisoners, and a few soldiers carrying the Zigador returned to Fort Vitora. Back at Fort Vitora, the Zigador was kept in the dungeon and nursed for a few days till he was fully mentally alert. When deemed healthy, he was presented in front of Kolakwa and the advisory council.

"Do you have anything to say in your defense?" Kolakwa asked him. The Zigador glared at Kolakwa and spat in his direction. He yelled, "You have no right to arrest me. I shall not answer you."

Kolakwa calmly repeated the question. Getting the same response, he looked at Saumitra. But Saumitra remained silent. As Kolakwa was about to pronounce the judgment on the criminal Zigador, a thought crossed his mind. *No one has given me the authority to sit in judgment of this man. Handing out small punishments for minor crimes in the villages of my Bunei was one thing. But this is a capital crime committed by an outsider, carrying a death sentence as a punishment. Would my father approve of my action when and if he ever returned?*

Kolakwa remembered an ancient adage. *The lion is called the king of the jungle, not because somebody has crowned him, but because he behaves like a king. Today, he has to be the lion to have order in society.*

The remembrance of his father added a sense of responsibility to Kolakwa. In his lessons, Saumitra had taught him the list of crimes deserving the death sentence unless there was a mitigating factor. *This monster has committed many crimes, each deserving the death penalty. His fate should be a lesson for all the future oppressors*. With a firm, loud voice, Kolakwa declared, "With the rising sun as our witness, I sentence this vile person to death by being thrown off the cliff. Let the wild animals have him. The entire world will know that this happens to the oppressors in Atmaraj. Even if the thought of committing atrocities on the weak and helpless surfaces in their minds, they will quake, knowing the punishment they will receive."

The guards tied and stuffed the Zigador into a large cloth bag. Then they flung the bag off the ramparts into the forest valley below, food for the wild beasts.

This was the first time Kolakwa had sentenced someone to death. Although this was his duty as the upholder of the law, his restlessness knew no bounds. Later that morning, he meditated, sitting on the floor before the Dramho shrine. In his father's absence, he prayed to his divine parent to become his support and guide.

The next day, preparations were made for Kolakwa's arrival at Fort Javli. He rode his favorite black horse to the main door of the Fort. Slogans of "Long live Atmaraj. Long live the Crimson flag. Long live Naresh Kolakwa" filled the atmosphere. As the main door was opened, flower petals were showered on the procession. Kolakwa carried the folded Crimson flag on his right arm.

After reaching the ramparts, he hoisted the Crimson flag on the ceremonial pole in the fort. Kolakwa gave the soldiers of the previous Zigador a choice to either return to their villages or stay in the fort to join him in establishing Atmaraj. A few left reluctantly, saying they had sworn loyalty to the Zigador and could not break their oaths. Most joined the budding Atmaraj army. Saumitra guided the men through a blood oath of allegiance to the Crimson flag and Atmaraj. Ordora privately instructed his men to watch those who had switched sides. The guard door used by Kolakwa's party to gain entry was sealed and ballasted.

Amidst the celebration, Mahadoo set up a table with his magic tricks. He borrowed a brass bracelet from an onlooking Mormo and motioned to put it in a box on the table. After waving his magic wand, the bracelet disappeared from the box. The Mormo frowned as everyone clapped and said the bracelet belonged to his departed father. Mahadoo asked him to close his eyes and say a prayer to Dramho. On opening his eyes, Mahadoo asked him to check his inner vest pocket. The Mormo found the bracelet and started laughing and clapping. Mahadoo also brought out a plump cat and a mouse who did tricks together. "If the cat and mouse can be friends, so can all of us," Mahadoo said to the mesmerized crowd.

Kolakwa devotedly looked at the Crimson flag waving in the breeze. Dramhodas strolled towards him and stood next to him. Observing the joyous soldiers, Kolakwa whispered to Dramhodas, "This conquest was too easy. I worry that the next one will require a heavy price."

Chapter–6

Striking When the Iron is Hot

One morning, Kolakwa summoned Saumitra and Krikaneel to his chamber. Kolakwa was enthusiastic. "The rainy season will be over soon. Let us begin the expansion of Atmaraj. Almost three months have passed since the capture of Javli."

Saumitra remained somber. "The Zigador of Javli had attacked a village in our realm. We were justified in attacking him back. Once we start aggression into the lands of the neighboring Zigadors, we will cross a line of no return. In the best circumstances, the Zigador, whose fort we attack, would fight with us alone. Things will get difficult if other Zigadors come to help him. The worst situation would be if Dingir ordered all the neighboring Zigadors to band together or if he sent the imperial army to attack us. That would mean the end of our dreams."

"But when will we start working on turning our dreams a reality?" Kolakwa asked, his tone filled with resentment.

As the days passed, Kolakwa grew increasingly short-tempered. His dejection was apparent. During one afternoon lunch, he pushed his dish away in frustation." Krikaneel, the capture of Javli had given rise to a hope that Atmaraj would soon start expanding. But this standstill is very frustrating. If we persist in waiting for the right moment, we will keep justifying our inaction and become comfortable in our situation."

Day after day, Mamalu, Saumitra, and Krikaneel kept assuring Kolakwa that the Atmaraj expansion would soon begin.

One day, sad news arrived of Ordora's passing due to a snake bite. Dramhodas was beside himself in grief. "My father wanted to die in battle with a sword in his hand," he lamented. After a month, Kolakwa officially gave command of twenty men to Dramhodas following a discussion with other senior Mormos. Dramhodas immediately proved his fighting skills to his men while leading them on missions to repulse marauding Daitya criminal bands around Atmaraj lands.

Soon, the post-rainy season period ended, and winter was slowly approaching. One dreary morning, Saumitra entered Kolakwa's quarters. "Our spies have brought news that one of his bodyguards made an assassination attempt on Dingir's life. The royal capital is in great upheaval, with a large Daitya faction revolting against Dingir and Gangwo. Many Zigadors and courtiers are being arrested, questioned, and executed. Your father Zigador Shamonda had sided with Dingir at a critical juncture against the rebellious Daitya faction, increasing his influence."

Kolakwa was ecstatic and said, "Let us make the most of the opportunity. We should attack the forts in our vicinity, controlled by the neighboring Zigadors. With Dingir and his advisers being distracted, the Ruler's Court won't be able to assist them." The Mormos earnestly began the preparations for the campaign. The Atmaraj army captured a few small forts in the lands of the neighboring Zigadors with relative ease. ManyMulkan Mormos and their soldiers from those forts willingly switched sides and joined the Atmaraj army. Many soldiers of the opposing Zigadors who had converted to the Daitya religion also joined Kolakwa's army. None were asked to return 'home' to their ancestral Mulkan way of worship. Those who returned did so freely, citing that the original conversion was under great duress.

The Zigadors did not help each other against Kolakwa. No help came when the Zigadors lodged complaints to the Ruler's court. More men joined Kolakwa's army as Atmaraj expanded. As the army grew and gained experience, they could conquer larger territories with frontal assaults. In many of these battles, Kolakwa led his men from the front. His skills and bravery were on full display. Kolakwa's alacrity with his sword while riding his black horse and defeating the enemy soldiers with apparent ease made his surrounding soldiers believe Kolakwa had Dramho's blessings.

Before attacking, Kolakwa always sent a letter to that Zigador:

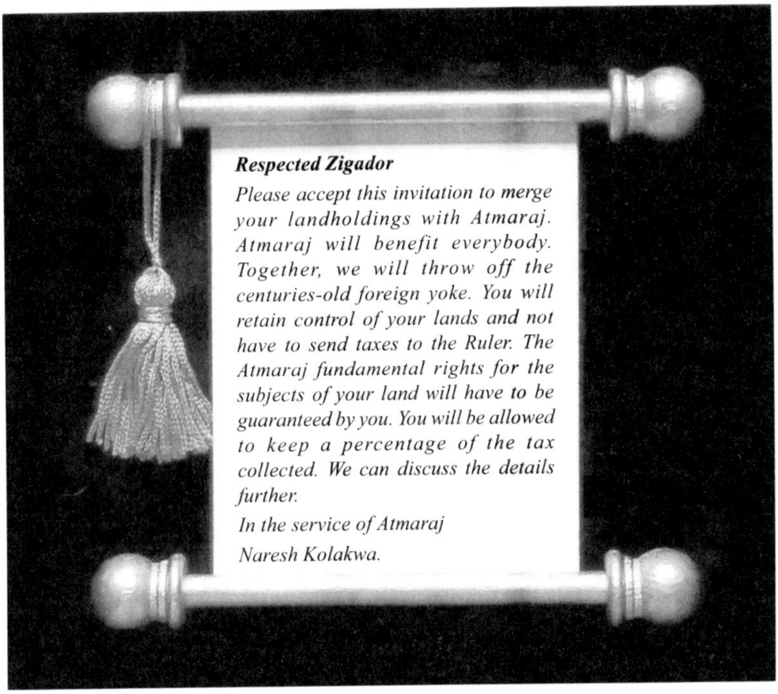

Respected Zigador

Please accept this invitation to merge your landholdings with Atmaraj. Atmaraj will benefit everybody. Together, we will throw off the centuries-old foreign yoke. You will retain control of your lands and not have to send taxes to the Ruler. The Atmaraj fundamental rights for the subjects of your land will have to be guaranteed by you. You will be allowed to keep a percentage of the tax collected. We can discuss the details further.

In the service of Atmaraj

Naresh Kolakwa.

Only a few minor Zigadors willingly joined Atmaraj. Most resisted and had to be subdued by force. During the ceremony of transfer of control of every fort, Kolakwa made a standard announcement,

"Every individual has the right to choose their method of worship, as long as they do not impede others. The choice of worship is not a criterion for the person's loyalty to the principle of Atmaraj. If someone does not want to worship, that issue is between that person and the Divine. Others have no right to interfere."

A Dramho shrine was established at each captured fort.No existing Daitya place of worship was disturbed.

Occasionally, Kolakwa heard worried murmurs about the future when the Ruler would return with full strength to reclaim the forts and the liberated lands.

Kolakwa observed that Dramhodas took too many risks with his life during the battles. Knowing Dramhodas since childhood, Kolakwa could guess the reason behind this behavior. Censuring him, Kolakwa said, "Dramhodas, we have many battles and wars in the future. Be careful when you fight. If you survive, there will be many more occasions to make your father's spirit proud." Dramhodas looked surprised.

On one of his frequent visits to Fort Vitora, Mahadoo shared some berries with Dramhodas. Enjoying the sweet and sour fruits, Dramhodas confided to him, "Since Kolakwa pays my salary, my job is to fight anyone he tells me. My family has done the same, serving as hired soldiers for many generations. Fighting for some king or a powerful person, we earned money by attacking whoever our master told us to attack. We have killed innumerable people who have personally done us no harm. But I don't want to be a mindless servant." After pausing for a moment, as he scrunched his face, biting into a particularly sour berry, "I believe that Kolakwa genuinely thinks of me as a friend and respects my opinion as a soldier. As a friend, I am prepared to do anything he says. But how can an ordinary soldier like me be a friend to the king? I am confused, Mahadoo!"

Mahadoo produced a sweeter fruit from his bag and handed it to Dramhodas. With great affection, he said, "Dramhodas, perform every action as an offering to Dramho. Only do acts which are fit to offer to Dramho. If you must kill someone, do it to uphold justice and the divine law. Then whoever pays you does not matter; you will only be Dramho's servant."

Some months later, Kolakwa attacked Fort Vishal (*Veeshaal*). The Daitya Zigador rode to the battlefield on his elephant, protected in a box made of a metal grill. The grill on the back and side had sections that could be opened to fire arrows but otherwise protected the Zigador. The box was more open in the front, with the grill having larger openings. However, the frontal approach to attacking the Zigador was impossible since the elephant would trample anyone in its way. The elephant's movement also made it hard to hit Zigador's weak spots with arrows.

Dramhodas reached the elephant after defeating many enemy soldiers. He recognized a few from the neighboring villages. With a heavy heart, he killed them, knowing any hesitation on his part would cost the lives of his men.

Dramhodas hurled a spear at the Zigador, which hit him on the chest, toppling him backward. But the spear did not penetrate the armor. Quickly recovering his poise, the Zigador shot his arrows. One stuck into Dramhodas's chest and severely injured him. After the extensive loss of life in the Atmaraj army, Kolakwa became anxious at the turn the battle had taken. At that moment, an old soldier suggested an idea used in ancient times. Using pieces of leather, they had a craftsman construct a leather mask with a long trunk and large elephant-like ears that would fit a horse.

This mask was attached to Kolakwa's horse. Kolakwa rode his horse to the front of the Zigador's elephant.

The Zigador recognized Kolakwa and shouted, "You have finally grown up. Let me see what kind of warrior you have become. It would give me immense pleasure to squish Shamonda's progeny."

He picked up his massive spear and ordered his elephant driver to trample Kolakwa and his horse. But suddenly, the elephant stopped in its path and refused to move. It saw Kolakwa's horse wearing the mask, thought it was a baby elephant, and declined to trample it. Kolakwa seized this opportunity and aimed his arrow, which found its mark at the junction of the helmet and chest part of the armor, instantaneously killing the Zigador.

Once the Zigador died, all the Atmaraj soldiers started chanting, "The Zigador is dead. Long live Atmaraj." Hearing their master was no more, the Zigador's soldiers stopped fighting and either ran away or surrendered.

After the battle, Kolakwa visited Dramhodas in the recovery tent. He sighedin relief on seeing Dramhodas smile at him. The Zigador's arrow had not penetrated Dramhodas's chest wall. A rib had stopped it from reaching his heart. The medicine man put a salve over his wound and braced the chest wall to decrease discomfort. Dramhodas tried to speak but winced as the broken rib caused excruciating pain when he inhaled. Kolakwa managed to whisper, "Please reward the soldier who suggested the idea for the baby elephant mask."

After commenting on the bravery of different soldiers and group leaders, Kolakwa sadly remarked, "We had to resort to trickery to eliminate the Zigador."

Krikaneel overheard this conversation as he walked into the tent to sit by Dramhodas's head. He replied, "My Naresh, this conflict is not for our gain but an ongoing struggle between good and evil. The Zigador chose the unjust side in this battle. On the universal balance scale of good versus evil, we are just weights put on the good side to restore balance against the evildoers. Deceit is wrong, but it becomes morally justified when used to establish the greater good. We must be vigilant that personal ambition and greed do not creep into our quest for Atmaraj and that our intentions remain pure. Remember your vow to Dramho. Atmaraj for all."

"Hail Dramho," Dramhodas joined, barely whispering due to the pain.

* * *

Fort Salher was one fort that the Atmaraj army approached during expansion. Kolakwa sent a messenger to invite the Mulkan Zigador Jaichand to join Atmaraj, as he had done with other opposing Zigadors.

After two days, a rider brought a reply from Zigador Jaichand saying that he was willing to join Atmaraj, citing their common Mulkan heritage. As a goodwill gesture, he sent a gift of a necklace made with many gold-capped small Dramhos and a pendant of a larger Dramho. He also had invited Kolakwa inside the Fort for a special dinner and celebration. There were no counter-demands or guarantees required.

Admiring the beautiful necklace, Kolakwa said, "I wish all other Mulkan Zigadors would be like Jaichand. Atmaraj in the entire Shantiprastha would become a reality sooner."

"This over-eagerness seems highly suspicious," Krikaneelremained doubtful, annoyed at Kolakwa's ogling at the necklace.

Soon, a caravan arrived with gifts and food delicacies. During the campaign, Kolakwa and the senior Mormos ate food with limited ingredients and equipment. The sight of the spread of exquisitely prepared food made all of them ravenous. But Krikaneel stopped them. He decided to test the food for poisoning by ordering a few food bearers who arrived with the caravan to sample the items from each vessel. They ate with no hesitation, and none seemed affected. Although Krikaneel permitted the servants to return, he ordered his guards to secretly arrest one food bearer who had consumed the food. This servant was hidden away and kept under observation.

Seeing that the food bearers were not affected, Kolakwa ordered his servant to serve him the food.

But Krikaneel stepped ahead and requested Kolakwa,"My Naresh, can we wait a few hours before we eat?"

"If you feel it necessary," agreed Kolakwa reluctantly, visibly irritated.

Krikaneel ordered his servant, "Bring me the plate, bowl, and spoons from the wooden box in my tent."

The servant brought the highly polished pure silver utensils.

"Rub samples from every food vessel onto the utensils," Krikaneel ordered.

Kolakwa and Krikaneel then went to Kolakwa's tent to figure out how to use Zigador Jaichand. After two hours, they returned to the food area. Krikaneel examined the silver dish, bowl, and spoon, which had all blackened.

Krikaneel exclaimed, "Manahshila[1]! I knew something was wrong. Manahshila is a deadly poison that takes effect after eight to twelve hours. The silver turns black when it contacts food containing this poison."

1. Arsenic disulfide, which reacts with silver to form black silver sulfide.

Kolakwa was furious. He roared, "The scoundrel Jaichand has tried to poison us. He agreed to friendship too easily. You were rightly suspicious."

Krikaneel remained calm."My Naresh, we can use this treachery for our benefit."He summoned a guard, "Spread the word Naresh has taken ill. Also, mention that we are not suspecting the food since the food bearers who tasted the food yesterday were fine."

The following day, Krikaneel checked on the arrested food bearer, who had become deathly ill with severe pain in the belly and violent loose motions. He died soon after."Most likely, the food bearers who tasted the food yesterday and returned would also be ill by now. Jaichand has sacrificed them for this ruse to work," Kolakwa surmised.

Krikaneel outlined his plan to Kolakwa."Since Zigador Jaichand thinks we are already poisoned and do not suspect him, we can invite him to our camp and then arrest him."

A message was sent to Zigador Jaichand.

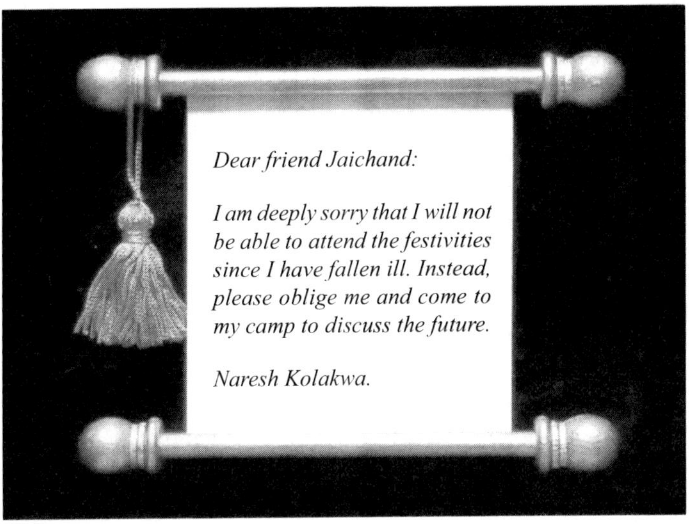

Dear friend Jaichand:

I am deeply sorry that I will not be able to attend the festivities since I have fallen ill. Instead, please oblige me and come to my camp to discuss the future.

Naresh Kolakwa.

The next day, a messenger arrived announcing that Jai chand was coming shortly but would not stay long since his mother was on her deathbed. Both Kolakwa and Krikaneel were surprised that Jaichand would risk coming. Kolakwa ordered that Jaichand be arrested after he arrived. However, when a man claiming to be Jaichand arrived with his companions, Kolakwa'sspy, who had seen the real Jaichand up-close, recognized the man as an imposter and secretly alerted Kolakwa.

Kolakwa ordered his men not to arrest the imposter and treated him with profound respect. He offered generous terms, letting Zigador keep Fort Salher and nearby lands and manage two more captured forts. They let the party go without the slightest hint that they were discovered. On returning to Fort Salher, the impostor Jaichand conveyed all the information to the real Jaichand, who was delighted that his ruse had worked. Rumors were spread that Kolakwa was deathly sick, and the campaign was returning to Fort Vitora.

Krikaneel, Dramhodas, and one hundred soldiers secretly hid in the neighboring Fort Salota. The next day, Kolakwa sent a message to Jaichand to take over Fort Salota. When he arrived at Fort Salota with his twenty-five troops, Jaichand was promptly arrested. His close servants confessed to the details of poisoning under the threat of being fed the leftover food. Afterward, Krikaneel and his soldiers went to Fort Salher with some of the captured Jaichand's soldiers in the lead, under Jaichand's flag. The guards of the fort readily admitted them. Upon entering, Krikaneel took control of the fort and declared that Fort Salher had joined Atmaraj.

The next day, Kolakwa proclaimed, "Zigador Jaichand, as a punishment for your treachery, you will spend the rest of your life in prison." Zigador Jaichand was housed in prison cells with his servants until a more permanent facility was found. Unbeknown to him, two of those servants were related to the food carriers who suffered a painful death as part of Jaichand's elaborate poisoning scheme. They had smuggled manahshila with them. At the next chance, they avenged their relatives by poisoning Jaichand's food, causing him to die a painful death.

* * *

The size of Atmaraj increased almost three to four times with these expeditions. Dramhodas's prominence in the army rose to nearly the levels of the senior commanders sent long ago by Kolakwa's father.

"My Naresh, our spies have brought information that the rebellion in the Ruler's capital has been subdued," Krikaneel reported one day.

Kolakwa nodded, "This means we will be the next item on their agenda." Scrutinizing the map on the table, he continued, "He will most likely order our surrounding Zigadors to attack us rather than come himself since we are too small of a threat."

"Nevertheless, we are keeping our ears to the ground. Our spies in the capitaland the lands of the neighboring Zigadors are on alert. They will promptly report any fresh development," Krikaneel assured.

Kolakwa sighed, an uncharacteristic display of worry, "Either way, the future of Atmaraj is on shaky grounds,"

Chapter–7

Dark Clouds Gathering

In the Ruler's capital, Dabrahoor, Gangwo had just returned home from the execution of the last rebel, Zigador. His successful suppression of the rebellion reaffirmed his position as the brain and muscle behind Dingir's throne. As his horse wagon entered the gates of his house, he waved at the crowd of beggars standing in line at the door of his compound.

Gangwo's palace was second only to the Ruler's size and majesty. Previously, it belonged to the commander-in-chief of Dingir's father's Daitya forces. After Gangwo installed Dingir as the Ruler, he executed the commander-in-chief and confiscated his palace. Besides the riches already present in the palace, Gangwo added many priceless artifacts he had stolen from the defeated enemies. The latest acquisition was the well-known ring of the founder of the Daitya faith, given to the ancestor of the just executed rebel Zigador. Hoping to be spared from the execution, the Zigador tried to bribe Gangwo with the ring. Gangwo took the ring but did not stop the execution. The ring had immense significance for the Daityas. They believed it conferreda special blessing on its wearer. In the privacy of his study, Gangwo fished out the ring from his pocket. After examining it, he tried to wear the ring himself. Given his gigantic fingers, it did not fit even his little finger. Gangwo tossed the ring on the table. Remembering the excruciatingly painful execution, Gangwo smiled. *This trinket did not help the traitor. It is a worthless piece of junk.* But after a moment's thought, he picked it up again and kept it in his desk drawer. *Maybe in the future, I will find some use.*

After a hearty meal, Gangwo took a stroll in his private park, and whistled, prompting his pet fox to hop over to him. The fox was missing his right front paw. Visitors to Gangwo's house always wondered how someone with Gangwo's character traits would keep a handicapped fox as a pet and shower it with so much love and care. Nobody believed that Gangwo could love another life form.

Gangwo gently picked up the fox, who looked tiny in his arms. Gangwo was a massive man. He rose above an ordinary person's height by at least a forearm's length. His broad frame could eclipse that of two fully grown men standing beside each other. Gangwo's face was fear-inducing with his large and protruding jaw, and the Daitya marking on his left cheek looked more prominent than it did on most others. He had mildly bulging eyes, and there were rumors he suffered from severe headaches and found relief only in hearing the screams of people being tortured.

As Gangwo scratched the fox behind his ears, he looked back on when he first found the creature. During one of his hunting trips, Gangwo found the fox trapped in a jaw coil spring trap. The fox had partially bitten off its leg to free itself from a trap. Such bravery by the fox had a profound impact on Gangwo. He spared the fox's life and ordered his servants to nurse it back to health. Foxes mark their territory by urinating on the borders. Gangwo considered the entire Shantiprastha his territory. He had symbolically urinated on the holy places of the Mulkans to defile them and mark them as his territory after he destroyed them.

Every day, Gangwo changed his strolling path to foil assassination attempts. After finishing, he went inside. At his desk, he picked up and glanced at another weekly spy report of Kolakwa's capture of forts, then tossed it on the pile of complaint letters of the defeated Zigadors. As he pushed the stack into a box, he mulled. *I can cut off the head of this baby*

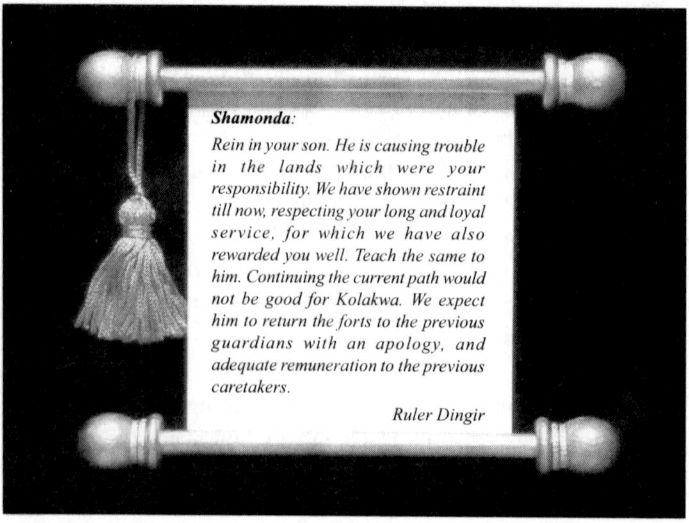

Shamonda:

Rein in your son. He is causing trouble in the lands which were your responsibility. We have shown restraint till now, respecting your long and loyal service, for which we have also rewarded you well. Teach the same to him. Continuing the current path would not be good for Kolakwa. We expect him to return the forts to the previous guardians with an apology, and adequate remuneration to the previous caretakers.

Ruler Dingir

snake Kolakwa anytime I want by setting a bunch of Zigador wild dogs to lay waste his land and cut him into tiny pieces. It may be cleaner but less spectacular to bribe one of his underlings to poison or murder him in his sleep.

Tenderly caressing the stump of the fox's leg, he whispered, "But for now, I need to let this baby snake grow large enough so that Dingir and the Zigadors develop some fear of him and let panic set in the Court. Then I will go as the great protector of the Ruler's throne and squash the vermin, thereby consolidating my superiority in the minds of everybody."

The fox rested his head on Gangwo's shoulder. Gangwo smiled cruelly and remembered Mulkans' earlier rebellion, which he had ruthlessly crushed so much that even the Daitya Zigadors were appalled by his orders.

Gangwo summoned his secretary. When he arrived, Gangwo ordered the man to write a letter. "Send it to Shamonda in the Dingir's name. Do not address him using any polite words," he instructed.

After Gangwo finished his dictation, he produced a box with the Ruler's seal, which he affixed to the letter. He ordered the secretary, "Bring me the map of Shantiprastha with the latest Zigador boundary markings." The secretary spread the map on the table, revealing details of the lands controlled by different Zigadors. It also had information on which areas were completely Daitya and which were Mulkan. "Everybody is a traitor if they get a chance and feel they can get away with it," Gangwo roared, for no particular reason. A shiver ran down the secretary's spine as he hoped the master was not talking about him. Gangwo rolled his index finger around the names of the five Zigadors near Kolakwa's new conquests. These dogs can hunt Kolakwa for me. Then, as if reconsidering, he ordered, "Take note of these names."

Within a month, Kolakwa captured more areas, which caused panic in the Court. Finally, Gangwo decided it was time to finish Kolakwa.

* * *

"O, Guardian of the world, I request your permission to speak," Gangwo presented himself to Dingir, bending at the waist while standing at the entrance of the presentation room of the Ruler's palace.

The presentation area was large and austere, the only focal point being a large portrait of Dingir on the wall above Dingir's throne, facing the door. There was no other seating arrangement in the room. Images of previous Rulers were affixed to the side walls, and the symbols of the Daitya faith hung between the paintings. A large, ornately decorated pot sat near the far wall. It contained water from the lake on whose banks the founder of thefaith was born. Vapors were piped into the room from the four corners, giving it a foggy appearance common in the lands where the Daityas originated. Hidden from the view of the visitors was a small door at the rear of the presentation room, which opened onto Dingir's residence.

As Dingir entered the room, he arched his neck to face Gangwo. Gangwo stared at the Dingir's feet per tradition, showing his subservience. Dingir was short, thin, and had a sallow skin complexion. Although Dingir had access to the most nutritious and tasty food in the world, a disease of his digestive system prevented the absorption of the nutrients. He suffered from premature hair loss. His deep-set eyes had an unceasing, cruel stare.

After an uneasy silence, Dingir spoke with the loudest voice he could muster, "Speak." He appeared very annoyed. He was on the way to see his favorite slave girl when the servant announced Gangwo's request to meet him. "*One day, I won't need him. But till then, even I, the almighty Dingir–Ruler of Shantiprastha, have to show this low-born cur too much respect,"* Dingir fretted.

"I seek your guidance, O light of this world," Gangwo addressed Dingir in the sweetest voice he could conjure.

Gangwo had ensured that all the courtiers knew about the drama of seeking guidance from Dingir. Everyone knew Gangwo was the decision-maker in the empire. However, Gangwo and Dingir would engage in an elaborate farcical ritual. Gangwo would decide on something. Then, he would narrate the topic to Dingir andseek guidance. Dingir would act as if he thought about it, ask cursory questions, and then ask Gangwo, "What do you think I would say?"

Gangwo would tell his decision.

"You guessed correctly. That is my decision." So technically, every order was the Ruler's decision. Dingir had never disagreed with anything Gangwo had suggested.

"Time has come to stomp the head of the snake, Kolakwa. I think you will send the Zigadors around his land to attack him together and lay waste to the realm he controls. Thestories of destruction will spread far and wide, and no one will ever dare to bring a thought of rebellion in their mind," Gangwo said in a hatred-filled voice.

"You guessed correctly. That is my decision." Dingir uttered."Can you guess why I waited so long to do this?" the Ruler asked, caressing the Daitya scars on his left cheek.

"You were giving Shamonda a chance to rein in his son. You could have attacked Shamonda and Kolakwa and finished both the troublesome father and son. But you know that Shamonda in the Northwestern Kingdom forms a buffer between the far west Barbarians and our realm. If we attacked

Shamonda, he could ally with the Barbarians and be difficult to destroy. With his failure to control his son, you have decided to take that risk and set preparations to attack Shamonda after we finish Kolakwa."

"You guessed right." Dingir smiled and walked away.

Gangwo walked backward to the door, turning around only after he was out of Dingir's sight. The protocol mandated that you should never show your backside to the Ruler.

On returning to his house, Gangwo's secretary showed him the letter from Shamonda in which he had profusely apologized for his son's behavior but expressed his inability to control him. Gangwo tore the letter and threw it away.

"Send this letter to each of the five Zigadors I showed you last month," Gangwo ordered.

To my loyal servant Zigador:

I hope that the almighty Ghumu has been kind to you.

It has reached my ears that the Mulkan dog Kolakwa is causing mischief in your portion of my realm. Therefore, I am ordering you to coordinate with other neigh boring Zigador servants and crush the head of this vile creature. After you capture all the forts, I will redistribute them to you.

If any one of you brings the broken but living Kolakwa back to me, I will give you a special reward. I am looking forward to giving him a long agonizing death.

Merciful
Dingir, the Ruler

"None of these cowardly Zigadors would not take on Kolakwa by themselves. But together, they should be able to defeat Kolakwa," Gangwo remarked to his secretary as he affixed the Ruler's seal.

* * *

"New pots have arrived," Saumitra announced to Kolakwa one morning at Fort Vitora.

A servant followed Saumitra, carrying three pots. After placing the pots securely, Saumitra ordered the servant, "Bring hot embers."

The servant went to the kitchen and picked glowing embers from the earthen stove, commenting to the cook, "Saumitra and Kolakwa are doing their magic again."

The servant left after he brought the embers. Saumitra closed the doors. He then placed the hot embers inside the pots. After waiting for a few instances, words appeared on the pot's outer surface.

Five Zigadors, Vishram, Kumbha, Panha, Basrud, and Loha, will attack you simultaneously in a month's time. My gift is in the usual place. May Dramho protect your mission. Always remember to make friends with your enemy's enemies.

"This never fails to amaze me. My father's secretary has sent us so much vital information by employing household items like the colorless onion juice as ink to write on the pots and coating the surface with shellac to protect the ink. The simple act of heating the pot by placing burning coals in them makes the invisible writing on the pot visible." Kolakwa remarked. The secretary was cautious and sent three pots to ensure that at least one reached intact.

"Remember, it took your father decades to infiltrate the Ruler's administration with spies. Hopefully, we will establish such a network in the future. He has also sent 50 gold coins in the saddle of the mule carrying the pots," Saumitra noted.

"I always wondered about the safety of the messenger," Kolakwa asked.

"The messenger is an old, deformed man your father has employed for ages. He somehow finds ugly mules whom no one would like to steal. The stench of the man and his mules keeps them safe," Saumitra laughed.

"This stench will sustain the future aroma of freedom," murmured Kolakwa as he imagined what disaster would have fallen on Atmaraj without this advanced warning.

Chapter–8

Many Developments

The next day, Kolakwa assembled the Advisory Council to discuss the news of the invasion. Additional information arrived from the spies in the Mleccha (Mley-Cchaa) lands that the Frang is had attacked the Mleccha capital, Fort Surat. The Advisory Council started wondering how these seemingly unrelated events would affect Atmaraj.

"Who are the Frangis?" Kolakwa asked, looking toward Saumitra.

"I knew little about them till last week," said Saumitra. "Our spy from the Mleccha lands told me about them. They look like Mlecchas and are from the land close to the Mleccha homeland. They compete with Mlecchas in business activities. In the past, they have invaded each other's homeland and are similar in strength."

Dramhodas sneered, "We already had the Mlecchas, who are like a disease of the skin. They appear as tiny dots and spread before you know it. And now we have these new parasites called Frangis!"

Saumitra saw Rokba looking at Dramhodas in a confused manner. He, therefore, volunteered, "Let me recount the Mleccha history. The Mlecchas came from a distant land called Maru. Maru is an immense desert with almost no resources. Since they could not grow crops, the Mlecchas evolved into skilled traders. In the early days, a group of Mlecchas ventured out of the desert and traveled to a kingdom known to manufacture good-quality weapons. The Mlecchas had nothing of value to exchange for these weapons. They asked the manufacturers to sell them the weapons on credit. To secure the credit, they left their children with the manufacturers as a promise to repay the money."

"Their own children!" a Mormo exclaimed.

"After securing the weapons, the Mlecchas approached the countries who were at war with each other. They sold them weapons in exchange for gold and other valuable commodities as partial payment. They, however, also stipulated that if the country buying the weapon won in the war, they would hand over the imprisoned defeated soldiers to the Mlecchas as the remaining payment. The Mlecchas sold weapons to both sides of the war. Hence, regardless of who won the war, they ended up with many imprisoned defeated soldiers who were enslaved and sold to another kingdom for immense profit. The Mlecchas then paid back the weapons manufacturers, and their children were released. After a few years, the Mlecchas became extremely wealthy and powerful."

Krikaneel asked, "Why are these traders a threat to us or the Ruler?"

Saumitra replied, "Initially, everyone considered the Mlecchas as a useful ally. They started establishing trading posts around the world. Slowly, the Mlecchas captured land around their trading posts and enslaved the locals. Their initial interest was controlling the areas that produced their best goods. Then, they started colonizing larger areas to corner the markets for their goods. As they acquired more land, they conflicted with the local powers. They help the weaker party in the wars between locals, and when the weaker party wins with their help, they dominate and control him."

"So, are they just like the Daityas?" asked Dramhodas.

"Both the Daityas and Mlecchas are foreign invaders on Shantiprastha. Daityas arrived three hundred years ago, while Mlecchas arrived one hundred years ago. But, in contrast to the Daityas, the Mlecchas were not interested in the enslaved people's ways of worship. As long as the enslaved people created wealth for the Mlecchas, they let them live as they wanted. They routinely do not destroy places of worship, but sometimes stole Dramho crystals and sold them as collectible items in foreign lands."

Krikaneel asked Saumitra, "Why has the Ruler not driven out the Mlecchas from Shantiprastha?"

Saumitra replied, "The Ruler considered the Mlecchas as a minor irritation occupying only a tiny amount of land on the coast. Few Daityas were seafaring traders. There was little competition between the Mlecchas and the Daityas on the sea. The Mlecchas in Shantiprastha declared themselves subordinate to the Ruler. They sent him foreign luxury goods, slaves, and money as a tribute. These offerings kept the Ruler happy. Fine goods imported by the Mlecchas keep courtiers' families comfortable. Hence,the Ruler has mostly ignored the Mlecchas. The situation changed at the time of the Great War when many Zigadors left with their armies to fight the war. The Mlecchas captured their unprotected forts, expanding their holdings. Fortunately for the Mleccha Queen, given the Great War's weakening of the Ruler's army and the subsequent rebellion of some of the Daitya Zigadors, the Ruler did not want to start another war immediately. As he was waiting to regain the battle strength of his men, over twenty years have passed with other distractions in the empire."

Dramhodas rose. He had lost interest in the Mlecchas and their war with the Frangis. "We need to plan our defense against these five Zigadors immediately. Our Mormos will keep our men on high alert. I will order all soldiers who have gone home on holiday to return. Our spies will promptly report any movement by the neighboring Zigadors."

* * *

"O, Guardian of the world, a large fleet of Frangis has landed and besieged Port Surat of the Mlecchas. The Mleccha queen is pleading for our help. The Mleccha native land, Maru, is too far to send immediate help." Gangwo said, presenting himself to the Ruler's presentation room early one morning. Gangwo chose early mornings when he wanted the meetings to be short, without the usual question-answer charade.

Dingir had a rough night because of his disease of the digestive tract. None of the usual medicines had helped. At last, as he was falling asleep early in the morning, Gangwo requested an audience. Despite being very cross, he did not dare to keep Gangwo waiting.

"Why should we help the thieves? They have been stealing our land. We should get rid of them!" asked Dingir.

Gangwo raised his thick eyebrow, "O Protector of my life, you remember who Mlecchas are!"

After pausing to gather his thoughts, Gangwo continued, "It is true that the Mlecchas have encroached on our land. We will crush them soon. But officially, the Mlecchas Queen is a protectorate under your mercy and annually pays you a considerable sum of money as a tribute. Therefore, we are obliged to send resources to help the Mleccha save Port Surat, the Mleccha capital, even after the treacherous behavior of the Mlecchas."

"Shouldn't we let the Frangis destroy the Mlecchas, and then we destroy the Frangis afterward?" Dingir asked.

Gangwo shuffled his feet. He straightened his back to show his actual height and assert his authority. His speech changed from slow sweetness to impatient terse.

"We do not want the Frangis to get a toe grip on this land, which would facilitate their bringing more of their kind. Mlecchas are a known entity for us. We do not know the strength of the Frangis. A known enemy is better than an unknown enemy."

"What do you think I would say?" Dingir asked.

Gangwo gave a long exhale as things went back to normal.

"I guess you would say that teaching lessons to Kolakwa and the Mlecchas could wait, but we should urgently get rid of the Frangis."

"You are right. Go ahead. That is my order," Dingir agreed.

Gangwo issued orders to the Zigadors around Atmaraj to take their forces to Port Surat instead of attacking Atmaraj.

Within a week, spies shared this news with Kolakwa, who was relieved at this unexpected windfall.

* * *

Soon after, there was an upbeat mood in the Queen's palace at the Mleccha capital of Fort Surat.

"This will teach a lesson to the Frangis," the Mleccha minister gave a hearty laugh. "The combined forces of our brave troops and the Ruler's Zigadors crushed the Frangis. Unfortunately, our men and the Ruler's forces have suffered heavy losses."

The Queen maintained a grim face. Even with that expression, any Mleccha would still call her beautiful. She was short and rotund. Her face was round, with a narrow forehead, rounded eyes, and a stubby nose. Ample, thick brown, tightly curled hairs were long and meticulously well-kept. Regardless of her physical characteristics, her person carried an elegance that transcended cultural norms. She could instantly manifest an entire spectrum of emotions on her face, totally unencumbered by her inner thoughts. Today, for once, she reflected her true feelings on her face.

"You don't look that happy with the news, my Queen?" the minister was surprised.

"I will be happy once Dingir's army leaves our land. There are many historical instances where guests come to help the owners, extend their stay, and eventually kick out the hosts. If I were Dingir, I would instruct my army to stay and permanently occupy our area, ejecting us. Our Mleccha forces are very weak from this war with the Frangis. But fortunately for us, the war has also significantly weakened Dingir's forces who have come here. Based on our spies, the Zigadors seem in no mood to fight further and want to return to their homelands without delay."

* * *

As was his everyday routine, Krikaneel woke up at sunrise and began performing his morning exercise when his guard alerted him that a "traveler from the coast" wanted to see him. Krikaneel immediately asked the man to come in, recognizing the code name for the spies from Mleccha land.

After being briefed on the latest developments at Fort Surat, Krikaneel hurried to Kolakwa's quarters. "My Naresh, the war with the Frangis has weakened the Mlecchas. We think the Ruler may desire the Zigadors to stay and eliminate the weakened Mleccha. However, our spies have determined that the Zigadors are unwilling to fight with Mlecchas because they lost too many men against the Frangis. We can expand Atmaraj and avoid the Ruler's attack by taking advantage of this situation with Mlecchas."

"What do you suggest?" asked Kolakwa.

"First, we should seek permission from Dingir to attack the Mlecchas on his behalf. I believe Dingir will agree, thinking he will get an enemy subdued at no cost. If we fail, he will deny permitting our invasion. While we are invading the Mlecchas on his behalf, the Ruler's Zigadors will not attack us." Krikaneel proposed to Kolakwa.

Kolakwa looked at Krikaneel with admiration at this brilliant idea. How Krikaneel developed a strategy fit for an experienced statesman was beyond his comprehension.

After pausing momentarily, Krikaneel continued, "What we really need is Fort Sangram. Anyone who controls Fort Sangram and the surrounding areas controls the access from the coast to the plateau. If we were masters

The Light of the World

I, Kolakwa Braznee, your humble servant, ask for forgiveness for the mistake of capturing the forts around Bunei. I am very young, and in my youthful ignorance, I committed this mistake. You are merciful and kind. Please forgive me.

As a gesture of repentance, I am offering to eliminate the Mleccha incursion into your lands using my men. There will be no expectations from you.

Forever your servant.

Kolakwa Braznee

of Fort Sangram, the Mlecchas could never attack Atmaraj. We may even be able to tax all the Mleccha goods passing through that way.

After consultation with the Advisory Council, Kolakwa dispatched an emissary to the Ruler with a letter.

The letter mentioned nothing about returning the annexed lands to the Ruler. Additionally, Kolakwa sent valuable gifts.

As usual, all correspondence with Dingir passed through Gangwo. On receiving the letter and gifts, Gangwo was pleased that Kolakwa had fallen in line without costing any lives of the Ruler's army. *Dingir can declare in court that he has mercifully forgiven Kolakwa. At a later date, I will strangle Kolakwa's throat when he is no longer useful*, Gangwo mused as he squeezed the Daitya medallion around his neck.

Chapter–9

Chetaki

Sangram province was at the frontier of the Mleccha and Ruler's land, right where the plateau dipped rapidly towards sea level. A tiny piece of Kolakwa's land also jutted into this area. Fort Sangram (Sun-graam), which guarded the major pathway extending from the plateau to the sea, was located on one of the steepest hills.

Kolakwa requested Mahadoo and Rokba to come to Fort Vitora to share their knowledge of Sangram and the surrounding lands.

"I have often been to Fort Sangram with my old master's show to entertain the Mlecchas at the Fort," Mahadoo said to Krikaneel and Kolakwa. "The Mlecchas liked the magic tricks and bought some small magical devices we were selling."

"How are the Mlecchas as people?" Krikaneel asked.

Mahadoo replied, "Mlecchas are unusual people. They liked our magic boxes. Usually, people buy our boxes and want to know how they work. Instead, the Mlecchas offered my master money to make copies of the magical boxes. They wanted to sell them. To keep them happy, we made some boxes and promised to return next year with more magic boxes to sell. My master was not interested in manufacturing but in performing. Therefore, we never returned. The Mlecchas were better customers compared to the Daityas. My master avoided the Daityas, who would get angry and break our equipment if they thought we made a fool of them with our magical tricks."

Rokba added, "Most of the inhabitants of the Sangram area are Mulkan, and some were mixed progeny between the local women and the Mleccha soldiers. Many locals are fishers by trade who leave their villages for part of the year to sail the seas and engage in fishing. They return during the rainy seasons and plant rice in small paddy fields. The men and women are simple, hard-working, and very brave."

Kolakwa noticed Mahadoo looking at Rokba with great admiration and affection. It felt odd, but he let the thought dissipate after exchanging glances with Krikaneel, who had also noticed.

Kolakwa was getting impatient. "What about the fort?"

Rokba continued, "I asked around and found that the local Zigador had originally stationed only a small group of soldiers under a Mormo because of the long peace with the Mlecchas. He had not provisioned the Fort to withstand a long siege. As a result, the Fort was left vulnerable after the Zigador and his men left to fight the Great War. When news came that the Zigador had perished in the war, the Mleccha army seized the opportunity to attack the fort. The Mormo in charge gave up the fort without a fight. Rumors circulated the Mlecchas had bribed him."

"How are the defenses of the fort now?" asked Kolakwa.

"A stonemason who worked on the Fort told me that the Mlecchas have upgraded the defenses and well-provisioned it with supplies and soldiers. With these changes, the Fort had become almost impregnable."

Mahadoo added, "After the Mleccha takeover, the people in the Sangram lands had quietly accepted one master for another, but recently, Mleccha soldiers had started robbing and harassing the local populace who, in retaliation, have started a low-level insurgency in the area. We increased the unrest by sending traveling storytellers to every village to tell stories of Atmaraj, where there is justice for all. A popular song is sung by men around night fires, describing the capture and punishment of the cruel Zigador of Javli. Many local young men want their lands to be part of Atmaraj."

Krikaneel added, "Our spies are training local rebel youths to fight andhave supplied arms. They occasionally attack Mleccha soldiers."

"Usually, the Mlecchas are not needlessly cruel like the Daityas, but recently, they are overreacting. To quieten the masses, they have unleashed a reign of terror," said Mahadoo.

"The Mleccha queen has posted her cousin Shaisto on Sangram. Shaisto is a giant man who performs feats of strength to impress people. He tortures captured local youths suspected of involvement in the insurgency and rips their limbs off with bare hands. Then, he sends the mangled bodies back to their villages. Because of this, instead of fear, the youths have developed maddening hatred towards the Mlecchas," added Rokba.

* * *

Even before Kolakwa's emissary returned from the Ruler, Saumitra requested Kolakwa to hold an advisory council. Kolakwa called Krikaneel,

Dramhodas, Rokba, Mahadoo, and a few trusted senior Mormos.

Mahadoo and Rokba sat on the floor while everyone else was given seats.

"In my court, all my advisors are equal. Everybody is free to present even the wildest idea. Please take your seats," Kolakwa said, looking at Rokba and Mahadoo. They got up and hesitantly sat on the chairs, trying to sit with minimal contact of their body to the furnishing.

Mahadoo looked around. His eyes briefly locked with Rokba. He tried to smile but stopped halfway as Rokba looked away in deep thought.

Kolakwa began the meeting by saying, "Fort Sangram is the key to the foray into Mleccha lands. If we have control of Fort Sangram, all the lands below will be ours. After that, expanding into the Mleccha territory would be easier."

Saumitra continued, "Once Fort Sangram falls, the local partisans will eliminate the Mleccha soldiers distributed in the territory. I have already smuggled more weapons, money, and provisions to the rebel youth. With our support, the rebels have rejuvenated, recruited more men, and trained with renewed vigor and zeal. We have asked them to await further instructions."

A Mormo whose relatives had visited Sangram said, "But the fort is impregnable. All the soldiers are Mlecchas. It will not be possible to turn any of them to our side."The Mormo added, "Shaisto and his superhuman feats of strength cause apprehension in our soldiers. Wild rumors about devil worship and human sacrifice are rampant. My relatives also shared that the main door is solid and has a robust mechanism on the inside. We cannot take a large battering hammer to attack the main gate because of the steepness of the approach pathway. Further, the door also has large, pointed spikes, making it impossible to use the war elephant captured during the battle of Fort Vishal to ram the gates."

Kolakwa scanned the faces of everyone around the room.

"What about scaling the walls?" asked Rokba.

"Impossibly steep," was the Mormo's reply.

A gloomy silence fell over the group.

"What if someone can fix the rope to the top of the cliff?" Mahadoo asked.

Rokba volunteered, "If there is a fixed rope, I can climb any wall. But who will take up the first rope?"

"I have someone," Mahadoo said. "A special someone – Chetaki (*Chey-tukee*)." Everyone except Rokba gave him an incredulous look.

The next day, the entire group went to Mahadoo's encampment. In the camp, many boys and girls fed and cared for various animals in cages. These children were orphans abandoned by their community whom Mahadoo had adopted and given shelter. They were a large family of humans and animals, unwanted by mainstream society, bonded by mutual care and love rather than blood relations. A Mormo made a snide comment that the children looked healthy and well-fed, better fed than his children.

As they walked, everyone admired the multiple giant catapults in various stages of construction.

"Please follow me." Mahadoo led the group to a large tent.

Inside, they crowded on the side of a large cage.

"Meet Chetaki," said Mahadoo.

Everyone stepped back as their eyes fell on the creature approaching them in the cage.

The nightmarish creature was a thousand times larger than the house lizard, with a six-foot-long body. It had a long muscular tail, thick neck, long claws, well-developed legs, and a forked tongue protruding from her mouth. A shiver ran through Rokba's spine who was closest to the cage.

"She is a young monitor lizard, not yet fully grown, but close," Mahadoo affectionately informed everybody.

Chetaki looked at Mahadoo as if she understood he was talking about her.

"We finished exercise early this morning," a nearby boy volunteered. Mahadoo took two metal pipes hung on the cage's wall and rhythmically struck them. She scampered towards him, knowing from habit that a treat was coming. He reached into a barrel sitting close by, picked up an enormous chunk of meat, and threw it at her. She caught the piece of meat and scampered away. After Chetaki had finished eating, Mahadoo struck the pipes together and summoned her back. He opened the cage door, letting her out. "Look at this beautiful crest running along her back," Mahadoo said, stroking her. Rokba gingerly touched her so as not to offend Mahadoo. Kolakwa came close, but did not touch her. Everybody else stayed far away.

"I raised her from her infancy. She cannot hear the human voice but is a metal percussion music lover." Mahadoo was the only one who laughed at his humor. "Monitor lizards cling tightly to rocks. They have powerful paws. Her grip is strong enough to support a light weight grown man," Mahadoo said, looking at Rokba. We can tie a rope to her waist, holding on to which Rokba can scale the cliff. One of my brothers likes to climb, and we always play the climbing game with her.

Mahadoo guided Chetaki into her rolling travel cage. He started pushing itover an uneven pathway towards a rocky hill with large boulders at the rear of the camp. Two soldiers helped him only after a fierce gaze from Kolakwa. As the group reached the base, Mahadoo let Chetaki out of the cage. He unwrapped the rope around his waist and tied one end to a harness he had attached to Chetaki. After caressing her momentarily, he rhythmically banged the metal tubes, which she knew meant 'run.' Chetaki scampered up the cliff to the top and then grabbed onto a large boulder.

Mahadoo handed the other end of the rope to an ear by Mormo. "Pull on this with all your strength." The Mormo pulled. Chetaki did not budge. Rokba grabbed the rope and pulled it with all his might. The rope did not give at all. Rokba started climbing the cliff, holding onto the rope for support. In about ten minutes, he was next to her. Then he climbed back down again. After Rokba was safely on the ground, Mahadoo banged the pipes in a different sequence, and Chetaki came scampering back to him. He fed her a piece of flesh from his bag. Rokba's attitude to Chetaki completely changed after his climb. He caressed her wholeheartedly. No one would have guessed at that moment how closely their names would be linked in the annals of the Mulkan people.

Chapter–10

Love Tangle

Back at Fort Vitora, Kolakwa declared that Rokba and Mahadoo were assigned to lead the mission to capture Fort Sangram. Kolakwa decided to attack the fort after the rainy season, when the rocks would not be slippery.

Rokba practiced working with Chetaki and Mahadoo. Mahadoo shared with him some trick weapons.

From that day, Mahadoo moved his camp closer to Sangram, and Rokba corralled his goats close to Mahadoo's enclosure. Afterward, Mahadoo accompanied Rokba to graze his goats closer to Fort Sangram.

"Rokba, you are brilliant. I remember the day when you solved the puzzle box." Mahadoo said to Rokba one evening as they had dinner together.

"That was the best day of my life." Rokba smiled. "Society has mistreated me as far as I can remember. That day, I felt that there was justice in this world. Our Naresh had valued my life and asked me to do something for him. Henceforward, my life had a purpose. His goals became my goals. Until that day, everybody, including me, considered my life less worthy than a goat. But Kolakwa saw value in me as a person. I will render him such service that one day, when I die, even a Naresh like him will shed a tear."

"Don't talk about death, Rokba," Mahadoo said softly.

"And also, I met you on that day, Mahadoo," said Rokba as he picked up his dish.

Mahadoo could barely conceal his smile.

As the sun set over the mountains every day, Rokba played haunting tunes on his small bamboo flute. The musical notes traveled with the wind blowing from his hut to Mahadoo's camp. As he lay in his bed, the music enveloped Mahadoo in a gentle embrace. Some nights, the drizzling rain added a rhythm to the music. Mahadoo closed his eyes every night with a serene smile on his face.

* * *

One day, while returning to their camp, Mahadoo said to Rokba, "In two days, Mlecchas will celebrate the Kwekwe Dayat the Fort. We can take my magic tricks and perform a show for the soldiers. You be my assistant, and we can scout the Fort closely."

Early morning on Kwekwe Day, they reached Fort Sangram. As they approached the gate, Rokba saw a Mleccha for the first time. The man was as short as Rokba. He wore a long gray tunic to his knees and a leather belt over the waist. He wore loose trousers under the tunic. His long, curly, brownish hair extended from his leather helmet. He was well-armed with a straight sword and a long pole spear. The Mleccha guard yelled at Mahadoo in broken Mulki, "Stop! Why have you come here?"

Mahadoo replied in Mleccha language, "We are doing a magic show for the soldiers," as he pointed at his bag of tricks. With a hand wave, Mahadoo produced five copper coins from the guard's left ear. He placed the coinsin the guard's hand and smiled. The guard let them pass.

Once inside, they roamed the Fort under the pretext of trying to find a suitable place for the show, gaining an overall idea of the layout. Rokba followed Mahadoo around carrying his stuff, pretending he was mentally disabled.

When they reached the main entryway, they pretended to be amazed by its immense size. One guard boasted, "This is the most secure gate in the whole Mleccha land."

"What if an army with elephants comes?" Rokba said childishly.

The guard showed him the spiked outer surface of the door. Rokba admiringly touched the door. To further impress him, the guard demonstrated the lock mechanism and explained how wooden logs reinforced the doors, making them impossible to force open from the outside.

Between the grazing trips and the excursion to the Fort, Rokba decided on the best place to approach and scale the cliffs.

One evening, as they were returning to their camp, Rokba sang a song as he herded the goats. Mahadoo tried to join in, barely humming in rhythm, as he followed him absent-mindedly. Their tranquility was broken as they heard screams and cries for help in a girl's voice from the nearby field. They rushed and found two Mleccha soldiers attacking a peasant girl. Rokba jumped and, using the sharp knives hidden in his forearm bands, swiftly cut the throat of both attackers. They hid the bodies of the soldiers in the nearby ravine.

The girl was around their age and looked like a poor villager. They enquired the direction of her village and started escorting her back. The girl refused to follow them. She just stood there and started crying.

Between her sobs, the girl managed to say, "When the Mlecchas attacked, my husband ran away. Now that I have been dishonored, he will not take me back. My life is ruined." She sat on the ground, clutching her head.

Mahadoo sat down next to her. In a gentle voice, he echoed one of Saumitra's teachings. "When bad things happen to us, it is like two arrows hitting us one after the other. The first arrow is the event that hurts us. This arrow is not in our control. The second arrow is our reaction to the event. This second arrow is in our grasp. Be brave and triumph over the second arrow."

The girl stopped sobbing and wiped her face with her skirt.

After a few breaths, her face slightly lit up, "You are right."

But immediately, she whispered dejectedly, "Where will I go?"

Mahadoo thought for a second.

"Can you cook? My family needs help with their care," he asked.

"I can cook and do all the work necessary to run a household," the girl said, hopefully looking at Mahadoo.

"If you help me take care of my brothers and sisters, I will give you a place for shelter," Mahadoo volunteered.

Wiping her tears, the girl uttered, "Thank you. I am very grateful."

During this entire conversation, Rokba stood silently, watching the girl. The gentle breeze blew her hair across her tearful face. She pushed back the lock of her hair with her right fourth finger. He opened his mouth, but no words came out. Instead, he just stood frozen, awkwardly smiling.

As they started walking again, Rokba asked the girl, trying to catch her gaze, "What is your name?"

"Bhumi (*the feminine aspect of the divine representing the earth*)," the girl replied timidly, looking at Rokba with an admiring but scared expression.

After they returned to their area, Rokba corralled his goats and came to Mahadoo's camp for dinner. Throughout dinner preparation, Rokba's eyes followed Bhumi as she walked around. Later, he started playing his flute, sitting on a nearby rock. The calming music of the flute gently laid a cozy blanket on the surrounding hills.

As the days passed, Rokba started spending more time at Mahadoo's camp. Usually, he brought flour and vegetables. Often, he enquired, "Bhumi, is there enough milk for the children?" He stood as close as possible to her in the small kitchen area. "Take as much milk as you need from the goats."

One evening, as he was walking by, Rokba noticed Bhumi in the kitchen shed kneading the flour for rolling the flatbread. The aroma of vegetable cooking permeated the camp. Mahadoo was nowhere to be seen. Rokba hesitated for a few moments and entered the kitchen shed. He stood just inside the doorway. He admired Bhumi for a few moments. Then, picking up courage, he whispered, "I like you."Relieved that she did not become angry, he continued, "But Mahadoo was first to offer you refuge in his camp. I do not want to take you from him." Bhumi laughed shyly and said, "Mahadoo does not want me in that way."

"How can you be so sure?" Rokba asked, looking surprised.

"Because he likes you, Rokba. Don't you know that?"

"I do not know what to say. I knew it but did not want to know it," Rokba mumbled. He picked up a flatbread and stuffed it in his mouth, absent-mindedly chewing it.

Both heard footsteps rapidly moving away from the door of the tent. Neither had heard Mahadoo walking towards the tent, too engrossed in their feelings.

In less than an hour, Bhumi called, "Mahadoo, food was ready.". Instead of the usual enthusiastic cheer, there was silence. Mahadoo came furtively and sat in a corner. He avoided looking at Rokba. They sat around the campfire. Bhumi cooked well and made delicious food from the minimal resources in the camp. Throughout the dinner, Bhumi maintained a banter, bringing up new topics to keep the conversation going. Mahadoo and Rokba replied in monosyllables and single sentences, staring at their food, unable to look up at each other.

After Rokba left, Mahadoo asked Bhumi sadly, "Did I lose my closest friend? What is wrong with me? How do you understand my feelings?"

Bhumi hugged him gently and said, "Dramho makes flowers in all different colors. They all have different shapes, colors, and aromas. No flower is better than another. Some flowers are rare and not like others. Different does not mean wrong. Do not worry."

Later at night, the musical notes of Rokba's flute lulled them to sleep.

As the days passed, discussing the attack plans and practicing with Chetaki, the unease between the men decreased. They returned to their previous interactions as if nothing had happened.

One evening after dinner, as they sat in the yard admiring the evening sky, Rokba told Mahadoo, “Last night, I dreamed I had died. A large crowd was saying my name and talking about how great I was. Such a death would make life worth living. I was born a no body and never knew my parents. The man who raised me never talked about how he found me. Our Naresh first made me feel like a person. Every time I pray, I implore Dramho to take me from ‘no one’ at birth to ‘someone’ at my death.”

“Do not talk about death. Under Kolakwa’s rule, Atmaraj will be heaven on earth,” Mahadoo said enthusiastically.

“Do you think so, Mahadoo? Everybody always mistreats people like you and me who are poor and weak. Most of the time, it is our people and not foreigners who have abused us. We rarely interact with the Daityas or Mlecchas. In Atmaraj, the foreign invaders will be gone, but will our people stop exploiting the helpless among them?” Rokba questioned wistfully.

Mahadoo was at a loss for words, but after thinking for a moment, he replied, “Hurt and the resultant pain will always be there. All I want to do in life is make everybody smile and help people forget their pain briefly. I believe that in Atmaraj, there will be more occasions to smile, even without my magic tricks,” Mahadoo said sadly.

“I will fight and lay down my life for Atmaraj only because Kolakwa yearns for it. He has made me feel proud of my existence. If forming Atmaraj will make him happy, I will complete any task needed to achieve it or die trying.” Rokba stopped talking abruptly. Then, looking at Mahadoo, he whispered, “I will always do everything to make you proud of me.” The air was thick with unexpressed emotions. For a moment, the universe was motionless.”Where are you guys?” the silence was broken by Bhumi stepping out into the yard.

Many days, Rokba stayed at Mahadoo’s camp when the conversations extended into late nights. Mahadoo accepted life as it was and took the joy of whatever Rokba’s company he would get as a gift from Dramho. Sometimes, he asked Chetaki, “W*hy did Dramho make me the way I am? Is suffering and loneliness my only fate in life*?” Both the lonely beings stared at each other.

A dream of the fluttering Crimson flag just before he arose the next day reminded him why he lived. *Life would be better in Atmaraj. I do not know how. But it had to be.*

Chapter–11

Sangram

After the rainy season passed, Kolakwa selected the first day after the new moon night in the coming fortnight for the expedition to Fort Sangram. As he mingled with soldiers during his visits to Fort Vitora, Mahadoo overheard two Mormos expressing doubts about the mission's success. He conveyed this information to Saumitra.

Seeking to rectify the decreasing morale, Saumitra suggested to Kolakwa, "We should ask Dramho for guidance on Sangram."

Kolakwa ordered the council members and many Mormos to gather at the Dramho shrine in Fort Vitora. Rokba and Mahadoo stood at the back of the room while Saumitra addressed everyone. "The verdict boxes on each side of Dramho have lamps with equal amounts of oil. As per our tradition, I will light them and lock the shrine. We will re-enter after one hour."

He continued, "If only the lamp on the right side is burning, then it will reveal that Dramho has blessed the mission. If only the lamp on the left side is burning, then Dramho does not favor the mission. If neither lamp is burning or if both are still lit, we will repeat the process on the next auspicious day."

After lighting the lamps, everybody walked out. After an hour of apprehension, the guards opened the doors, and everybody followed Kolakwa inside the sanctum. Only the lamp on the right side was burning.Kolakwa exclaimed, "Dramho has spoken, and there is a blessing for the mission."

Everybody cheered, "Hail Dramho, hail Atmaraj."

After everyone left, Saumitra prayed fervently to Dramho, asking for forgiveness. Unbeknownst to everyone, Saumitra had slipped a few drops of a special liquid into the oil of the lamp on the right side to keep it burning longer. The liquid slowed the speed with which the oil traveled up the wick.

* * *

The week before the mission, Kolakwa, Rokba, and the few selected Mormos finalized the plan. Indicating at two younger Mormos, Rokba said, "These two Mormos and their fifty men will accompany me in the climb. They have trained with me for a long time. We have practiced fighting daily at night with the blades of the swords blackened with soot. They are also familiar with the fort layout and gate mechanism,"

Nodding to the remaining four Mormos, Kolakwa continued, "With your two hundred men, you will march to the front gate," He added, "Five men should smear their bodies with black soot and scout along the road to the gate after nightfall to ensure that there are no sentries along the path. If there are sentries, the scouts should finish them."

"Rokba and fifty soldiers will climb the cliff, overpower the guards, and open the gate before the main contingent of Mleccha troops is alerted. Then the two hundred will come in through the main entrance to fight the entire Mleccha contingent stationed there," Kolakwa summarized at the end of the meeting.

On the eve of the mission, spies brought news that a company of Mleccha soldiers had stopped by Sangram on the way to another fort. Kolakwa added fifty more men to the two hundred soldiers who would enter the main gate.

"You should add more soldiers to your group," Kolakwa suggested to Rokba.

"We have no more soldiers who can complete the perilous, exhausting climb and still have the stamina to fight," Rokba replied.

* * *

The night was pitch black. However, because of their frequent excursions, Rokba and Mahadoo were comfortable leading their men along the path through the hilly region. Four porters carried Chetaki in a cage covered with a cloth suspended on two poles. On reaching their pre-chosen spot, Mahadoo took Chetaki out of her cage. The nearby soldiers stepped back in shock, looking at her in the darkness. Mahadoo tied the rope to her harness, petted her, and gently banged the two steel pipes. Chetaki slowly climbed the sheer cliff wall and reached the top. Rokba gave a solid pull to the rope and felt a go. So, he swung the rope, and Chetaki adjusted herself. He pulled again, and this time the rope held firm. "Hail Dramho, long live Atmaraj," Rokba murmured. He removed his footwear and started climbing up the sheer face of the rock with a roll of stouter rope around his shoulders. He also carried anchors and a hammer covered with soft leather to minimize the sound while hammering. In the darkness, Mahadoo arched his neck, straining his eyes to penetrate the night, trying to see Rokba on the rock face as he scaled the sheer cliff. Mahadoo continuously murmured a prayer to Dramho as he took shallow breaths. His throat and lips were dry.

After what seemed like an eternity to Mahadoo, the stouter rope rolled down the cliff. Mahadoo started breathing more easily and backed away from the wall. Two soldiers climbed the rope carrying stouter ropes, tying them at the top and throwing them down the other ends. As more soldiers reached the top, fixing stouter ropes, more soldiers could start climbing up two or three at a time. Many soldiers gagged themselves so that screams would not come out of their mouths if they slipped and fell to their deaths.

Mahadoo moved to the side and banged the two metal pipes together. Then, waiting for Chetaki, he intermittently continued to hit the pipes to reveal his location to Chetaki.

As most climbers crossed the ramparts into the Fort, Chetaki crawled to him. Mahadoo continuously murmured prayers to Dramho, imploring him for Rokba's safe return.

"O, Chetaki, I wish I was a fighter and could join my Rokba," Mahadoo petted Chetaki. Unknown to all, Mahadoo also had a paralyzing fear of heights. The yelling and screaming from the fort alerted Mahadoo that the battle was starting. After one long glance at the summit, Mahadoo returned to his camp with the four porters carrying Chetaki.

Back at the camp, Bhumi was anxiously waiting. "Did the climb go well?" she asked. Mahadoo shook his head in the affirmative. Then, both hugged, repeatedly assuring each other about Rokba's safety.

Early the next day, Bhumi packed Mahadoo a heavy lunch, and he started walking on the path toward the main entrance of Fort Sangram. As he reached the bottom of the mountain, the Crimson flag was visible, flying over the ramparts. Tears of joy and pride rose in his heart. He ran along the path and reached the main entrance in half an hour.

He met some soldiers Rokba had trained at the main gate. Mahadoo felt sick to his stomach as they averted their glances with sad faces instead of beaming with joy at the victory. Mahadoo stopped, his feet stuck to the ground. After taking a few breaths and praying to Dramho, he passed through the open gates. The soldiers on the way fell silent and gazed sadly at him as he walked towards the part of the fort where Rokba and others had climbed the cliff. In the distance, he could see the Crimson flag draped over an outline of a human body on the parapet.

Mahadoo dragged himself towards the flag. As he pulled back the edge of the flag to expose Rokba's face, he bit his lower lip, muffling a moan escaping his mouth. He laid his head on Rokba's chest. This was their first touch. Many nights, he had imagined the warmth of Rokba's chest. Today, the cold stiffness of Rokba's body sent a sorrowful chill through Mahadoo. Mahadoo drenched Rokba's blood-stained shirt with his warm tears.

The soothing morning draft of the breeze made Mahadoo conscious that bystanders should not look upon his grieving as more than that of a dear friend.

Many bystanders had collected around them at a respectful distance. Mahadoo got up and started walking towards the gate of the Fort. As he descended the pathway, he noticed a young soldier calling his name and running toward him. Mahadoo wiped his face and stopped for him. Without waiting to catch his breath, looking straight into Mahadoo's eyes, the man said, "These are yours." He handed two knives to Mahadoo, whose throat tightened as he recognized them. Waiting for another two breaths, the young soldier whispered, "I know what you are going through. I am one of the few who can understand." He signaled to Mahadoo to walk and continued with him, narrating yesterday's happenings.

"After Rokba dropped the ropes, I was one of the first who ascended the cliff. As more men climbed over the wall, the Mleccha guards were alerted and raised the alarm. We easily overpowered the few Mlecchas we encountered. But as more Mleccha soldiers showed up, we realized that the traveling Mleccha soldiers who had come to the fort were no ordinary soldiers but elite crack troops of the Mleccha army. They immediately got into formation and started fighting back."

Seeing a flat-top large boulder by the path, Mahadoo suggested, "Let us sit down."

The man looked exhausted from yesterday's night fight. Mahadoo opened the food package that Bhumi had sent with him. Thinking of Bhumi again brought tears to his eyes.

After eating a few pieces of the flatbread, the man continued, "Nearly fifty of us who had reached the top were now facing over two hundred Mlecchas, many of them elite fighters. This abysmal situation disheartened our soldiers. Some started running towards the ropes, hoping to climb down and escape. Rokba rushed toward the ropes. I saw someone spit, grunting, 'The goat herder is running away.'."

Rokba ran to the ropes and cut them. Then, he yelled, "Hail Dramho, long live Atmaraj, we either win or die here. Nobody will retreat."

"There was no option for retreat. We now redoubled our determination and started fighting in earnest. I was fighting near Rokba. After I finished one Mleccha, I cut down the one just behind Rokba, preventing him from stabbing Rokba in the back. On my left side, I saw a giant of a man covered with leather armor and a helmet, killing our men with a single stroke of his giant sword, unaffected by their cuts. I realized that this was Shaisto. Rokba confronted him and began fighting. His stabs and cuts could not pierce Shaisto's armor. As they dueled, Rokba vainly tried to pierce the Shaisto's armor from all sides. Because of his agility, Rokba avoided Shaisto's powerful strokes. Unfortunately, Rokba tripped on a fallen helmet. Shaisto brought down his massive sword on Rokba. Rokba's sword broke as he tried to block the blow."

Mahadoo's breath stuck in his throat. Cold sweat emanated from his head, and a slew of tears from his eyes intermingled on his cheeks.

"Instead of running his sword through Rokba, Shaisto grabbed Rokba and lifted him by his throat to make a spectacle out of his killing Rokba. Shaisto let out a mighty roar. Everybody stopped fighting and started looking towards Rokba, flailing in the air. Suddenly, Rokba spat something from his mouth into Shaisto's eyes, causing them to burn. Still, his hands would not let go of Rokba's neck. With whatever tiny fragment of life left in him, Rokba clutched these precious knives in both arms and stabbed Shaisto's temples through the slit in his helmet. Shaisto dropped Rokba and fell backward to the ground." The young soldier's words sounded distant to Mahadoo. He did not want to hear about Rokba's heroism. He just wanted Rokba back.

"I ran my sword through the Mleccha and rushed to Rokba. As I cradled his head, he uttered, 'Long live Atmaraj. Hail Dramho,' as he left us to go to Dramho's abode." The soldier became silent. Both sat quietly, looking toward Fort Sangram. Pulling himself together, Mahadoo coaxed the young soldier to eat more and drink the buttermilk.

The young man continued, "Shaisto' scollapse caused utter confusion, during which our men reached the gate and opened it. With the new two hundred and fifty troops coming in, the tide of the battle changed direction. In a short time, we defeated the Mlecchas. Afterward, I removed the knives from Shaisto and cleaned them."

Mahadoo thanked the man for his kindness. Mahadoo wished him well, praying that he may find someone with whom he could live his life the way he wanted.

As he approached his camp, Mahadoo saw Bhumi waiting, staring toward Sangram. As he came near, she could see his face. Her face turned from anxious to grief-stricken. She rushed toward him. They held each other in a long embrace. In the privacy of their camp, they could grieve openly, intermittently trying to console each other. Mahadoo gave both knives to Bhumi. Bhumi held them tightly and clutched them to her chest. Afterward, she took one knife, put it in Mahadoo's palm, and closed his fist. They stood silently, holding each other's hands.

After a few days, Mahadoo came to Fort Vitora. For a long time, he sat with Kolakwa, Krikaneel, and Dramhodas in the Dramho shrine, where they shed tears and grieved Rokba's loss.

Later that day, Kolakwa issued an official decree, "From today, Fort Sangram would be called Fort Rokba in honor of the noble warrior and all other unnamed warriors who sacrificed themselves on Sangram."

As he watched the somber ceremony, Mahadoo palpated Rokba's knife in his pocket. *Rokba, my friend, you are somebody. People will never forgetyou as a pillar on whom Atmaraj was built.* Silent tears swelled up in his eyes.

"My Naresh, the local partisan men with help from the Atmaraj army, has cleared Mlecchas from the entire region of Sangram," Dramhodas updated Kolakwa.

* * *

After a few weeks, an emissary from the Ruler reached Fort Vitora, demanding that Kolakwa hand over Fort Sangram and the entire territory in the Mleccha region to the Ruler's army.

Kolakwa called the advisory council of Saumitra, Krikaneel, Mamalu, and a few senior Mormos.Kolakwa looked around the room. "How do you think we should respond?"

"Let us request Dingir to let us hold on to the Fort and lands to complete our conquest of the Mleccha. In addition, we should send a gift of gold coins and other valuables to Dingir to sweeten the deal. A letter will not be respectful enough. I can take the gifts himself and try to convince Dingir and Gangwo." Krikaneel volunteered.

"After the Mleccha conquest, we may turn more Zigadors to our side," Dramhodas added.

A senior Mormo asked, "What if Dingir does not agree with our proposal?"

"We will seek guidance from Dramho then," Saumitra closed his eyes in prayer.

* * *

On a crisp, early winter morning, two months after the victory at Sangram, Bhumi came to Mahadoo and stood quietly. Mahadoo studied her face. After a few moments of silence, he knowingly smiled. "A new life is coming, right?" For a few weeks, he had noticed a change in Bhumi.

An unusual radiance had developed on her face. She looked healthier than before. He had seen similar changes in animals. Bhumi silently nodded. Mahadoo waited expectantly. Since Bhumi volunteered no more information, he asked, "Do you know the father's name?"

"This is Rokba's baby," she whispered. Mahadoo smiled and stepped forward, tightly hugging her. "Rokba is back with us." Then, wiping his tears, he uttered, "We will have to look after you. No more heavy work."

"I am worried that if anyone in the surrounding villages learned that I have become an unwed mother, they would mistreat me and not allow me at the village well where we get our water."

"I will marry you, Bhumi, and claim the child as my own," Mahadoo smiled, gingerly touching her belly. That night, Bhumi cooked Rokba's favorite sweet dish of coarse brown sugar milk pudding. Both ate simultaneously, crying and smiling.

"I am getting married to Bhumi," Mahadoo announced to Kolakwa and Krikaneel. Both looked surprised but smiled, expressing their joy. The wedding was a small affair attended by Kolakwa, Krikaneel, and Dramhodas. In addition, Mahadoo invited the chiefs of the surrounding three villages and prominent villagers to witness the marriage.

"Bhumi is part of my family. She is a sister to me. I want to ensure she is cared for very well." Kolakwa announced to the guests as he blessed the couple. Kolakwa gifted Bhumi the lands adjoining Mahadoo's camp enclosure and the tax income from three surrounding villages. Bhumi joyfully thanked Kolakwa, "We can now have a permanent place to house more orphans."Although nobody said anything, everybody felt Rokba was with them, showering his blessings.

Chapter–12

Journey to Dabrahoor

As Krikaneel started preparation to go to the Ruler's capital, Saumitra taught him the protocol of the Ruler's court. They also revised lessons in the Daitya language. Kolakwa made the tribute to the Ruler appear bountiful by combining the treasury collected from Fort Rokba, gold coins obtained as ransom money from the Mleccha Queen for the Mleccha prisoners of war, and coins from Kolakwa's treasury. In addition, new clothes were sewn for Krikaneel in the style of the Daitya ruling class.

Before leaving for Dabrahoor, Krikaneel met his mother to pay respects. Her face was strained. Her worry lines looked more prominent than usual. He paid respect by touching the ground before her feet. "Don't worry,Mother;Dramho will care for me." Krikaneel tried to assuage her anxiety. "Krikaneel, my son, you have an excellent opportunity to present yourself in the Ruler's Court and showcase your brilliant mind. I sincerely believe you would become a top courtier of the most powerful Court in the world. This little rebellion will be crushed by the Ruler, eventually. I don't want my precious child, my only hope in the world, to be a sacrificial lamb in these games of the powerful people. They use people like us for their whims, and when they tire of that game, they move on, discarding us into the trash pile." She started crying. Krikaneelwas thunderstruck at this unexpected reaction from his mother. He hugged her tightly, wiping her tears. "I promise I will be back, Mother." Krikaneel dragged himself outside his quarters, breathing deeply, trying to calm the tempest in his mind.

After a brisk walk reciting the one-hundred-eight names of Dramho, Krikaneel went and paid respect to Mamalu and Saumitra. Both showered him with the benediction of a long, illustrious life and the success of this mission. A messenger rode ahead to convey information about his journey to the court.

The day before his departure, news arrived that Shamonda had died because of illness, worsening the already sad mood at Fort Vitora over Rokba's martyrdom. As he walked on the ramparts of the Fort in the cool evening breeze, Krikaneel expressed his conflicting feelings to no one in particular. *Why am I sad? Maybe because Shamonda caused my birth, although unacknowledged. He is the official father of my brother, who is mourning. Mamalu, who is like my mother, is now widowed and heart broken. Should I hate him for causing pain to my mother?*

He finished his stroll and walked towards his quarters. Before retiring for the night, he debated, *Should I ask my mother about Shamonda? I am uncertain whether she was a willing or unwilling participant in my conception. Moreover, I do not know whether she considered Shamonda the cause of ruining her life or if she had affectionate feelings towards him. Any knowledge in those matters will only distract me from the mission.*

Krikaneel got up after a few hours, unable to sleep. He stood outside, gazing at the stars in the skies and wondering *how it would have been to have a father. Kolakwa had a father only in name. As a child, I would feel jealous of Dramhodas when Ordora playfully carried him on his shoulders. There were other boys in the fort whose fathers indulged in intoxicants and beat their mothers. Is no father better than a terrible father?*

"I would have preferred a terrible father over nobody," he mumbled.

There are more pressing things to think about. Krikaneel forced his thoughts to the journey ahead to pull himself out of his melancholy.

* * *

The following day, Saumitra took Krikaneel to visit Kolakwa and express his condolences. Reflexively, Krikaneel hugged Kolakwa. Neither said a word. As he stepped away, Krikaneel was surprised by the tears pooling in his own eyes.

Surprisingly, Kolakwa addressed them in a steady voice."Our father's death is detrimental to Atmaraj's future, removing his indirect protection. The Zigadors who hate us are now unencumbered to plot our downfall."

Looking at his father's portrait, he continued, "My two brothers in the West seem uninterested in developing a relationship with me. This reluctance is understandable. Who in their right mind will side with us? Our relationship with the Ruler is like poking a wild beast with a sharp stick. Dingir may decide to snuff our existence. If he judged the stepbrothers were siding with me, he would also attack them."

Krikaneel started on his journey to Dabrahoor the following day. As expected, the trip was uneventful. Saumitra had told him, "The Zigadors through whose realms your group will pass will ensure your safety. The Ruler will be upset if anyone robs the tribute being taken to him."

After they safely reached Dabrahoor, Krikaneel rented a residence in the city. His secretary applied for an appointment for a presentation at the court of the Ruler.

* * *

"We should try to scare the Mleccha queen into offering terms for capitulation instead of engaging in actual warfare. Then, we will not have to fight with the Mlecchas and lose resources," Kolakwa expressed to Saumitra as they had lunch together at Fort Vitora.

"I will instruct our spies to leak information to the known Mleccha spies, exaggerating the Atmaraj army's strength and spreading false news of a large number of Zigadors joining us on Ruler's order. They will also boast of the imaginary massive aid we are receiving from the Ruler for the invasion. In addition, we will spread rumors of potential invasion dates," Saumitra replied.

"I will order the Mormos to increase the number of soldiers and war equipment near our borders with the Mlecchas," Kolakwa said.

* * *

A few days passed as Krikaneel waited for the appointment. One morning, there was a commotion outside the residence. Krikaneel went out and noticed a hunchback woman beggar asking the guard at the front door to let her in. She was insistent about wanting to see the master of the house. The guard was trying to drive her away. Krikaneel came to the front yard and noticed the beggar lady winking at him. He asked the guard to let her in and took her to a private corner of the courtyard.

After ensuring no one was overhearing them, the lady cleared her throat. She spoke in a man's voice, "My handler has instructed me to share information with you. Every few days, I will come begging in front of your house early in the morning. Get a small zavba plant and plant it in your front yard. Offer water and prayer to the plant every day in the morning. Whenever you see me begging, let me in and share the sacraments from the offerings to the zavba plant. I will drop you a note with any relevant information. Do not try to find out about me. That would not be good for either of us."

Krikaneel offered the disguised man a glass of water, which he drank before he continued. "I am unaware of who my real master is, but my handler told me to do this." Then, the man pointed to the left ear and continued, "He wishes you success in your mission."

How does this man know of the Braznee clan's skin deformity? Does he know that I have one too? Since Shamonda is dead, the informant's handler must have been close to our family. Krikaneel knew he would never find out. He hoped that the informant and his handler were benefactors, not enemies.

After the initial meeting, the informant visited Krikaneel's house every few days. On some occasions, the informant, dressed as a beggar lady, would sit under a tree in the yard and act as if he were having a religious discussion with Krikaneel. He shared, "Many of Gangwo's spies report on every aspect of the life of people visiting or living in the capital. In this manner, Gangwo has prevented multiple revolts and assassination attempts on him and Dingir by getting early information. Potential powerful and well-connected rivals to Gangwo have been assassinated by poisoning or carefully orchestrated accidents. Weaker enemies were publicly killed to make a spectacle to act as a deterrent to others. Gangwo is reputed to have a supernatural ability to read people's thoughts because of the information he collects routinely."

Krikaneel also connected with a few spies Kolakwa had in the capital community. Some were well-established merchants, while others did menial jobs at the palace. Many low-level information gatherers did not know for whom they worked and just gathered information for money.

After a week, Krikaneel received an appointment at the Ruler's court.

As he prepared for his presentation at the Ruler's Court, Krikaneel's thoughts turned to Gangwo. He remembered the interaction he had with Saumitra a few weeks ago.

Saumitra had sat him down and shared, "The most dangerous person on Dingir's side is Gangwo. Most people do not know about Gangwo's origin. Those few who know prefer to keep it to themselves, fearing for their own life."

Saumitra had taken a deep breath with a look on his face as if he were somewhere else, describing something he was seeing. "Gangwo was not born a Daitya. He was the son of a Mulkan Zigador, who led a rebellion against the then Ruler, Dingir's father. When the Ruler's forces attacked, the other Mulkan Zigadors, who had initially sided with Gangwo's father, turned their backs and abandoned him. As a result, Gangwo's father was defeated. It is said that young Gangwo hid in a concealed closet and witnessed the horrible death of his parents at the hands of the Daitya soldiers. Later, as the Ruler walked through the captured palace with his princes and generals, Gangwo came out of hiding. He stood before the Ruler, saying, 'I hate my people and everything which was mine. I prayed to Dramho, but he did not help my father. I pray you to let me want to join your people'."

Krikaneel could sympathize with the child Gangwo.

Saumitra continued, "Seeing the deep misdirected hatred in the Gangwo's eyes, the then Ruler must have realized that he had found a weapon that would be very useful for him and destructive for the Mulkans. He took the little boy with him. He instructed the Daitya preachers to make Daitya markings on Gangwo's face and teach him the tenets of the Daitya faith. Nobody knows if Gangwo truly internalized the Daitya dogmaorif he functions with pure hatred against the Mulkan people."

Saumitra paused before adding, "For the first few years, the Ruler treated Gangwo as a domestic personal slave. Later, this changed."

Krikaneel remembered how he had tried to visualize Gangwo's appearance. "I have heard that Gangwo is of colossal stature," he said.

Saumitra nodded. "Yes. It is said that in his early teenage years, Gangwo met a wandering medicine man who shared with him a powder that, when drunk with milk, resulted in exaggerated muscle size. Gangwo routinely took the powder, which caused him to gain excessive height and tremendous strength. It also gave him uncontrollable rage and caused him to lose the ability to have children. He never married, and none of his female slaves ever became pregnant. Seeing his tremendous strength and cunning, the then Ruler kept Gangwo with him on his trips and asked him to beat, torture, and kill people."

"How did Gangwo become so politically powerful when he was a mere hunting dog for the Ruler?" Krikaneel's curiosity got ahead of his patience.

Saumitra replied, "Over time, the Ruler observed Gangwo was strong, ruthlessly devious, and very smart. He started giving him increasingly important assignments and politically sheltered him from other courtiers. Slowly, Gangwo must have observed and internalized the inner workings of politics in the palace."

"Some people create their destiny, regardless of where they came from," Krikaneel commented with a face beaming with admiration, forgetting for an instance that this man wanted to destroy everything he cherished.

Saumitra smiled slightly, looking at Krikaneel's face, and continued, "In his early youth, Gangwo protected Dingir, one of the Ruler's physically and intellectually weaker sons. In the turmoil that followed the Ruler's illness and death, Gangwo neutralized all the elder brothers and other rivals of Dingir. Using his political acumen, inhuman strength, and animal instincts, Gangwo installed Dingir as the new Ruler. Gangwo became the muscle and brain running the empire, with Dingir sitting on the throne. Even after Dingir became an adult, he greatly feared Gangwo, having seen his physical power, intellect, rage, cruelty, and the infiltration of his loyal people within the administration and the army. Dingir understood that his ability to stick to power and survive depended completely on Gangwo."

As he remembered his teacher's radiant face, Krikaneel recalled that after narrating this information, Saumitra appeared uncomfortable. He had let that feeling pass without dwelling on it. But now, Krikaneel wondered, *how does Saumitra, for a Mulkan monk, know so many details of the Ruler's history?*

On the appointment day, a guard guided Krikaneel into the Court. Krikaneel could not help but marvel at the scene before him. The Court of the Ruler was in a vast, majestic hall. Music poured from the fenestrated walls, behind which musicians played various instruments. There were massive crystal chandeliers imported from faraway lands suspended from the ceiling. Beautiful colored glass scones were fixed to the walls. There was a display of exotic weapons mounted on the walls. Large paintings glorified the exploits of Dingir's ancestors, some trueand many exaggerated. The hall had enormous, decorated pillars supporting the roof.

Previously, Krikaneel learned from one of his spies that there were underground passages under the great hall with spiral stairs going up the bases of the immense hollow pillars. Spies with excellent hearing abilities sat inside the pillars, monitoring the discussion of the Zigadors and other dignitaries as they socialized in the hall before Dingir's arrival. The walls of the pillars also had tiny holes to watch the people.

As Krikaneel awaited the Dingir's arrival, a courtier beside him started making small talk. Krikaneel volunteered that this was his first time at the Court. The courtier got excited and started sharing, "The official reason for the throne to be on that very high pedestal is to symbolize the stature of the Ruler and his nearness to the heavens above." Then, whispering, he continued, "The real reason for the elevated position is for the Ruler's safety and ability to see everybody in the court. Below the Ruler's throne, hidden inside the large pedestal, are guards who are watching us through tiny slits. If anybody attempts to attack the Ruler, there are doors on the pedestal which can be flung open, and the guards can jump out and protect the Ruler."

After checking around, he furtively pointed to the slightly lower level, to the right of the Ruler's throne, "Gangwo will sit on that chair from where he can be close to Dingir."

Krikaneel thanked the man, acting overly impressed by his knowledge.

After one hour, Dingir arrived. Various administrative matters were handled, and many dignitaries were presented. Subsequently, the announcement was made for Krikaneel's presentation.

As practiced earlier, Krikaneel addressed Dingir. "O, protector of the world, your radiance greater than the midday sun." He presented the tribute. Although not very dazzling, it was enough to please Dingir, as Krikaneel could guess from his smile.

"My master, Kolakwa, has begun the conquest of Mleccha lands on your behalf. He sent me here to request that you let him keep Fort Sangram, which will make capturing the rest of the Mleccha lands easier. After we eradicate the Mlecchas, you can decide on the future fate of that land."

After hearing the petition, Gangwo requested Dingir to delay his decision for a day.

Early the following day, a monk came to Krikaneel's residence. After Krikaneel gave him food, they had some 'philosophic discussion.' The monk was the same informant who had changed his appearance. He shared that his sources in the court told him that Gangwo's spymaster had confirmed Krikaneel's identity and the rumors of the circumstances around his birth. Later, one of Kolakwa's spies told Krikaneel that a friend who fanned Dingir overheard Gangwo comment that Krikaneel had an uncanny resemblance to Shamonda.

* * *

"Why don't we stomp the Mulkan baby snake while he is here and kill off the other snake in the south afterward?" Dingir asked, admiring his reflection in the giant mirrors adorning the audience room.

Gangwo replied. "O wise one, I want to keep this snake here so that he gets used to the wealth and feeling of power, stoking ambition to be a Zigador in him. After a year, when he goes back, we will supply him with men and weapons. The two brothers will fight and divide the Mulkans, causing disillusionment in any other Mulkan snake thinking of raising his hood against us. If we kill them both, there is a risk that someone else will continue the struggle."

"You rightly guessed my thinking."

"We can eliminate Kolakwa anytime we deem necessary and in such a way that no one ever will dare to rise against you," Gangwo remarked as he departed.

The next day, when Krikaneel was again presented to Dingir, Gangwo announced, "The Ruler has decreed that he will let Kolakwa keep the Fort and the territories till the Mleccha territory is won. Until then, he desires

Krikaneel to stay in the capital until the Sangram area is returned to the Ruler. Since Shamonda has left the world, the Ruler expects Kolakwa to, over time, achieve his father's status. By his stay at the court, Krikaneel will learn the ways of the court and better advise Kolakwa."

Back in his house, as he paced in his room, Krikaneel thought, *Gangwo is using me as a surety that Kolakwa would follow through on his promise of returning the lands. Gangwo must have deduced that Kolakwa considered me his brother and would not risk my life. I am more than willing to die for Atmaraj. We won Fort Rokba by paying a steep price of too many lives. To lose them in exchange for my single life is not a good bargain.*

Krikaneel's men carefully leaked false information to Gangwo's spies, who were watching his house. They describe how happy he was to stay in the capital and that he may soon look for a wife. They also planted misleading stories of his admiration for Gangwo and his jealousy of Kolakwa.

A fortnight passed with Krikaneel spending his time learning about the Daitya faith and their thinking. He improved the spy network by recruiting new informants. He tried to evaluate the loyalty of different Mulkan Zigadors to the Ruler. However, as days passed, Krikaneel started getting very restless.

I had suggested to Kolakwa the plan to come here, thinking that either Dingir would accept or reject the offer. I did not expect to become a prisoner and be held at ransom. My thoughtlessness is causing problems for Atmaraj, Krikaneel brooded in a dark mood.

Maybe I deserve to die. Why not kill Gangwo or Dingir before dying myself? I can meet Gangwo and stab him. Perhaps I will invite him for dinner and poison him. One day, they are going to kill me. I should do as much damage as possible before I die, Krikaneel brooded as he stared at the darkness outside his window.

If not Dingir or Gangwo, I could get easier targets like the Daitya priests who preach hatred against Mulkans. Maybe I can slip manahshila into the food at the feasts for Zigadors in the Ruler's palace. The more I kill before I die, the better for Atmaraj, Krikaneel thought.

I promised my mother that I would come back. He remembered his mother's crying face.

Every day, dark thoughts kept on bubbling in his mind. Now, all alone, sleeping demons were waking up in his mind. *Was my mother, right? Is Kolakwa intentionally keeping me here permanently, hoping Gangwo will eventually kill me? He may still believe that I am his competitor.*

Escaping was impossible, given the round-the-clock watch on his residence by Gangwo's men. Further, he did not want to leave until Kolakwa signaled him to do so. Every day, Krikaneel alternated between positive and negative thoughts.

One day, the informant, disguised as a monk, stopped by his house. After talking to Krikaneel briefly, the man said, "I can tell that you are suffering."

Krikaneel was silent. "I can help you," the man continued.

"I am not sick," Krikaneel shouted as his face flushed.

"You are the same age as my son. A couple of years ago, my son had similar changes. He tried to harm himself. Luckily, I got there at the last moment and saved him. A medicine man gave him a powder which helped him. I will get you medicine from him. You must take care of yourself. Atmaraj needs you. We all need you," the man pleaded with kindness in his eyes.

When the man returned the next day, he handed Krikaneel a powder packet, instructing, "Divide the powder into eight parts. Take the powder with warm milk every day before meditating on Dramho."

Krikaneel drank the powder with milk the following morning, meditating on Dramho. As the medicine took effect, Krikaneel closed his eyes. He felt his surroundings blur. The Dramho in front of him transformed into a red ball of fire and started talking in Saumitra's voice.

"You are my son, my instrument of restoring justice and balancing good and evil. Never forget that I am always in you. Respond to every situation after careful thought. Do not involuntarily react."

Krikaneel experienced a similar state every day after ingesting the powder. After one week, the spy noticed Krikaneel had improved. His face shone with fresh determination. The spy advised Krikaneel to decrease the powder he added to the milk for the next week and later stop taking it. Simultaneously, Krikaneel increased his meditation and physical exercise.

Krikaneel's mind cleared after the medicines. He started calmly evaluating the escape options.

I am going to escape soon or die trying, Krikaneel thought.

Chapter–13

Escape from Dabrahoor

One day, a strange, unsightly beggar arrived at Krikaneel's house. He looked like he was afflicted by leprosy. The guards tried to drive him away, but his condition filled Krikaneel with compassion, and he ordered his guards to let him in and feed him.

"Kolakwa sent me to bring you home," the beggar murmured to Krikaneel. Immediately, Krikaneel took the beggar inside. Once they were in the privacy of the meditation room, the monk removed his beard, fake hair, fake warts, and false teeth, revealing that he was Mahadoo.

After hugging each other tightly, Mahadoo said, smiling, "I knew my kind-hearted Krikaneel would never drive away a suffering soul."

"I have been begging in this area for over one week and have studied the routine of the spies," Mahadoo shared with Krikaneel during lunch. After lunch, Mahadoo proposed an escape plan. Since the Ruler's soldiers and Gangwo's spies constantly watched the house, any escape would be immediately noticed, and they would be chased and caught. Mahadoo's plan would give them a head start before the chasers got on their trail. To prepare for the escape, Krikaneel started feigning severe headaches and screaming that the light was bothering him. He started losing his temper frequently and fired all the locally hired help and most of the trusted servants who had come with him from Fort Vitora, accusing everyone of stealing and plotting to kill him. He secretly ordered the trusted servants to go home. Only two servants remained with him.

Krikaneel also started shutting all the house's curtains during the daytime to stop sunlight from coming in. In the evenings, the Gangwo's spies could see Krikaneel's shadow and the shadow of a few remaining servants moving across the curtains of the windows.

Meanwhile, Mahadoo prepared cutouts that matched the profiles of Krikaneel and the remaining servants. He suspended them with ropes that were twisted to provide clockwork motion. The cutouts periodically moved across the lights when the operator released the mechanism. As a backup, a few cutouts also had a floatation system mechanism for movement, with the gradually falling water level caused by slow dripping moving the cutouts. Long-capacity lamps with large oil reservoirs were also constructed to cast shadows of the cutouts over the windows.

For fifteen days, Mahadoo ensured that there would be no chance of failure in his systems. Then, Krikaneel and the two servants shaved off their heads and facial hair and adorned clothing worn by monks. The shaved heads and absence of facial hair were a sign of an order of monks who extensively traveled, preaching about complete surrender and devotion to the Divine without using any physical representation.

"When we interact with people, slightly stoop and round your shoulders. Also, hang your jaw and pull it back. It will be difficult to disguise your warrior physique and square-jawed rugged feature," Mahadoo smiled as he punched Krikaneel's shoulder. "You look like a well-fed beggar yourself," Krikaneel quipped as Mahadoo put on his leper disguise, hinting at Mahadoo gaining weight since Bhumi had taken over the kitchen of his encampment.

In the middle of the night, Mahadoo left through the front door toward the Ruler's spies, watching the house from across the street. He started coughing, asking them if they had any intoxicants. Mahadoo's horrible, disfigured face and hands were so repulsive that the spies rapidly walked away. The disguised Krikaneel and servants seized the opportunity and slipped out the back door. Walking through the shadows, they reached one of the smaller exit gates of the city. A person from Krikaneel's group approached the guards. "Our sick colleague needs intoxicants to fall asleep. We have run out of our supply and are leaving the city to find more in the surrounding villages."

After one look at the disfigured disguise of Mahadoo, the guards stepped away and waved their hands,asking them to leave the city. Outside the city, in the nearby broken village shrine compound, Krikaneel's men had arranged and paid a local Mulkan man to meet them and bring four horses, weapons, and provisions for further travel. It was dark when they reached the predetermined spot. The place looked deserted. As they huddled together, discussing the next action plan, they were startled as twenty soldiers surrounded them. The soldiers grabbed them and tied their handsbehind their backs. The group leader was barely an adult Mulkan man with a prematurely hardened face. He had a prominent crimson circle on his forehead. He got down from his horse and, sneering at Krikaneel, said, "Traitors! I will cut off your heads and present them to the Ruler as a gift from my brother. I am sure he will be so pleased that he will make me a Zigador."

Krikaneel realized they were betrayed by the man who was supposed to help them. Such behavior had been the repeated story of Mulkans, wherein throughout history, men had broken their promises and betrayed their kind for money and other material consideration. He stood with a dejected face. *How has my noble race degenerated into this wretched state? I am responsible for Mahadoo and these two soldiers losing their lives for my rescue.*

Krikaneel silently prayed, "Dramho, let the Mulkans regain their self-respect and sense of self-worth."

"Master Rana, should I pay him off?" a soldier asked the leader, pointing to the traitor partly hiding in the shadows. The name 'Rana' perked Krikaneel's ears. His spies had told him that Rana was the name of one of the two sons that Shamonda had begotten in the Northwestern Kingdom.

Maybe I should engage with the man and try to discourage him from killing us, Krikaneel thought. *However, it looks like he knows we are Kolakwa's people and still wants to turn over our cut-off heads to the Ruler.*

Rana grabbed Krikaneel's neck and held a sword to his throat, screaming abusive words. Krikaneel could feel the sharp edge on his skin and expected a quick slash. Rana's companion soldier brought the flame of the torch close. Suddenly, Rana's face froze, and his facial expression changed. "Baba," he muttered. *Baba* is the baby word for father in Mulki.

He has recognized our father's features in my face, Krikaneel thought. Old soldiers who had been around since before Shamonda grew his beard stared at the familial skin deformity on Krikaneel's face. When he grew facial hair in his teenage years, he quickly hid the deformity by growing a beard and purposefully styling his beard differently from what he had seen in Shamonda's portrait. Now clean-shaven, the skin deformity was exposed. Further, without the beard, his facial features looked prominent.

"I cannot do this. You are my blood," Rana murmured in Krikaneel's ear.

Then, he lowered his sword and yelled to his soldiers, "Looks like these guys are just mendicants. Let them go. You will not repeat this, or I will cut off your tongue and nail it toyour horse's hooves." His soldiers knew their master could do that and worse, to their family members.

"May Dramho protect you, my brother," the leader whispered to Krikaneel. The four horses, hidden behind the temple, were given to Krikaneel's party. Rana also gave some money to Mahadoo for their journey. Without delay, the Krikaneel, Mahadoo, and the two soldiers climbed the horses and started riding south at great speed.

After riding overnight, the group made camp in the jungle. As the two soldiers were cooking food over the fire, Krikaneel noticed Mahadoo was staring at him as he cared for the horses.

"I wonder why they let us go. Did you play a mind trick on the leader or recite a magic spell that Saumitra taught you?" Mahadoo asked after he finished. Krikaneel just smiled, not wanting to lie. *Why did neither Mahadoo, Rokba, nor Dramhodas ask about Kolakwa and his shared skin deformity when we were growing up? Maybe everyone knew*. The two other soldiers never asked questions. They were just happy to be alive and going home.

Mahadoo had designed his cutout-and-light contraption to give them three days' advantage before Gangwo's spies would notice their escape. But, in a stroke of luck, it gave them a lead of five days. The spies watching the house had changed after three days. The new spies took anothertwo days to notice that the shadows had stopped moving. When the spies entered the house, they found a note Krikaneel had left addressed to Dingir.

"O Great Master of the world

I must take leave of your hospitality due to my ill health. I was also scared of the men who watched my house day and night. I wanted to take your leave personally, but I fear Gangwo. Thank you for your hospitality.

Your faithful servant

Krikaneel

The party mainly traveled in the early morning hours and at dusk when there was less likelihood of meeting other travelers. They avoided larger villages and cities, stopping at small hamlets where simple village folks fed them and offered shelter. The rainy season had started, making travel difficult. Fortunately, the rivers had not flooded yet.

After riding for ten days, Krikaneel's group reached Fort Vitora safely. Kolakwa was beside himself with joy. They all hugged and went to the Dramho shrine to offer their gratitude. Late into the night, Krikaneel and Mahadoo shared their adventures. It was over two months since Krikaneel had heard Kolakwa's voice. Krikaneel realized that in their entire life, they had never been apart for more than a few days. It felt nice to hear Kolakwa's laughter after so long. They had not laughed heartily forever. Krikaneel mentally debated. *Should I share with Kolakwa that I had met our half-brother? Maybe later.* Mahadoo shared that the enemy soldiers let them go because Krikaneel recited some magical spells that confused them. Kolakwa did not press the issue. Such free laughter was rare in the life of the three friends.

Kolakwa shared with Krikaneel the extensive fake preparation they had made for invading the Mleccha. The same troops arrived at the border multiple times with extensive fanfare, creating an illusion of a massive buildup of the army. Tents were erected with empty boxes, supposedly containing arms from the Ruler for helping the invasion. A plan was leaked to the Mleccha spies that the invasion would start after the rainy season.

Kolakwa and Krikaneel prayed that the Mleccha's would fall for this gambit. An actual invasion would cost too many lives and considerably weaken the Atmaraj army.

Chapter–14

Securing the Sea

One summer evening a decade earlier, a little girl around eight was making a sandcastle on one of the many beautiful beaches of the Sangram area. She crouched as she decorated the castle with colorful shells. Nearby, a boy of similar age sat on a boulder. He had paused his quest of collecting seas hells to watch the girl. Three other boys were roughhousing nearby, pushing each other in the sand. The quiet girl caught their attention. They surrounded the girl. "What are you doing?"

She replied, "I am building this fort to fight the foreign invaders."

The boys laughed. Their leader, a somewhat bigger boy, kicked the castle, breaking it. "I am a Mleccha soldier, and I destroyed your castle."

The boy sitting on the rock watching the scene unfold curled his fingers into tight fists and rushed to the girl's rescue. He abruptly halted as he noticed the girl pick up a fistful of sand and throw it into the face of the bully. Then she briskly got up and, clutching a giant seashell, crashed it on the boy's head. The boy screamed and ran away, crying. The girl turned towards the other two of his friends, who started screaming and running away.

Brushing the sand off her clothes, the girl sat down and started rebuilding her castle. After waiting for a few instances, the boy rose from the rock and started walking toward the girl. The girl stood up, the seashell in hand, ready to strike again, but the boy said, "I mean no harm. I am just bringing you these colorful shells for your castle."

Gently smiling, he opened his fists, showing the colorful seashells, "My name is Daryaveer (*brave of the sea*). What is your name?"

"I am Veershri (*spirit of courage*). I live over there," she pointed at a nearby hamlet.

Daryaveer sat down next to her and started helping her rebuild her castle. He suggested adding large pointy rocks under the sand covering.

"If someone kicks the fort after you are gone, they will break their legs, hitting the hidden rocks."

The girl shook her head in agreement.

"You are smart. I was going to hide pointy sticks in the sand," she replied with a mischievous smile.

"Let us use both," the boy agreed.

They decorated the fort with colorful shells. Happy with their joint project, the girl smiled at the boy.

Now, after over ten years, the girl was still smiling at the boy as they held hands and walked on the same beach in the moonlight. They were an unusual couple. For the last three years, along with their band of friends, they had been attacking Mlecchas outposts using the weapons supplied by Kolakwa's spies. Daryaveer and his friends learned to fight from an old sailor who had worked most of his life as a pirate. The old sailor had cared for Daryaveer since his early childhood. Daryaveer's father had perished in an attack by marauding Mlecchas, who had also carried away his mother. Occasionally, Daryaveer would wander to the remains of his old destroyed house and rummage through the ruins. On those days, his adopted father would discern the despair in his eyes. "Daryaveer, our life is a sailboat. We may want to sail in one direction. But therewill always be winds pushing us in the opposite direction. If you blame the wind and do nothing, you will be flung far away from your desired destination. Learn the skill to tack your boat. Navigate your life in a zig-zag manner to beat the opposing forces of circumstances." Daryaveer never submitted to the vagaries of circumstances.

The girl's father trained Veershri, and Veershri's father was one of the men who had worked on the ships of a neighboring Zigador of Basrud. As soon as she was old enough, she joined her father on his fishing expeditions and learned the art of sailing. He had taken her to visit the Zigador's ships and familiarized her with the workings of various equipment. Many other fathers used to laugh at Veershri and her father when they saw them practice sword fighting. They jeered. "The only weapon a woman needs to learn to handle is a rolling pin with which she can beat her husband."

As they reached adulthood, Daryaveer and Veershri's parents wanted them to get married and settle down. The couple discussed their future together on their many late-night romantic walks on the beach.

"Let us wait some more time. Based on the stories of Kolakwa that I have heard from the traveling storytellers, I believe he is not just any ambitious Zigador but is truly striving to establish Atmaraj," Veershri said.

"We should contribute to the creation of Atmaraj," Daryaveer agreed.

Two weeks after the newly named Fort Rokba became part of Atmaraj, a group of twenty youths led by Daryaveer came to Fort Vitora. They wore traditional fishermen's clothes but weapons similar to Kolakwa's soldiers. Nobody noticed that there was a woman in the group dressed in a man's clothes.

"My Naresh, we are from the Sangram and adjacent coastal parts. With your help, we liberated our land from the last of the Mlecchas. Please accept us in the Atmaraj forces," requested Daryaveer."We are traditionally fishermen and are more comfortable on the sea than on the land. My men are brave and will fight to protect our motherland and the generous sea. We need your guidance and resources. With your support, we can build warships and arm them with weapons so that no foreigner might dare to come toward our motherland from the sea." Daryaveer fell to his knees to show his complete submission.

Kolakwa took a step forward and lifted Daryaveer with his shoulders. "We need people like you and these men to protect our most vulnerable coastline. Our ancient Mulkan kings had large navies for war and trading with faraway lands. Over the last few centuries, this tradition has been forgotten. Do you have anyone who knows deep sea-worthy shipbuilding?"

"Unfortunately, no. All our boats are small to mid-sized boats, which are used mostly for fishing and traveling between coastal villages," Daryaveer said.

"I will grant you men and resources to build ships. But first, we will find boat builders and sailing trainers," Kolakwa promised.

"My soldiers will also teach these men fighting techniques," Dramhod as added, looking at Daryaveer.

"Fighting on ships requires shorter swords and smaller shields. Our teacher who worked on ships of foreign pirates has few of these weapons." Daryaveer requested. "We already have the longer swords for fighting on the land, given by your men," he added.

Kolakwa ordered a meeting of Daryaveer with the head of the iron smiths. A new design for short swords was created. The blades were slightly longer than the distance between the elbow and the fingertip and broader than usual, with a sharpened portion extending from the midpoint to the tip. The proximal half was left blunt. It would block the strikes from the opponent's sword, while the sharp part would cut the opponent. A hook was attached to the hand guard that could catch onto the opponent's handguard and pull his sword from his hand. This hook could also pierce the opponent's face if it got close.

"Assign two Mormos and their men willing to relocate to the coastal villages to safeguard the ship-building site. Send a senior Mormo to scout for suitable coastal areas where we could build forts as safe harbors for holding the ships," Kolakwa told Daryaveer and Krikaneel.

After the men had retired for the evening meal, Krikaneel approached Kolakwa. "My Naresh, I always follow our teacher's advice of 'trust but verify.' Some men with Daryaveer have Mleccha features. Our spies will strike friendship with the group for the few days they were on Vitora and observe them closely."

"I have looked into the eyes of those young men and saw the fire for freedom burning in their souls," Kolakwa replied.

Krikaneel had his men continually eavesdrop on the coastal men in their lodging rooms. There were four guest lodging rooms in the fort. These rooms had secret double walls with a narrow corridor between the two sets of walls on all sides. Kolakwa's spies would enter the corridor through a hidden door and overhear the happenings inside the rooms. The spies were rotated every few hours so they did not doze off. Through this system, they continuously monitored the guests.

After a couple of days, Krikaneel reported, "My Naresh, the men with Mleccha features are offspring of relationships between the marauding Mlecchas and the local women. These men are fiercely loyal to the land since their local mothers raised them. The men are genuinely interested in working for Atmaraj, liberating themselves from the yoke of foreign rulers and becoming a bulwark against any seafaring invaders."

Over the months, the building of multiple ships started. Kolakwa hired a Frangi shipbuilder and his son to bring the best knowledge and naval technology.

Simultaneously, work started to build a fortress in the adjacent area. It was named Swaminidurg — fort of the Swamini Sea.

One day Krikaneel came to Kolakwa. "A Frangi emissary has arrived asking to meet us." After necessary precautions, the guards let in the emissary. The Frangi emissary spoke broken Mulki and came with excellent gifts of weapons and clothing material.

After bowing to Kolakwa, the emissary said, "My Naresh, the Frangi government has instructed an arms trader to give you a good discount on weapons and equipment to build your ships and volunteer services of naval warfare strategy teachers to you. We are your friends. Please remember our help when you become the masters of your coasts and grant us trading permission."

"We will remember your help," Kolakwa said.

How will we keep these foreigners at arm's length once their utility is completed? Already, Shantiprastha has Daityas and Mlecchas. Now, these Frangis have come.

After the emissary was gone, Krikaneel remarked to Kolakwa,"I believe that the Frangi calculation is that the stronger our navy, the more we could fight and neutralize the Mlecchas in this part of the world. Worldwide, the Mlecchas and Frangi are similar in strength, with competing ambitions to control lands and trades. They think we would never be strong enough to fight the Frangi navy. Any conflict between us and Mleccha navies will keep both our fleets weak in this region, so it would be easy for them to subdue us in the future."

Daryaveer visited Fort Vitora every few months to update Kolakwa on his progress.

Daryaveer's men enthusiastically absorbed the knowledge provided by the Frangi teachers, which added to their previous knowledge of the sea accumulated during generations of fishing. The men had been instructed that if they had information that the spies from Mlecchas or the neighboring Zigadors were nearby, they would purposefully make it appear that they could not handle the weapons on the ships. The spies sent messages to their masters that Kolakwa's navy was a joke with bumbling fools playing with ships; hence, they were not a threat to the masters.

Over time, Atmaraj carpenters built multiple ships. Kolakwa instructed Daryaveer, "Make sure our men work closely with foreign craftsmen and learn their techniques. One day, the hired Frangis will leave. We will need local skilled labor to sustain and raise the navy to its future glory. The Frangis are friends today but will look to colonize us in the future, just like the Mlecchas."

Chapter-15

Triya

One cloudy morning (incidentally, the eleventh day of the month, considered auspicious by Mulkan tradition when most fasted and led a day of religious activities), Krikaneel went to the Dramho shrine on the fort to offer his morning prayers. He ran part of the way to avoid being soaked by the drizzling rain. That morning, he had smiled looking in the mirror. His hair and beard had grown back in the last month, thanks to nutritious food intake and the medicated hair oil his mother applied to his head before retiring each night.

He held the doorframe of the shrine as he tried to catch his breath. However, he forgot to breathe as he saw a partially drenched girl who looked like she was finishing her prayer. He quietly stood at the entrance, watching, mesmerized by her profile as she gracefully recited a prayer and offered sweets to Dramho. Her jet-black hair was fashioned into a long, single braid extending to below her waist. She had entwined yellow-orange flowers in her hair.

He wanted her praying to continue for eternity. Eventually, she turned around and smiled. She stepped forward and shared the blessed sweets with him. A pleasant feeling of lightness came over him. He nearly dropped the flowers he was carrying in his right hand. He leaned against a pillar and tried to regain his composure. Mesmerized by her almond-shaped face, he felt the urge to offer her the flowers he had brought for Dramho. The girl had a prominent linear scar on her forehead, which added to her allure of unsophisticated, raw beauty.

Krikaneel usually addressed all the girls as 'Sisters.' But somehow, drowning in the girl's sparkling black eyes, the thoughts in his mind were not brotherly. "Who are you? We have never met before," he asked, trying to sound casual.

"I am Triya (*Tree-ya, one who smiles*), Dramhodas's younger sister. Today, I visited the Fort with my brother to pray to Dramho."

Krikaneel wondered why she would visit the Fort to pray at the Dramho shrine while there was one in Dramhodas's village. Notwithstanding, looking at her face, he wished she would come to pray here every day.

"My name is Krikaneel. I work with your brother."

The instant he mentioned his name, he could have sworn that her eyes widened for a moment. She blushed and started looking everywhere except at Krikaneel. He was unsure what caused this sudden change in her behavior.

As he attempted to talk to the girl, a string of garbled sounds came from his mouth. He felt the blood rush to his face as a sudden warmth overcame him. His heart raced. He had never felt this way.

The two just stood there, with Krikaneel's eyes lingering on her down-turned face while she stared at the ground. A bird chirped overhead, breaking their trance. The rain had stopped. Triya coyly smiled and hurriedly left the shrine.

His morning prayers were less devout than usual. The girl's face would not leave his thoughts.

After a few days, there was a festival of Goddess Shreeti. All the women from the families of soldiers living in the nearby villages were invited for the celebration at the fort. The women wore elaborate festival clothes and adorned themselves with jewelry. As he walked to Kolakwa's quarters, Krikaneel came across a familiar face, walking with Dramhodas's mother. "Hail Shreeti," he bent his head to greet the lady. "Hail Dramho, Krikaneel." She returned his greeting with a slight nod. Then, with a shy smile, he greeted Triya, who silently gave abash fulgrin.

She is so beautiful Krikaneel felt pleasantly lighthearted as he continued on his way. Thoughts of Triya kept surfacing in his mind every few hours. He soon realized this distraction was not good and tried to concentrate on the political matters at hand.

A week later, around noon, Krikaneel saw someone at a distance who looked like Triya, carrying a bundle of utensils on her head, dressed in work clothes. She was drenched in sweat, dust covering her face and exposed skin.

"Triya," he greeted her from a distance. Walking briskly, he barely caught up with her. "Nice to see you again." He smiled. Triya's face carried a look of embarrassment. "How is your mother?" Krikaneel tried to engage her in small talk to delay her leaving, but Triya pulled herself away. "I need to get these utensils home. Mother is waiting."

As he stood watching Triya walk away, he decided to act on his emotions. He went to Saumitra and matter-of-factually told him what had happened. Saumitra's response was a slight smile. At dinnertime, Krikaneel went home and confessed to his mother. After moments of thought, his mother pleasantly replied, "She would be a good wife for you, coming from a warrior family. She would understand the sacrifices required of a warrior's wife. You will be a good husband, as you are kind and understanding. My baby has grown into a strong, very handsome man." But immediately, her countenance changed. She turned and appeared busy with her housework. After Krikaneel retired to sleep, his mother prayed at the Shreeti shrine in the corner, "Mother Shreeti, please help us. My son has no official lineage. Which self-respecting family would welcome a relationship with us? Krikaneel will be heartbroken if the girl's family refuses our proposal." She wept silently.

Saumitra visited Krikaneel's mother the following morning, and they left together. When Krikaneel came home that evening, his mother jubilantly told him, "My son, I have good news. You are to marry Triya, Ordora's youngest daughter and Dramhodas's younger sister."

His mother continued, "Saumitra took me to Mamalu and explained the situation. Mamalu immediately called for one of Triya's older brothers from the village and Dramhodas. Fortunately, they were available to come. After they arrived, Mamalu made us sit in the adjoining room. She wanted us to hear everything so there would not be any misunderstanding. After Mamalu asked the men to sit down and offered them snacks, she breached the subject of the possible wedding."

Krikaneel's mother stopped talking. Krikaneel got worried as she dabbed her eyes. *Did someone insult her?*

She continued, "After the initial formalities, Mamalu told the men, 'Krikaneel is my son, same as Kolakwa. Would you please do the honor of allowing him to wed your little sister?'"

"Because I think Dramhodas's elder brother must have looked hesitant. Mamalu declared, 'Krikaneel is Kolakwa's blood. Even if he was a vagrant child not related to any noble family, his actions till now make him the noblest humans we know.'"

Krikaneel's mother's eyes were now profusely watering as she described the events. "Krikaneel, even if you forget me as your mother, never forget Mamalu."

Gaining her composure, she continued, "Dramhodas's elder brother stated, 'My father has taught us to judge people based on their actions, not their birth. I am willing and privileged to have this relationship. I was hesitant because I still think of Triya as a little girl. Please give mea few days to ask her opinion.'"

"What did Dramhodas say?" questioned Krikaneel asked anxiously.

"I saw him happily smiling when we entered the room," his mother replied.

In a few weeks, Triya and Krikaneel were married in a ceremony at the bride's village. Mamalu wanted the wedding to occur in the Fort on a grand scale. But Dramhodas's elder brothers prayed to her to permit them to conduct the wedding in their village, as Ordora wished. Dramhodas ensured that the marriage between his beloved sister and best friend would be so extravagant that everyone would remember it for their lifetime. They politely refused any monetary help from Mamalu and Kolakwa.

Like her name, Triya always smiled and brought joy everywhere she went.

Sadly, the joyous days were over soon. After four weeks, Saumitra suddenly fell gravely ill. He requested Mamalu, Kolakwa, and Krikaneel to his bed. Saumitra motioned with his hand and addressed Kolakwa, "My Naresh, I request you to appoint Krikaneel as my replacement to advise you. He is ready and will ensure you will never miss my presence."

Then, as his breath strained, he uttered with extreme effort, "I want you to understand that the true enemies of our people are not the Daityas or the Mlecchas. The real enemy is the divisions among us. No force can defeat and enslave us if we are united. Even if you successfully drive out the Daityas and the Mlecchas, if we cannot unite, another conqueror may enslave us in the future. Think about this. Hail Dramho. Long live Atmaraj." Saumitra permanently closed his eyes with a peaceful smile.

* * *

"The rainy season is over," the General of the Mleccha armyflared his already bulbous nose. "Let Kolakwa come. We are ready to crush him, my Queen. We are not some local Zigadors who can be swatted like insects by these upstarts and wannabes."

The Admiral of the Mleccha navy nodded, agreeing with his colleague.

These great soldiers have led the Mleccha armed forces through many successes, yet they lack political foresight. Well, that is why I am the Queen, the Queen thought as she gently smiled. She sat on the throne dressed in a shimmering white dress, looking elegant and cultured.

"We are the rulers of the seas. If the rainy season had not made the seafaring so hazardous, we could have got help from our motherland," the Admiral said.

The Queen looked at both commanders with the facial expression of a mother disappointed with her children. She rose and walked towards them. "My brave warriors, we should think long term. We are traders who bring cheap goods from other countries and flood the markets of this land. Our goods are cheap and do not last long. Our cheap goods made the local people abandon their more expensive locally made products. The reason for having this entire colony is that we found an opportunity. We recently lost so many men in our fight with the Frangis. That was for our survival. We may win the fight to protect our lands from Kolakwa, but we will lose too many men in a head-on fight. We always choose battles in which we have a distinct advantage."

The Queen picked up a fistful of nut samples in the presentation dish in the corner and poured them back."These lands we control are like the goods we carry from port to port. While the goods are on our ships, they are ours. Every merchant knows he should not get attached to his goods, and when a buyer comes along, he should be happy to sell the goods at a profit and move on to find better deals. If the merchant is alive, the trade able goods can come and go. These lands are just like those tradeable goods."

She looked on the wall at the painting of her cousin Shaisto with Fort Sangram in the background, putting on a facial expression of immense sadness."We cannot sacrifice too many of our men for these goods. Today, if we lose the land, we can have it back at the next opportunity, but if we lose too many of our people, getting their numbers back will need years of procreation and nurturing to mature the babies. Can you calculate how much time and resources will be wasted? The profit balance makes little sense. I cannot afford to lose fully grown Mlecchas for acres of a trade able commodity. No, we will not fight them."

She waited in silence for a few seconds. Both the men stood uncomfortably, shifting their weights from one leg to the other, avoiding the Queen's penetrating gaze. Hearing no counterargument, she continued. "Let us devise a plan to minimize the loss of money and goods, and then we will wait for an opportunity to recuperate our losses. Meanwhile, we shall seek other opportunities. Time will always bring more opportunities. Every storm that starts will always end. We only need to outlast it. Remember, the good sailing season is much longer than the dangerous stormy season." The Queen finished her berating in a calm voice. She then left the room.

"The demons in hell must be feeling lonely," said the General. "Their mother is here with us." The Admiral shook his head in agreement.

The two men then joined two surveyors and two accountants the Queen had instructed to determine which lands made the least profit and could be surrendered to the Ruler with negligible loss.

Later, in the treasury room, servants prepared to pack the tribute and gifts to be sent to the Ruler with the treaty of capitulation. They packed heaps of gold coins, precious jewels, perfumes, fine clothes, and art objects. A much smaller second pile was in the other corner of the room. Seeing the Queen enter, the servants stood up. "Pack the Ruler's share in carved expensive boxes," she ordered. "Kolakwa's share can be packed in ordinary boxes. Tell the armory chief to pack enough superior-quality weapons for Kolakwa to arm five thousand men. Also, throw in a few samples of the newer weapons, which might entice him to buy more."

The treasury minister looked at her in a shocked manner. "My Queen, why do you want to give weapons to our enemy?"

The Queen was very annoyed but maintained a calm face. In a pleasant tone, she assured him, "My trusted wise minister, Kolakwa, will not fight us anymore. His next fight will be with the Ruler."

She took a long breath and continued, "We give Kolakwa weapons so he can hold the Ruler at bay. As they become equal in strength, they will fight each other for a longer time and leave us alone. The stronger Kolakwa becomes, the more wealth he has and the more weapons and goods he will buy from us. The weaker Dingir becomes, the more weapons he will buy from us to keep supplying his troops to fight Kolakwa. To grow crops, you must plant seeds that are not used as food but give returns many times over," she narrated in a single breath.

Looking pleased by the awestruck expression on the minister's face, she continued, "As we are his suppliers, Kolakwa will make sure that nobody attacks our trading posts. And we will not have to attack him since he is our customer."

She smiled ominously. "Until the profit balance makes sense."

Chapter-16

Kolakwa's Wedding

A few months passed, and one morning, a small party arrived at Fort Vitora requesting to meet Mamalu. After the guards conducted the necessary security precautions, Mamalu granted them a private audience. The party's leader was a lady who was the sister of a Mulkan Zigador in the southeast portion of Kolakwa's lands. Mamalu welcomed the lady with appropriate respect.

"Sister Mamalu, I have come to you with a proposal. My brother has a sixteen-year-old daughter, and we propose a wedding with your son, Kolakwa."

The party had brought gifts of clothes and jewelry for Mamalu and Kolakwa. They also presented sweets and flowers as an offering for Dramho. Mamalu asked her servants to lodge the party comfortably in the Fort.

That evening, Mamalu requested Kolakwa's presence in her chamber. As usual, she was sitting on her wooden swing, gently swaying. This swaying helped her think clearly, reminiscent of her childhood when she played on this swing next to her father, listening as he discussed politics with his Mormos and sons. Kolakwa saluted her as he walked into the room. He remained respectfully standing. "Mother?"

She called him near and made him sit beside her on the swing. Caressing his face, Mamalu said, "My son, the time has come for you to get married." Kolakwa declined respectfully. "Mother, I am sorry, but this is not an appropriate time. There is so much work needed to expand Atmaraj. Our work is risky. I do not want to tie any other person's life to my life, which is in constant grave danger."

"My son, the primary function of marriage for people like you is the production of an heir for continuity of line, increasing the number of warriors, and facilitating geopolitical alignment of powerful families. The other party also has similar ideas when they enter this contract," she explained.

"What about the girl's wishes?" Kolakwa asked.

"Both you and the girl can, of course, say no, but usually, the bride and groom are just the pieces in the political board game." Mamalu sighed and ran her hand on Kolakwa's back, gently patting him.

"The girl's age is appropriate. The aunt is good-looking, so hopefully, the niece will be too. A relationship with a powerful Zigador in the south would also help you with military support and future expansion in the south."She glanced at Shamonda's portrait and continued, "If the person with whom we marry turns out to be good, that is a gift from Dramho. I married your father because that was the best thing for my people since I had lost my father and brothers. My people needed a powerful protector. Fortunately, your father was a good man. Hopefully, this girl will be beautiful and kind, becoming a dutiful wife and mother to your heirs."

"Mother, if you think this is the right decision, I am ready to do whatever you say." The practical wisdom and reality of life were clear to Kolakwa.

There was no portrait of the future bride. They did not discuss her abilities, likes, or personal wishes. It was a geopolitical treaty. *Ironically, sometimes ordinary people had more say in how their lives progressed than the rich and the powerful*, Kolakwa wistfully thought. Mamalu ordered a servant to convey a message to the visiting lady guest requesting an audience.

Mamalu met the girl's aunt with sweets and gifts in her chamber. She shared the good news with the visiting family. Soon after, guests departedin a hurry for further preparation. Mamalu asked Kolakwa to call the Advisory Council. They debated whether to send invitations for the wedding to the Zigadors outside the Atmaraj, the Ruler's Court, and the Mleccha queen. The presence of many foreigners in Fort Vitora would increase the risk of spies and saboteurs. "It would be difficult to have our people minding so many guests' whereabouts and activities," Dramhodas said. They decided to make the wedding a small-scale affair. Further, Kolakwa insisted on not having a frivolous display of wealth to conserve resources. Mamalu fixed the date on an auspicious day in two months.

* * *

As the date drew closer, the wedding preparation was in full swing. Two weeks before the auspicious day, a bird catcher arrived at Fort Vitora and asked for the Brago. He had heard that there were many pigeons in the Fort's granary whose droppings made lots of mess. Since there was a wedding in two weeks, he offered to get rid of these pigeons. After the bird-catcher quoted a reasonable price, the Brago accepted the service proposal. The bird-catcher returned the next day with his two assistants and pieces of equipment. They caught all the pigeons and took them away in a few hours.

A week before the wedding day, the large marriage party arrived with extensive gifts of jewelry, clothes, food, and weapons. A reception party waited at the gate to welcome the guests. The bride was carried in a special palanquin. Her father and two brothers accompanied her. The bride's favorite sturdy black horse followed the palanquin. She had also brought along her pet cheetah.

The servants decorated Fort Vitora with flower garlands. In the Mulkan tradition, geometric designs were drawn on the ground with colored rice flour in the center of large open areas. These designs decorated the space and added to the festive mood. In addition, this tradition shared the joy of the festival with even the insects by feeding them. After the festivities, the servants swept the flour into corners where ants and insects could feed on it. These areas were cordoned off later by spraying clove and peppermint oil around them so the insects did not spread to the other parts of the Fort. Domestic animals were given extra feedings of their favorite foods during the festivities.

Krikaneel ensured the guests were looked after and meticulously watched for untoward actions. Triya was foremost in helping Mamalu, who treated her like a daughter and shared some of her clothes and jewelry. Krikaneel arranged extensive donations from the royal treasury to the Dramho shrines. Food and money were distributed to disabled veterans. Free meals were organized at both Mulkan and Daitya places of worship. There were feasts on all the forts of Atmaraj. In most villages, the priest conducted special worship services to bless the newly married.

A delegation arrived from the Mleccha Queen with gifts. This arrival was surprising, as Kolakwa had not sent an invitation to the Mleccha Queen.

The Mleccha Queen sent presents comprising a beautifully decorated wooden bed, a carved armoire, and a chair swing. These pieces of furniture were from faraway lands across the seas. But the most valuable gift was a chain mail coat. Tiny metal rings were interconnected to make a flexible metal sheet that was put together as a long-sleeved undershirt extending up to the neck on the backside, with a detachable portion wrapped around the head. Separate pieces, which could be wrapped around the waist and thighs, were also included. Because of its flexibility, the mail chain armor did not obstruct any movement. Further, it was lightweight and did not make the wearer appear bulky.

As everyone was admiring the gifts, Dramhodas was poking the chain mail coat as if not sure as to the quality of the armor. As if guessing the thoughts in Dramhodas's mind, the leader of the Mleccha party asked permission to prove the strength of the armor. He donned the armor and wore his shirt over it. Then, he requested Dramhodas to attack him with his sword. Dramhodas stepped forward and, for the first attempt, gingerly took a swipe at the man. His shirt was torn, but the man was still smiling. Dramhodas significantly increased the strength of his blow, to no avail. Frustrated, Dramhodas slashed the man with all his might. The man flew back a few feet, falling to the ground because of the impact from the considerable strength of Dramhodas. However, after removing his clothes and armor, there was no injury to his skin. Dramhodas and the other Mormos were highly impressed. "The only weakness of this armor is a powerful stab with substantial force," warned the leader.

Turning to Kolakwa, the representative stated, "My Naresh, this armor was made by artisans from a faraway country and took almost one year to make. Each ring was handcrafted and intertwined with other rings. The metal is also an alloy of secret composition."

He took two slender knives from another box wrapped in a beautifully embroidered, jewel-encrusted cloth.

"For their thinness, the knives are strong and extremely sharp. The craftsmen made these from the same alloy as the chain-mail armor. The knives hide inside these sleeves, and the sleeves go around your forearms. They are for emergency use."

The representative also delivered a personal letter from the Queen addressed to Kolakwa, reminding him of their friendly relationship and requesting Kolakwa to be true to the friendship when the need arises.

The Mleccha party was given good hospitality and sent back with appropriate return gifts.

"I wonder how the Mlecchas knew about the wedding," Kolakwa asked Krikaneel.

Krikaneel replied, "My Naresh, most likely, our servants were traveling the countryside to purchase flowers and other decorative materials for the wedding. The news of such a major event must have spread through the villagers to the Mulkan traveling traders. The traders are intricately connected with the Mleccha traders, who must have alerted the Queen."

"We need to learn from them how to improve our network."

Three days before the wedding, Kolakwa was on his evening stroll. He saw a figure mounted on a tall black horse coming from the dwelling of the bride's party. Kolakwa recognized his future bride's horse. *Could this be my bride? But brides traditionally do not venture out doors for a few days before the wedding,* he wondered. The rider had typical riding clothes. He pretended to look in another direction but watched from the corner of his eyes. Even in the few strides of the horse, he realized the person was an expert rider. The rider trotted towards him and, in a girl's voice, asked, "In which direction is the best path for a short stroll?" He tried to appear as nonchalant as possible as he faced the confident, pleasant voice. "This way to your left goes to the eastern lookout post. The ride is pleasant and goes by the Dramho shrine."*She is beautiful*. Kolakwa was pleased, looking at her oval face with a cute nose, piercing light brown eyes, and curly hair peeking from her turban. He was surprised at the sword hanging from her side on her supposed pleasure ride.

As the girl thanked him and continued her trot, Kolakwa admired her seated profile from the back. *She has an authoritative voice. A straight back and square shoulders, and that sword. Our life together will be interesting*. He smiled as he headed back to his chambers. *I should have confirmed her identity*. Kolakwa cursed himself.

* * *

On the morning before the wedding day, a guard noticed two pigeons sitting on the roof of the granary. That part of the granary was on fire. The guards tried to extinguish the fire by throwing water. Seeing something suspicious, a guard brought down one of the pigeons by shooting an arrow. The guard found that someone had tied a fuel-soaked cloth ribbon to the leg of the pigeon. This ribbon had been set on fire and lit everything the bird sat on. Flocks of pigeons were seen flying towards the roof, each with flames arising from their feet. The guard frantically tried to extinguish the fires, starting in multiple places. There were too many pigeons flying in for archers to shoot. One guard rushed to Krikaneel's house and explained what was happening. Kolakwa also ran outside and saw the pigeons approaching the granary.

Many tents, decorations, flags, and banners throughout the Fort caught fire. Everyone, including the guests, was frantically throwing water to extinguish the flames.

Krikaneel started coordinating the firefighting and ordering archers to spread around the fort to prevent the pigeons from landing.

Kolakwa ordered his sentries to instruct the guards at the gate and on the fort's various lookout points to ensure that no enemy soldiers were attacking the fort, using the fires as a diversion to distract the security arrangements.

A guard announced that Mahadoo had arrived at the fort. He was panting and could barely speak. "Let out the royal falcons." It looked like he had run a very long distance. Mahadoo tried to steady himself but passed out. Kolakwa ordered a servant to run and tell the royal falconer to free all the falcons. He ran to the falconry himself to ensure that the order was followed. Then, seeing the falconer argue with the servant, he shouted, "Open all the falcon cages. Free the birds." The falconer was surprised but opened all the cages of the aviary.

The Falcons flew into the skies and, seeing the pigeons flying toward the Fort, started attacking them. On seeing the Falcons flying toward them, the pigeons flew away from the Fort towards the forest. Luckily, the trees were green, and the fires on the feet of the pigeons were extinguished. In the meantime, Kolakwa ran back to check on Mahadoo. Mahadoo was regaining his consciousness as Krikaneel sprayed water on his face. Kolakwa hugged him.

"Even the falcons are willing fighters for Atmaraj. The falcons saved our Fort today, Naresh," Krikaneel said, petting a falcon who had returned to Kolakwa. "Looks like the bird catcher was working for one of our enemies. Pigeons have a strong homing instinct. When released, they fly back to their nesting area carrying the burning stripes of cloth the bird catcher had tied to their legs. Such horrible cruelty to animals." The Brago then came and kneeled before Kolakwa. "It was my fault. I agreed for a bird catcher to clear the pigeons' nests." Kolakwa forgave the man.

"My Naresh, fortunately, no human life was lost in this attack. So many pigeons, however, have perished," Krikaneel reported to Kolakwa.

Krikaneel sent some men and spies to figure out who the bird catcher and his master were. But the men had disappeared from the area.

Kolakwa ordered, "Do not replace the burned decorations. Let everyone realize we must be ever vigilant for danger to Atmaraj from outside and inside."

* * *

The marriage ceremony proceeded at the auspicious hour, even though small fires were still smoldering at a few locations. The priests conducted the ceremony according to ancient traditional rituals. There were many symbolic components in the rituals. A garment on the shoulders of the bride was tied to the garment on the shoulder of the groom, symbolizing the holy bond. The couple made circles around the sacred fire, reciting their vows, with the fire representing the Divine as a witness. The priest reminded the groom and bride of their duties to each other, their parents, family, and society. The bride and groom took oaths of supporting each other and lifelong loyalty. Both tied gold necklaces around each other's necks. The bride's brothers lifted the bride to reach the height of Kolakwa's neck, symbolizing the lifetime support of the brothers for their sister. The brothers also carried the groom around the matrimonial tent to signify his inclusion in their family. Mamalu gifted the bride a fragment of her original wedding dress, tied to another strip from Mamalu's mother-in-law's wedding dress. In some families, long, unbroken chains of garment pieces were passed for generations. At the pre-decided auspicious time, guests rained flowers and grains upon the couple, symbolizing the societal approval and support of the union. The irony of singing and dancing in the background of damaged decorations and the smell of burned cloth and wood was not lost on the guests.

* * *

After the marriage ceremony, Kolakwa went to his decorated sleeping quarters to meet his new wife. Sitting next to her on the bed, he could hear a low-pitched growl and hissing coming from the corner of the room. Surprised, his hand reflexly went to his sword as he noticed a cheetah ready to pounce on him. The bride instantly shouted, "Tipki, no!"

The cheetah reluctantly settled down. The bride raised Tipki (spot) after being found as an orphaned cub in the forest near her home. The bride got up and walked towards the cheetah. Gesturing by her hand, she asked Kolakwa to come closer. She gently petted Tipki and introduced Kolakwa to her. Kolakwa extended his left hand, protecting his dominant right. Tipki licked his palm. As she settled in the corner, the young couple returned to bed.

Looking at his bride, Kolakwa asked, "Are you happy about the wedding?"

The girl, Savitri (Saa-vee-tree, *ray of light*), coyly looked at him. "I had told my aunt to ask for your hand in marriage. My father and brothers were not keen on this relationship since you are known as a troublemaker. They are worried you may be short-lived because of your aggression against the Ruler. Further, your activities would also cause trouble for my family. I have heard about you and your mission. I insisted on this proposal. Since I am the youngest child and sister, my father and brothers have never denied my wishes and demands, however foolhardy they may be. Hence, here I am." Kolakwa's eyes widened as he tried to clench his gaping mouth.

Most women in his life appeared subservient to their husbands and brothers. An exception was his mother. There were warrior female goddesses in the Mulkan pantheon and female warriors in Mulkan history. *This girl was special.*

"My Naresh, I have one request for you, which I pray you will grant me," Savitri gently asked.

"Yes, I shall grant you whatever you ask," Kolakwa whispered.

"Let me continue my weapons training and horsemanship." Savitri smiled in a demurred manner.

Kolakwa was stunned by the person who was now his wife. He was glad that he agreed to Mamalu's idea of marriage.

"Do whatever you want; I will never stop you," he uttered as he cradled her hand.

Chapter-17

Savitri

Savitri's father was a Mulkan Zigador in the southern parts of the plateau. They were an ancient family. The Zigador treated his people fairly, and the subjects lived happily under his leadership. He was blessed with a girl child later in age. She was named Savitri, bringing freshness and new hope to the family. Sadly, his wife died five years after the birth of the baby. The Zigador's mother and sister helped him raise the child. The girl was brilliant and inquisitive. Her upbringing was unusual, thanks to her grandmother.

During childhood, her grandma told her stories of great female warriors in history. All the stories had the hero using not only her physical strength but also her wit and organizational skills to defeat opponents with greater advantages. Savitri's favorite hero was Queen Amma, whose father, brothers, and husband died fighting the Daityas. She continued leading her people and fighting the Daitya invaders for many years by uniting allies who otherwise would not work together. Queen Amma maintained her freedom throughout her life. Woefully, after her death, her son surrendered and became a Zigador for the Daityas.

As she approached her early teens, Savitri started hearing from her friends the stories of atrocities committed by the Zigadors of the surrounding lands.

"Grandma, I want to become a fighter to protect the people."

Her Grandma sadly replied, "You are a girl. Fighting is not for you. When you get married, have many sons who will fight the bad people."

"No, Grandma, I want to fight myself. Goddess Vitora is a girl, too." Goddess Vitora, after whom the famous fort was named, was a female deity in the mythological times of Mulkan folklore that Shreeti created to kill evil demons harassing the people on earth. "I want to be just like Vitora. I will ask Father to teach me to fight."

"Father, I want to learn to fight with a sword," Savitri requested of her father one day. Her father never refused the demands of his unusual darling daughter. He laughed. "You will stop this nonsensical demand after a few days of practice when you realize how difficult it is to wield a sword."

Every morning, Savitri showed up at the arms teacher's place wearing her brother's old clothes from a younger age, which were more proper for sword fighting. The weapons master found her a smaller sword, given that she was a girl. But in a few weeks, she proved her strength, graduating to using a standard-sized weapon. Savitri's father was surprised when the arms teacher approached him after a few weeks, expressing great admiration for Savitri's skill and strength. "She is among the best I have taught. She makes up in speed and cunning what she lacks in strength."

"You mean one of the best girl students?" asked her incredulous father.

"No, my esteemed Zigador, of all my students are boys except her," the teacher replied. He then asked permission to teach her archery and unarmed combat.

Savitri, being a child, especially a girl, was not allowed into the room where her father, brothers, and Mormos discussed political maneuvers. However, she had found a place in the adjoining corridor where she sat and overheard discussions, resulting in a detailed understanding of the political layout of the local area and the Ruler's empire. Over the years, she learned from hearing the discussions of those experienced and politically shrewd men. Her father knew about her eavesdropping but did not stop her. Her aunt and arms instructor would answer queries on unfamiliar words and concepts.

Savitri's aunt, who lived with them, was also an intelligent woman who was widowed at an early age. She lived vicariously through her niece. She taught her as much as possible from books and the knowledge she had gathered over her life.

Years passed, and Savitri knew unless she took the initiative to do otherwise, she would be married off to some Zigador's son, who, after marriage, would relegate her to child-rearing and kitchen supervision. As she matured, her friends, the daughters of her father's Mormos, shared the stories of an unusual young man, Kolakwa, who was addressed as Naresh, not a servile title of Mormo or even Zigador. They told her about his quest to establish Atmaraj. Over a few years, she gained as much information as possible through her friends and the traders who came to sell their wares at her father's fort. She decided to take matters into her own hands and took her aunt into confidence.

* * *

Savitri could barely contain her smile as she trotted away from the young man. Over the last few days, she had confirmed the identity of a young man walking near her dwelling. Kolakwa was not only a hero dedicated to the cause dear to her heart, but was also an attractive, robust man with prominent cheekbones and narrow, keen eyes. She was at a loss for words to describe his presence to herself, other than his few facial features. But whatever she felt in those few instances of their interaction was very desirable. As the evening wind blew from the west, she tucked her locks into the turban. As she basked in the golden glow of the setting sun, surveying the golden mist across the landscape of her future home, she thanked Shreeti for making her prayers come true.

* * *

Savitri's father called her into his chamber the day before the wedding. He unwrapped a red silken cloth bag and presented her with a sword. "Savitri, this sword belonged to Queen Amma. It was abandoned in the junk after her passing. I managed to get this sword from her son, who did not seem to value it. I trust you will keep it safe and, if needed, use it one day at Shreeti's service."

Savitri picked up the weapon and admired it. It had many nicks and dents from many battles. Sliding her fingers on the handle, she could sense an energy wave flowing through her palm into her whole body. She closed her eyes and reverently touched the flat part of the blade to her forehead. The father and daughter locked their eyes, unaware of the significance of that moment.

Everybody wants a hero to be born, but in the neighbors' household and not in their own house, her father pondered. *Life is hard for heroes and the people who love them.*

Chapter–18

Danger to the Newly Blooming Atmaraj

Back in Dabrahoor, Gangwo was preparing to meet Dingir. As his servant was helping him get dressed, he admired the exquisite silver sculptures in his room, which the Sond people had recently gifted to him.

Immediately after the Mleccha Queen had capitulated, trouble started on the Northeastern side of the Ruler's realm. The Zigadors at the border had come together to invade the adjacent Sond kingdom. The Sonds had long accepted the Ruler as their overlord and sent a yearly tribute. Their land was densely forested and not suitable for agriculture. They lived off the forest and were economically backward and poor. There was a recent discovery of silver ore in their lands. The bordering Zigadors considered the Sonds an easy target and invaded the Sond kingdom, wanting to capture the mines. But the Sonds not only defeated the Zigadors but also invaded and captured their land. Nearly six months had passed, negotiating with the Sonds and returning of the seized land.

As Gangwo waited in the Ruler's audience room, he looked at the reflective surface of the wall. Incidentally, his reflection and the reflection of the adjacent Dingir's portrait coincided, such that it looked like he was on the throne. He half-smiled. He knew he was being observed by the bodyguard hiding in a recess of the wall. The bodyguard was deaf and whose only function was to jump out to protect the Ruler if someone attacked him. Beyond the ornate door were the Dingir's private quarters, which had everything any sensuous person would ever desire.

Gangwo had entered the private quarters many times as a child slave during the rule of Dingir's father. The childhood exposure to violence towards women, eunuchs, and young girls in that area had scarred his mind. He lost the ability to value human life and relationships.

The rooms contained exotic furniture, woolen carpets, and exquisite chandeliers. There were perforated urns containing aromatic herbs. Deaf slaves sat in separate rooms and pulled ropes that operated fans for cool air. If needed, a pull of a bell summoned hearing slaves. Dingir had a large assortment of female slaves and eunuchs for his pleasure, who were imported from far-off lands. He behaved in a sadistic manner towards them, taking out his inferiority in masculinity by abusing them.

There were silver baskets with fruits and delicacies from faraway nations. Exotic fresh flowers were placed in every corner and replaced every few hours. Fierce guards whom Gangwo had hand picked sealed the area. Each guard was very well compensated. Their family and loved ones were also closely watched. They knew that any dereliction of duty would cause a horrible death for themselves and their loved ones. Completely absent from the room were any display of weapons.

Every day, poets visited the Dingir's residence and recited poems composed to praise him. Preachers of the Daitya faith also called on him. They recited those portions of the Daitya religious books, which were intolerant of other modes of worship. Overtime, Dingir became increasingly fanatical, openly declaring that he would eliminate all the people from the earth who did not follow the Daitya faith.

As Dingir stepped into the audience room, Gangwo bowed low. Dingir nodded his head, acknowledging Gangwo, and put on a forced smile. The expression of fear and contempt interplayed on Dingir's face. Gangwo's smile was a fixed expression every time he met Dingir. Till Dingir ascended the throne, Gangwo had treated him like a young boy under his care. A drastic change occurred in the demeanor after the boy became the Ruler.

"My Ruler, now that the Mleccha necks are under our feet, it is time to crush the head of the snake, Kolakwa. You should give him a horrible death so that no other Mulkan snake will ever think of raising his hood again. I want to boil him alive." Gangwo seethed.

"Yes, Gangwo, I agree with you. Boil his body, part by part, so he stays alive, suffering for many days. I want to watch that myself. It is a pity to waste his talent. If he had accepted becoming our servants like his father and grandfather, we could have put him to good use," Dingir nodded.

Gangwo tightened his massive fists. "I realize that my Ruler. But we do not want this tiny snake to become a ferocious, fire-breathing serpent from hell and start swallowing more of our land."

As Dingir continued chanting the name of the Ghumu, rolling the prayer beads on a silken thread, he asked, per his usual style, "What do you think I am going to say?"

"O merciful one, you will say, order the Zigadors to crush the snake's head."

"You are right, Gangwo," the Ruler murmured.

"My Ruler, your mercy keeps everyone alive." Gangwo bowed low. Dingir started walking away, but abruptly turned.

"I heard Kolakwa's brother escaped from right under your nose," he sneered.

Gangwo looked shocked at how Dingir learned this information. He surmised that his enemies may have shared this humiliating development with Dingir.

"I let him escape, O wise one. This escape from us would enhance his image among his people so that he can project himself as a better leader than Kolakwa," Gangwo replied, making up this lie.

Dingir continued his sneering and walked away.

I will nail Krikaneel to the wall for this humiliation. Gangwo walked backward to the door.

Back at his house, Gangwo handed out alms to beggars lined up in front of his home, as they did daily before lunchtime. Gangwo stood, smiling as they blessed him and praised Ghumu. After the last of the beggars had left, Gangwo ate spicy meat mixed with dry fruits and rice. Gangwo never drank or smoked any intoxicants. Instead, he had used his enemy's proclivity for vices against them. After his meal, Gangwo whistled for his pet fox. After picking him up, Gangwo started pacing in the garden.

He murmured into the fox's ear, "I get angry at the stupid fools who praise Ghumu when I give them food. I want to grab them by the throat and tell them to praise me. If Ghumu wanted to give them food, he would have given it to them at their house, and they wouldn't be standing outside my house in the scorching afternoon sun."

The fox looked at Gangwo's face, making a low purring sound.

"In this world, it is just you and me. You bit off your leg trying to save your life while I always had to care for myself. Neither Ghumu nor Dramho showed up to save us. They are just imaginary crutches of weak people who cannot handle the brutal realities of life. The preachers and other religious leaders are crooks. With my bribes, threats, and small carrots of power-sharing, they dance to my music. You and I were born as accidents of nature and one day, we will be gone. Till then, we will live our life as we want."He gently put the fox on the table as he sat on a chair.

"You should see me during the prayer meetings," he continued. "You would have applauded my show of religiosity." Gangwo laughed loudly as he toyed with a large religious medallion on his neck. At that very moment, one servant saw Gangwo from the kitchen window. The image of Gangwo laughing and talking to the fox terrified him and confirmed that Gangwo was the devil incarnate.

The next day, Gangwo sent messengers to the five Zigadors whose lands surrounded Atmaraj to act on the previous order to coordinate an invasion of Kolakwa's land so that Kolakwa's forces would be divided and easily crushed.

Once the five Zigadors received the orders from Dingir's messenger, they started preparation. Although each Zigador feared confronting Kolakwa, they knew the five would be an overwhelming force together since Kolakwa's army would be divided and fighting on five different frontiers.

As the Zigadors coordinated their attacks on Kolakwa, they schemed how to trip and back-stab each other once they eliminated Kolakwa.

One Zigador suggested a day after a Daitya festival in two months, when they would attack early at sunrise. All the Zigadors agreed. Each hoped to capture Kolakwa but did not want to be the first to face Kolakwa's army.

Chapter–19

Offense is the Best Defense

The astute foresight of Mamalu in settling trusted people in different lands again paid dividends. In these Zigadors' lands, the orphans whom Mamalu had settled in their childhood with adoptive parents were now grown up. Because of the education and support Mamalu provided, they rose in prominence in their lands. They established a network of spies within the inner circle of their respective Zigadors. These spies gained and forwarded detailed news about the attack plans to Krikaneel and Kolakwa.

With this grave news, Kolakwa called the council with Krikaneel, Dramhodas, Mahadoo, Savitri, and a few senior Mormos. He also ordered Daryaveer to take a break from the naval exercises and visit Fort Vitora.

One senior Mormos commented, "I know many Mormos working for the money in the armies of the attacking Zigadors. They believe the Ruler will crush us eventually and do not want to be on the losing side."

Krikaneel uttered, "The wind is the enemy of a small lamp and will extinguish the flame. But when the flame becomes a huge forest fire, the same wind becomes its friend and helps it spread. We are small, and even our kind wants to help destroy us. We will become mighty one day, and even our enemies will want to become our friends."

Kolakwa spread the map of Atmaraj on the table and pointed out the routes each of the five Zigadors would take. Each of the participants in the council started thinking of ways to counteract this development. Together, they prayed to Dramho for guidance and protection.

"My Naresh, an attack is the best defense. We should make a preemptive strike," Dramhodas suggested. Everyone nodded in agreement. A decision was made to attack the strongest four of the five Zigadors, hoping that the news would scare the fifth Zigador into abandoning any plans of aggression.

After considerable discussion late into the night, they finalized the complex plan for the defensive offense.

* * *

A few days after the meeting, Kolakwa requested Krikaneel's presence in his chamber. "I am feeling restless, Krikaneel. As I prayed to Dramho today, I felt sad that we used deceit, betrayal, and other dishonorable means to defeat our enemies. As I was growing up, Mamalu talked about our great ancestors who adhered to the moral code during warfare. Now, we are behaving just like our enemies. What is the difference between our enemies and us?" Kolakwa sat down, cupping his face in his palm. He continued, "Krikaneel, you have been fortunate to have spent more time with Saumitra. You are my elder. Please guide me."

Hearing this question, Krikaneel remembered Saumitra had warned him to expect this question from Kolakwa a few weeks before he died. Saumitra had said, "Although Kolakwa is a great warrior with a tough, hardened exterior, in his heart are aspirations of a monk. If Kolakwa had been born in another situation, he would have renounced material possessions and led a life of learning and teaching about the Divine. But Dramho had a different plan. Given where and when he was born, Kolakwa's duty is to be a warrior, be a man of action, and that is what he has become."

As Krikaneel stood before Kolakwa, he spoke. "The violence and deceits of our enemies towards our people for centuries were with an evil intention of subjugation. The violence and tricks we engage are to establish the good." Krikaneel continued, "The act is always neutral. It is the intention that makes it right or wrong. For example, suppose an enemy soldier cuts off the right hand of a farmer. It is an evil act that will deprive the farmer of his working and defending hand. But the same act becomes noble if the medicine man performs it to treat a horrible disease developing in the farmer's hand."

Krikaneel sat down next to Kolakwa for the first time, placing his hand on Kolakwa's shoulder from behind him. Feeling his touch, Kolakwa felt relief in the presence of his elder brother next to him.

"My Naresh, we are not attacking the Zigadors for selfish motives or revenge. We are not attacking them for glory or wealth. We are not even attacking them to save our own lives or wealth. The war is necessary to defeat the oppressors to establish and protect Atmaraj. Atmaraj, in which innocent and defenseless people can have a peaceful and prosperous future. Our war is not with the Daityas but against every oppressor, whether Daitya, Mleccha, Frangi, Mulkan, or even against you and me if we become tyrannical. In the future, you and I may not be alive. Still, if good, brave, and smart warriors take upon themselves to sacrifice everything for its protection, Atmaraj shall sustain."

Krikaneel stood up and took his earlier position, somewhat stooping in respect. "Our hands may appear to be smeared with filth of violence, but our hearts should remain pure." He bowed and began retreating from the room.

Kolakwa nodded in acquiescence. Saumitra was no more. But through his wisdom, he would forever be around.

Chapter–20

Stealth Battles I

In preparation to attack Fort Vishram, Krikaneel collected every information possible about the fort through his spies. Krikaneel briefed Kolakwa. "Fort Vishram is on a tall mountain. There is a long path to reach the main door with guarded barriers. It is impossible to scale the walls. If anyone attempts to climb, the guards can pour hot sand and boiling water on the climbers from above. Sharp metal spikes embedded in the walls are directed downwards to impale anyone attempting to scale the walls. The guards always boast that capturing this Fort is impossible."

"If true, how did the current master capture it?" Kolakwa asked.

Krikaneel sighed. "A familiar story; a few coins led to the betrayal of the fort master. They leaked the information to the enemy that the master's son was visiting a relative in a nearby village. The current Zigador's ancestors kidnapped the son of the previous master. They ambushed the master of the fort and his men on the way to rescue his son. For over two generations, the current Zigador's family has controlled the fort and the area under it."

"Are we trying a similar tactic?" Kolakwa hunched his back as he walked towards the window.

Krikaneel avoided a direct answer. He replied, "The Zigador of Fort Vishram is very ruthless. Many of his subjects and Mormos were very unhappy. Two of his Mormos had previously sent out feelers to our Mormos wanting to support Atmaraj. I have met with them secretly and discussed various plans to capture the fort."

After a moment's pause, he continued, "We can ride to Vishram at night, and our friendly Mormos would open the Fort's doors and let our men enter the Fort. Hopefully, we can overwhelm the garrison inside after entering the Fort. I have spies monitoring the two Mormos for the last few months for any possibility of them double-crossing us."

On the day before the expedition, Krikaneel stopped at Kolakwa's quarters. He hesitantly asked, "My Naresh, please permit me to accompany you to Fort Vishram. I can use my left hand to throw a spear and use my knives to attack. I will not be an extra burden on your shoulder."

"You must be safe and stay back. We cannot afford to lose both of us at this moment of our struggle. If I get killed during our attack on Fort Vishram, you can lead our men in our quest," Kolakwa firmly replied.

"Just let me come this time. This mission seems most likely to succeed. The chance of us both getting killed seems remote." Krikaneel pleaded. He had a night mare the previous night that Kolakwa was grievously injured in the battle. He wanted to be there to protect Kolakwa.

Kolakwa could not bear to see the tears in Krikaneel's eyes. He agreed with a heavy heart but warned Krikaneel to remain close to him.

Kolakwa ensured that every soldier of the party knew his exact role, what to do, in what sequence, and what orders he would give.

The Mormo, who had promised to support Kolakwa, spread false information among the guards at the gate, claiming that a particularly nasty Daitya Zigador and his troops were expected to arrive tonight. The other Mormo who had pledged alliance to Kolakwa confirmed that he had infuriated his men and the other Mulkan Mormos against the Zigador by recently raising the topic of the insults and injustice occurring under the Zigador's rule. He assured Krikaneel, "I firmly believe that the Mulkan Mormos and their soldiers are furious at the Daitya Zigador and are ready to rebel at the slightest provocation."

"I hope it is true. Without the Mulkans rebelling, the mission has no chance of succeeding," Krikaneel said.

The guards of the fort did not wear any uniform. Only the visiting Ruler's troops, temporarily stationed on the fort, wore the standard blue uniform.

On the day of the attack, Kolakwa, Krikaneel, and one hundred men on horseback rode towards Fort Vishram under the flag of the Ruler. They were wearing blue clothes that were identical to the uniform of the Ruler's army. They started from the border village in the late afternoon, entering the Fort Vishram Zigador lands. On the mountainous path to the fort, Krikaneel could not help but admire the beauty of villages sprinkled throughout the valley below. The interplay between the mountain peaks' long shadows and the vista was mesmerizing. They reached the first guard post after dusk. With a partially covered face, Krikaneel took the lead and yelled at the guards in the Daitya language, "Move aside, you Mulkan imbecile!" Usually, the guards would ask for some documents before granting passage. However, they were currently lax because of an increase in the traffic of soldiers at odd hours in preparation for the attack on Kolakwa.

Krikaneel used similar tactics at the subsequent guard houses. Kolakwa's men reached the fort's entrance with no challenges. Observing the defensive architecture of the entryway, Krikaneel thought *there was no way we could capture this fort with a head-on invasion*. The friendly Mormo was present at the main gate and opened the door. Once inside the fort, he guided Kolakwa and his men to the barracks, where the other assembled Mormos and their men had sleeping quarters. Kolakwa's men tore off their outer clothes of the Ruler's color. Their inner clothes were ordinary clothes, like the local guards of the Fort.The men dispersed around the fort, trying to stay in the shadows. Then they waited.

* * *

About the time Kolakwa and Krikaneel had reached Fort Vishram, Dramhodas and five of his men had reached the village of Mulund. They could see Fort Kumbha in the fading light, built on tall cliffs with soaring ramparts. Kumbha is considered the most well-defended Fort in the Ruler's realm. The Zigador also has a lot of fighting experience and a well-trained army.

Dramhodas remembered the planning meeting with Kolakwa and the Advisory Council. A senior Mormo, a close friend of Dramhodas's father, had suggested a plan. He volunteered, "A Mormo on Fort Kumbha from the village of Mulundhas a daughter married to my relative. During a family get-together, I described our mission of establishing Atmaraj. He shared he had heard the stories and greatly respected our Naresh. He confessed that because of the proximity of his lands to Fort Kumbha, he could not openly support Kolakwa but was ready to help in any other way. I can contact this Mormo with a plan that some of our soldiers will ride with his men and enter Fort Kumbha when he gets summoned to prepare for the Zigador's planned invasion of Atmaraj. We will not share our planned actions inside the Fort with him, nor do I believe he will want to know about them."

Then, cryptically looking at Dramhodas, he continued, "My Naresh, will it be out of place if I request you to let Dramhodas lead this party?" Kolakwa did not understand the reason behind this odd request but replied with an affirmative nod.

On arrival at Mulund, Dramhodas paid his respects to the Mormo, who was his father's age. The men riding with Dramhodas were surprised to see the Mormo hug Dramhodas with great affection. The Mormo had informed his men that some men working for another Mormo would join them on their journey and that they should not ask them questions. Given the good things they had heard, his men hated the current mission against Atmaraj. Not attending their Mormo voice, a single word of discontent against the mission to attack Atmaraj made them suspicious that something was afloat. They left Dramhodas and his men alone.

Dramhodas had chosen fierce fighters as his companions for this mission. They were from the pool of men who knew the risk and still had volunteered for this seemingly suicidal mission. Unknown to him, three were from a group Rokba had trained to climb walls.

Dramhodas whispered to his men, "There is a high chance that we will be betrayed and slaughtered by the Mormo and his men even before we reach Fort Kumbha. Be on high alert. Please do not eat any offered food until somebody outside our party eats the food from the same utensil. Stay close and watch each other's backs."

While resting for the night, each of the six took turns remaining awake for one and a half hours each, and thus the rest had an uneventful sleep. As he sat during his guard duty, Dramhodas pondered his life. His ancestors fought for the rewards of land and titles. Was he like them? No, this was his fight. He was not a servant fighting for money. He was fighting for Atmaraj.

The following morning, as the group waited before their journey towards Fort Kumbha, Dramhodas shared the story of the current Zigador of Kumbha with his men. "Many years ago, when the Zigador was a young Daitya warrior, he was sent by his Zigador stepfather to capture Fort Kumbha. The stepfather had married his mother and wanted the stepson out of the picture. Capturing Kumbha was thought to be an impossible task. The stepfather hoped the young man would perish on this mission. Fort Kumbha had been in the family of the previous Mulkan Zigador for many generations. He had five sons, two of whom had perished in warfare, and one had died because of illness. The remaining two had no interest in fighting. When the invader laid siege, spies uncovered that the two sons would abandon their father in return for a significant amount of gold coins. After the Zigador delivered the gold coins to both sons, they left the fort to settle in Mleccha territory. The father was heartbroken. He handed over the fort to the invader without a fight. Thus, this proud, impregnable fort was lost without a fight."

Dramhodas became cautious as two men from the Mormo's troops passed by. He continued in a muted voice, "After the Daityas took over, many of the previous soldiers stayed on to serve under the new master.

However, over time, the humiliating treatment by the new master and the Daitya soldiers started gnawing at the insides of the Mulkan soldiers. The Mulkan soldiers in Fort Kumbha are like a box of explosive powder praying for a spark. The Zigador himself is older now. One of his two sons lives permanently in Dabrahoor, working at the Ruler's court. Our spies informed Naresh that the second son was also visiting his brother. Most likely, both will plan to be on the way to Fort Kumbha to help their father attack Atmaraj."

After a few hours, the party reached the foot of Fort Kumbha. Dramhodas's men marveled at the majesty of the fort. On the mountain's long, winding road, there were several fortified sentry stations. The tall stone ramparts were mute witnesses to innumerable previous invaders who failed to capture Kumbha. The fluttering yellow flag of the Ruler caused deep sadness in Dramhodas's mind. Unknown to others, Dramhodas had a deep connection to Kumbha. As a young man, his father, Ordora, worked as an assistant Brago on Kumbha under the previous Zigador. Ordorainitially stayed after the Daityas took over. However, after they destroyed the Dramho shrine in the fort, he could not tolerate working there and moved to Fort Vitora. Dramhodas spent his very early years in this fort. As he entered the gates of Fort Kumbha, sadness and anger simultaneously enveloped him. As the group rode through the main entrance, one of the Daitya leaders of the guards made a snide, insulting comment about the Mormo and his men. They did not respond but kept on riding toward the barracks area.

After settling in their resting area, Dramhodas peered through the window. Everything seemed familiar. He could remember himself as a toddler, his mother lovingly calling him, "*Draaamhooo*, where are you hiding?" She acted like she could not see him, although he hid his head under a basket with his body in plain sight. He barely remembered his mother. She had died in labor, giving birth to his younger sister.

He stirred himself out of his pleasant memories. The Mormo who had led the party went to the Zigador's residence to pay his respects. While doing so, he also noted the guards' position and memorized the building's general layout. After returning to the barracks, he stepped out of the rooms to smoke his pipe. Dramhodas strolled over and sat at his feet, acting like an ordinary foot soldier. The Mormo started whispering information about the layout of the Zigador's sleeping quarters and the details of the security. The Mormo also told Dramhodas about the height of the Zigador and his overall build. Based on this information, Dramhodas decided on the best way to kill him without excessive noise.

Chapter–21

Stealth Battles II

"Doors," Kolakwa whispered. The few Kolakwa's men who had stayed with him barricaded the sturdy doors of the barracks from the outside so no one sleeping inside could come out.

Fighting erupted when the patrolling guards realized the newly arrived soldiers were not the Ruler's men. Kolakwa's men attacked the soldiers in blue uniforms, ignoring the plain clothes-wearing Mulkan soldiers. The Zigador's Mulkan men discerned that the intruders were solely targeting the Ruler's men, and hence refrained from joining the fight. Instead, some of them attacked the Daitya soldiers to exact revenge for past insults.

Kolakwa and Krikaneel met the second Mormo, who had promised them assistance. He guided them toward the residence of the Zigador. The outside guard fled without engaging in a fight. As he climbed the stairs, Kolakwa hoped no women folk were inside the bedchamber, as their presence could complicate the fighting. Daityas were known to hide behind women, exploiting the ancient Mulkan warrior honor code forbiding injury to non-combatant women. The visibility inside the residence was limited. The Zigador had woken up and strategically positioned himself to avoid being surrounded. He was prepared to face the three intruders.

"Traitor dog," the Zigador yelled at the Mormo leading Kolakwa.

Suddenly, four men emerged from the other door. The Mormo altered his stance and shouted, "Kill both the Daitya demon and the snake Kolakwa."

Kolakwa realized that the Mormo had double-crossed him. The traitorous Mormo announced to his men, "We will claim that Kolakwa killed the Zigador. The Ruler will reward me for eliminating Kolakwa by appointing me the Zigador of Vishram. Then I will triple your pay."

The Mormo scornfully shoved Krikaneel to the side, "Move over, cripple. I will deal with you later."

He lunged to stab Kolakwa in the back, who was distracted while fighting with the Zigador. Before the traitor could react, Krikaneel swiftly drew his sword from the scabbard with his left hand and severed the treacherous Mormo's arm. Krikaneel then propelled his spear into the chest of another man. He engaged the other three men, whom the traitor Mormo had informed that Krikaneel was a disabled person with one functioning hand. They did not expect a highly skilled left-handed swordsman.

The Zigador was a very experienced and brave fighter. But he was distraught because of his Mormo's betrayal and made mistakes while fighting. Kolakwa was fighting, keeping his emotions at bay, and considered himself a tool of Dramho. This calmness and control over feelings allowed him to win the gruesome fight. After Kolakwa vanquished the Zigador, he turned to confront the other soldiers. Fighting in unison, using the same style of fighting taught by Saumitra, both Kolakwa and Krikaneel finished the three men and the traitor Mormo. Even without his right-hand thumb, Krikaneel could hold the shield in four fingers and a palm. Kolakwa was astonished at the sword-fighting skills of Krikaneel's left hand. Among the deceased Mormos men, Krikaneel recognized the soldier who was supposed to spy on his master.

They left the chamber and emerged onto the balcony. After taking a deep breath, Krikaneel loudly proclaimed, "The Zigador was dead, and the Fort was now part of Atmaraj." Most of the Mulkan soldiers in the Zigador's employ had joined Kolakwa's men in combat against the Ruler's soldiers. The Ruler's Daitya soldiers realized they were vastly out numbered and surrendered. The Mormos and soldiers trapped earlier in the sleeping quarters were informed of the Zigador's demise. They were escorted out and given the choice to stay after pledging support to Atmaraj or leave. Most of the Zigador's Mulkan soldiers and some Daitya men preferred to stay. One Daitya soldier expressed, "My ancestors and I were born and raised in Shantiprastha. This is my home. I will no longer be a traitor to my people just because my way of worship has changed."

As they inspected the fort, Krikaneeltold Kolakwa, "Sorry, my Naresh. I was bound by oath from Saumitra not to let anyone see my sword fighting. After offering my right thumb to Dramho, Saumitra made me intensely train with my left hand for years. My left hand has now become strong and nimble. I never intended to use my it, but when your life was endangered, and I had to break my oath to Saumitra."

As Krikaneel unsheathed his sword with his right hand, motioning to strike it against his left hand, Kolakwa blocked him and grasped his hand. He pleaded, "Stop this madness. I need you and your left hand for Atmaraj.

This secret will remain between you and me. An appropriate time will come to show your true strength."

Kolakwa and Krikaneel prayed to Dramho for the safety of the other three missions. Kolakwa gave the leadership of the fort to the Mormo, who had offered help. They unfurled the Crimson flag over Vishram at dawn.

* * *

On Fort Kumbha, Dramhodas and his five soldiers had their evening meal and retired to the far corner of the barracks. As the night progressed, they slipped out of the back door. Dramhodas anxiously surveyed the gibbous moon in the sky. Fortunately, there were clouds passing over the moon, the weather was windy, and the night was noisy because of the fluttering flags. Dramhodas led the party, creeping along the walls. Reaching base of the tower of the Zigador's sleeping quarters, they did not find the outside guard. They patiently awaited his return. Upon arrival, the guard knocked on the door. A small window in the fortified gate opened. The outside guard told the inside guard that he had returned. The inside guard shut the small window. Dramhodas realized there was no way to open the door by forcing it or tricking the guard inside. One of the Dramhodas's men crept behind the outside guard and slashed his neck. They dragged his body into a corner and tucked it in the shadows.

Dramhodas pointed at the tower window in the wall built on a cliff and whispered to the soldier next to him, "The only way to go inside would be for someone to climb through that open window, overpower the guard, and then climb down the stairs to open the door from inside." After pausing as he surveyed the tower, he uttered, "But that is impossible. A slip of the finger would cause the climber to fall hundreds of feet and get dashed against the rock below."

Incidentally, the soldier he spoke to wasa climber trained by Rokba. He immediately volunteered. The man expressed, "When I volunteered for this mission, I did not plan on returning alive. Whether my life becomes an offering to Atmaraj by falling into the valley or a sword piercing my chest makes no difference."

He gagged himself with the end of his turban to stifle involuntary screams if he fell down the valley. Securing a knife to his waist, he started climbing, gripping the rocks of the wall. Everyday practice and faith in the divine nature of the mission helped him endure the pain in his hands. There was no fear in his eyes. Each of the other five murmured a prayer to Dramho for the climber's safety and the mission's success.

With bated breath, Dramhodas and others watched, as the climber reached the window ledge. Fortunately, the inside guard was standing with his back towards the window. The climber entered through the window and slit the guard's throat, then he rushed down the stairs and opened the door. All the men rapidly climbed the stairs after locking the door behind them. They quickly overcame the guards, as most were sleepy. However, one guard outside Zigador's bedroom was heftier than expected and put up a fight, banging his hands on the wall before he was put down. This commotion woke the Zigador, who opened his bedroom door and came out of his room yelling, "Shut up, whining swine!"

Just then, Dramhodas, hiding behind the other side of the door, passed a thick braided wire around the Zigador's neck. With years of hatred and pent-up anger, Dramhodas used his enormous strength to strangle the Zigador. Dramhodas had seen the Daityas use slow strangulation to torture people to death. His father had told Dramhodas about a friend who was killed in this manner when he resisted a Daitya Mormo who was insulting his daughter. When the Zigador stopped struggling, he pulled him back and put him on his bed. To add insult to injury, Dramhodas shaved off the dead Zigador's mustache with his sword and stuffed it in his mouth. Unknown to Dramhodas, after he turned, another of his soldiers sliced off the Zigador's nose, defacing him, "Calling other people swine, eh! Now, who looks like a swine?" The soldier smirked.

The party got out of the Zigador's sleeping quarters and slowly crept back to the area of their residence. They changed their clothes, which had streaks of blood and tossed them over the ramparts. The following day, the Zigador's soldiers discovered that the Zigador and the guards had been assassinated. The Daitya Mormos started accusing random Mulkan Mormos of the crime. Tempers ran high, and fights between Daitya and Mulkan soldiers broke out. Long pending hatred boiled up to the surface, and an open battle started among the Daitya and Mulkan soldiers. The in-fighting between the Mulkan and Daitya soldiers continued throughout the day. Dramhodas and his men occasionally joined to help where the Mulkans were disadvantaged. By afternoon, most of the Daityas were dead or had fled the Fort. The soldiers tossed the body of the dead Zigador over the ramparts and yelled, "Let the wild dogs feed on one of their kind!"

All the Mormos and their soldiers gathered in the evening to decide the next step. The Mormo who had brought Dramhodas stood up and said, "The wisest and safest path ahead would be to merge the Fort with Atmaraj. This would be the best for us and our villagers. Finally, after a long time, we could live with self-respect."

There was a murmur of agreement. Then, Dramhodas gave a loud slogan, "Long live Atmaraj." Everybody joined, "Long live Atmaraj, long live Atmaraj."

The following day, as Dramhodas and the five riders rode to Fort Vitora with the good news, he wondered what was happening in the other battles. "Dramho, please help all of us, but especially Mahadoo. He has already lost Rokba. The failure of his catapults will kill him."

Chapter–22

Open Warfare I

The day after the planning meeting, Kolakwa gave the order that Mahadoo would lead the Panha mission. After a few days, Mahadoo assembled the Mormos under his command. The Mormos were surprised at how a magician would lead the soldiers, but trusted the wisdom of Kolakwa.

"Although Fort Panha is on flat land, it is very well-built. Therefore, it is impossible to capture. The last time Panha was captured was after it was surrounded for more than a year. After the food stock was exhausted, many people inside died of starvation, and the rest surrendered. Other times, the invaders captured it because of betrayal by someone on the inside who opened the doors. Both options are not available to us," Mahadoo briefed the Mormos.

As he paused to catch his breath, Mahadoo tried to grasp what the Mormos felt about him. They were at least a decade older than him, very strong, and battle-hardened after years of warfare. They had been fighting battles for longer than he was alive. He had not even taken part in a fistfight.

He pushed the thought aside. He drew with a piece of charcoal on the wall, "What the Panha lacks in height and inaccessibility, it makes up for in its intricate design. The Fort is built in the shape of an eight-pointed star. Because of the angle between the walls, there are no dead zones where attackers can hide. Archers can shoot arrows from adjacent angled walls with the enemy trapped in the middle. I have been told that the archers on Panha are well known for their accuracy. There are also dry moats surrounding the entire fort. Trying to climb the walls is not an option since the ramparts are well stocked with stoves and fuel used to heat liquids, sand, and stones to high temperatures, which is thrown on the invading soldiers trying to scale the walls." The Mormos shuddered to imagine the hot stones and scalding oil being poured.

Mahadoo paused for a moment, scanning the dejected faces of the Mormos. Then, suddenly upbeat, he said, gesturing with his arm, "We are going to set everything in the fort on fire by throwing fireballs into the fort using my large catapults."

Hearing Mahadoo's description of the fort, the bushy eyebrows of the battle-hardened Mormos had become deeply furrowed. On hearing about the catapults, the eyebrows suddenly jumped up as their jaws dropped together. Their expressions turned from doubt to surprise to admiration.

Mahadoo felt bashful. He stared at his hands and continued, "My catapults can throw stones long distances. For this expedition, we shall wrap stones with cloth smeared with fuel, plant resin, and yellow mud instead of ordinary rocks, which we will set on fire before launching. These fireballs stay lit longer and will fly over the ramparts of the Fort, setting everything on fire. Having visited the Fort multiple times, I know the locations of the wooden buildings. We will also aim at the stores where they stock-pile food and animal fodder. To stop the catapults, the enemy will come out of the fort to attack us. Then we can engage them."

"The soldiers I have already trained will lead each team of catapult crews. They have the maps of the fort that I have drawn to know where to direct the fireball. The crew will begin practicing starting tomorrow," Mahadoo shared with them.

"How do you know so much about the fort?" the Mormos expressed amazement at the depth of Mahadoo's knowledge. Mahadoo just humbly smiled. He had been moving around this region and had struck up conversations with soldiers and menial servants of the Zigador for many years. His straight for ward demeanor, slight body frame, coarse language, and, most importantly, easy smile put people at ease. They let down their guard and were eager to gossip with him and impress him by sharing their knowledge.

As they talked, an older Mormos in Mahadoo's team added, "Panha was built long before the Daitya invasion. When the ancestors of the current Daitya Zigador conquered the fort, they destroyed the massive Dramho shrine. He threw the broken pieces of the Dramho crystal over the outside walls to remind the Mulkans of their servitude and humiliation. The local Mulkan farmers collected broken pieces and built small shrines in the surrounding villages. Unfortunately, passing Daitya soldiers routinely damage these shrines and harass worshipers."

"Arrange for dispatching soldiers in small groups and house them in the villages at the border of Atmaraj lands with Panha," Mahadoo instructed the Mormos. "This would ensure that the scouts from Panha would not detect any invading force before our catapults were in place. If he figured out the invasion, the Zigador would send his troops to stop us on the way."

Weeks passed as Mahadoo's assistant strained the bombardment teams. A week before the invasion, Mahadoo called the Mormo in charge of the catapult crew, "It is time to disassemble the catapults and prepare them for transportation."

The Mormo smiled, "Our brightly colored wagons indeed look like circus wagons. No one will suspect that the boxes with pictures of monkeys and bears have hidden compartments with swords, spears, shields, and other weapons."

Later at night, Mahadoo prayed, "Dramho, I have asked you very few things in this life. The first time I prayed for Rokba's safe return, you took him away. Your actions are hard to understand. Please make these machines perform as they are supposed to. I will be able to contribute meaningfully to the formation of Atmaraj."

On the decided day, Mahadoo and his group started in the morning. They traveled through the Atmaraj lands during the day and through the Panha Zigador's land at night. Fortunately, no one stopped them. The sentries in the border villages were too sleepy to look thoroughly at the circus equipment.

By early morning, they arrived at the selected location facing the fort. The Brago of the fort sent scouts to investigate. Mahadoo showed them the animals and circus equipment, convincing them he was setting up a show to earn money. The elephant captured during the battle of Fort Vishal was the star attraction. Mahadoo bribed the scouts with intoxicant balls, sweets, and silver pieces. There were promises of dancing women on their way to conduct a show soon. Over the daytime, the scouts hung around to watch the work. They saw the partially assembled catapult, which appeared like structures for large tents and a trapeze support system. The Zigador was busy preparing for the attack on Kolakwa and was not concerned about the outside activity.

"Do not engage with the scouts and appear very busy," Mahadoo instructed his men. After a while, the scouts got bored and left the area.

At nightfall, Mahadoo and his men rapidly completed the final assembly to form the high-tension catapults. Four catapults were constructed and moved closer to the Fort. Mahadoo walked around the catapults, lovingly caressing them. He wanted to give them human names but decided against it and labeled them by numbers. *Attachment causes pain*, he thought. "Will anyone feel pain if I don't make it back?" he murmured, talking to catapult number four, the newest and the most advanced catapult he had built. "I hope someone will," he murmured, smiling sadly.

* * *

While Mahadoo's campaign was being assembled, Daryaveer's navy prepared to face the fourth adversary - the Zigador of Basrud. After accepting the responsibility for the mission to invade Fort Basrud during the planning meeting, Daryaveer returned to Fort Swaminidurg, where the newly built ships were docked. He hashed out detailed plans with senior navy officers.

"Invasion of Fort Basrud has its unique difficulties," Daryaveer stated. All the officers nodded their heads in agreement.

Daryaveer continued, "Fort Basrud is south of Atmaraj and on a cape jutting into the Swamini Sea. It has water on three sides and is connected to land on one. The Zigador knew it would be easy for the enemy to surround it. Hence, the Fort is always well-stocked with provisions and armaments. He has employed many Daityas, Mulkans, and mixed progeny of Mleccha with local women whom he uses on his private ships to conduct trade on his behalf to augment his wealth."

"A frontal attack on the fortress from the sea would be hazardous for our fledgling Navy. Basrud naval force is small but operated by sailors with decades of experience," a senior sailor who had previously worked from the Zigador's ships gave his opinion.

"We will take a multi-pronged approach," Daryaveer produced a map of the coast, "We will launch a two-sided attack. Three of our warships will sail and wait at sea within sight of Fort Basrud. Our ships have been constructed under the supervision of the Frangi ship builder and have a similar appearance to the Frangi navy vessels. Instead of the Crimson, we will fly Frangi Flags on these ships to give an illusion that the Frangis have allied with us and will attack the fort from the sea. Our Frangi naval battle strategy teacher taught us that the Frangi navy attacks with at least seven to eight ships. Hopefully, the Basrud Zigador also knows that and will assume that our three fake Frangi ships are waiting for reinforcements."

Smiling at the confused look on everyone's face, he continued, "The actual force would attack from the land and try to take over the Fort. The projected spectacle would be that the Frangis have joined forces with us to attack the Fort from the sea. As a backup, the fake-out ships will be ready for sea battle if needed. They will also have just enough soldiers with ladders and grappling hooks with ropes to attack the fort and reinforce the land soldiers if needed." Daryaveer placed seashells of various shapes from his pocket on the table to illustrate his plan.

A young officer was jubilant. "I hope we get to take on the Zigador's navy. We have learned a lot and practiced hard."

In a grave tone, Dramhodas replied, "I have a plan to disable the Zigador's navy. If the plan fails and their entire navy attacks our ships, I am ordering the captains of all three ships to flee. There will be no foolhardy heroics that may destroy our fledgling navy. There will be more occasions to test our strength with a more equal foe." Daryaveer concluded his narrative and looked around. Everybody agreed with the plan.

Days before the expedition on Basrud, a few of Kolakwa's men secretly proceeded ahead. They found a beach along the coast just south of the Mleccha Fort Vasai and north of Fort Basrud, which would be the place to land the troops. The sea approach was also outside the shipping lanes of Fort Basrud and Fort Vasai. They also constructed a makeshift wood-burning lighthouse on the beach as a beacon for the landing boats.

Kolakwa assigned four hundred land soldiers for the Basrud mission. Most had never traveled on a ship before. A few of the old sailors showed them how to use the pressure points on their wrists to decrease the incidence of seasickness. In addition, the Mormos provided the soldiers with dried sugar-coated strips of ginger root to chew on as a remedy for seasickness.

The last night before the new moon day was very dark. The flotilla of eight ships docked at Fort Swaminidurg presented an impressive sight to the soldiers patrolling the docks. Creeping in the shadow, Veershri approached the water. Praying to Dramho, she offered a coconut into the sea. She asked Dramho for the mission's success, protecting Atmaraj, and a long life for Daryaveer. Using the mooring rope, she climbed aboard one ship, which appeared somewhat different from the others. Walking around the deck, she appreciated the unusual smell. She disembarked in the same way. Afterward, she went to Daryaveer's house and reported how she could approach the ships undetected. "If I was an enemy saboteur, this could have been the end of the Atmaraj navy!"

Daryaveer was furious and summoned the head of the guards. He ordered him to double the security presence, especially around the odd-looking ship. Looking at Daryaveer, who never lost his temper, the head-guard trembled. He immediately ordered more guards to report to duty, and throughout the night, he monitored the port himself. Before falling asleep, Daryaveer wondered if this was the last time he would talk to Veershri.

* * *

In the morning, four ships, each with one hundred soldiers, sailed to the landing site. Daryaveer captained one of them. The vessels took a circuitous route to avoid the Mleccha shipping lanes. They sailed for almost eighteen hours and reached the mooring point close to the landing site at midnight. Daryaveer's soldiers, fishers for generations, were experts in navigation at night using stars and constellations. He had instructed the soldiers on all four vessels to lie down if the lookout person saw any Mleccha vessel nearby. The Mlecchas would not see the soldiers and assume that the ships were sailing for practice. The boats from Fort Basrud usually avoided the sea lanes frequented by Mleccha ships. It was unlikely that any Basrud ships would detect Daryaveer's four ships as they sailed toward the landing site.

At the landing site, Daryaveer's men had ensured that the sea was deep enough without hidden sandbars on the seabed.

From the mooring point, the men landed on the beach using small boats, aided by the lighting of the small lighthouse fire. The landing was uneventful. After drying themselves, Daryaveer ordered the men to eat and go to sleep. The following morning, Daryaveer led the men, who cautiously traveled in small groups through interconnected ravines extending from the area of the landing spot to a spot near the Fort. Daryaveer's men had scouted the route beforehand and posted guards to ensure no unexpected encounter with locals or men from Basrud. The men then waited for nightfall. Daryaveer had taught them to chant the one thousand-eight names of Dramho, synchronized with breathing, to pass the time while they were waiting and not be fidgety. This technique worked for the soldiers who were Dramho's devotees and those who were not. The devotees believed that chanting the names would get them Dramho's blessings. The non-devotees considered it a mental exercise for memory improvement and calming nervousness.

As darkness fell, the men moved closer to the fort, waiting for the signal from the sea to start the attack.

* * *

About the time the soldiers landed, the three fake Frangi warships with thirty soldiers each, some wearing clothes like Frang is and a fourth fire ship, sailed from Fort Swaminidurg toward Fort Basrud, hoisting the Crimson flag. They decided the timing so the ships would arrive at the point of waiting by mid-late afternoon. This point was estimated to be just below the horizon, beyond the visual distance from Fort Basrud, and outside the Basrud shipping lanes. After arriving at the waiting point, all the ships lowered their Crimson flags and dropped their anchors.

Before leaving Swaminidurg, the fire ship was carefully loaded with explosives and highly combustible fuel. Two long fuses extended to the explosives stored in the fireship's hold. The sails of the fireship were painted black to avoid detection. The crew of the fire ship was volunteer-only because of the possible suicidal nature of their duty. Even a single spark would light the ship and roast the entire team alive. Using fire ships was a trade mark of the Frangis, which they had effectively used to cause extensive damage to the Mleccha fleet during the attack on Port Surat.

The fireship crew was led by Veershri.

Chapter–23

Open Warfare II

As the sun arose on Fort Panha, over three hundred soldiers hiding in the border villages suddenly materialized. The high-powered catapults started bombarding the fort with balls filled with explosives and combustible fluids. The crew could change the range of the catapults based on the counterweight placed on the throwing arm. Each had different ranges and bombarded various parts of the fort. On the first volley, the hollow projectile carried flammable liquid. It burst after falling on the target, spraying the liquid over the target area. Then, the second projectile was launched with a burning fireball that ignited the earlier liquid, causing a massive conflagration.

Mahadoo had instructed the catapult crew, "Aim for the storehouse of weapons, fuel, and hay. Avoid the residential areas."

Groups of men pushed the catapult base in a semicircle, helping aim the projectiles at the different parts of the fort.

Suddenly, from the rampart rose a loud boom. A shower of metal bars and balls fell near the catapults. The soldiers started panicking at this new weapon. Mahadoo stared in the direction of the sound. He clasped his hands, cursing himself for his negligence. In the last few weeks of preparation for the catapults, he had not visited the fort to collect the latest information. The Zigador had deployed a new weapon, unheard of in these lands. "My mistake will cost us his battle and the lives of all my men."

Mahadoo urged the catapult team to work faster. After a long gap, there was another loud boom, and the projectiles hit one catapult, destroying it and killing most of the crew.

To avoid needless injury to non-combatants, till now, the catapult teams had avoided throwing the projectiles toward the residential area of the Zigador. This complex lodged the Zigador's family, including his children and the families of senior Mormos serving in the Fort. However, after the damage caused by this new weapon, the irate captain of the men loading the other catapults gave the coordinates so that the next projectile hit the Zigador's palace. Multiple fireballs landed on the residential buildings.

A third boom hit close a catapult, killing many soldiers. Meanwhile, Mahadoo had noticed increased activity on one side of the ramparts and assumed it to be the location of the new weapon. He ordered the catapults to throw the projectiles at that location.

As the catapults concentrated the fireballs toward the presumed location of the weapon, Mahadoo stared in that direction, praying they had hit it. There were no further booms from the fort.

As Mahadoo was trying to bring back order in his ranks, the door of the Fort flew open. Mahadoo saw the Zigador leading his Mormos and their men, screaming, "Revenge, revenge." They rushed towards Mahadoo's position at great speed. Mahadoo's men were not expecting this attack but hastily got ready, and a savage battle ensued. Both sides were fighting with intense hatred, not just as a duty. The Zigador was strong, brave, and a highly skilled fighter. He was urging his men to fight, assuring them of victory. He killed many of Mahadoo's men fighting on foot from his tall battle horse.

After deciding that it was impossible to stop the Zigador, Mahadoo ordered, "Load the crossbow." His men loaded a giant crossbow from which multiple spears could be fired. They cranked the crossbow and fired it toward the Zigador, although many of Mahadoo's men were nearby. One spear hitZigador's horse, which collapsed. As the Zigador fell to the ground, he was surrounded by Mahadoo's men and killed. Unfortunately, some spears also hit Mahadoo's men, who died in this friendly fire. After the Zigador fell, the tide of the fight turned. Some of the Zigador's soldiers started retreating into the fort, closely pursued by Mahadoo's men. The fight now extended into the fort through the open door. Mahadoo stopped the bombardment. The battle was over in a few hours.

As the adrenaline rush of the battle subsided, Mahadoo was overcome with melancholy. He was shaken by the death and destruction. The years of hatred and anger from memories of how the Daityas had treated the Mulkan people had urged Mahadoo's men to with great ferocity.

As Mahadoo walked around the Fort, he saw the charred remains of the Zigador's palace and multiple other buildings. The fuel storage area had caught fire, spreading to the horse stables and the cattle shed. The stink of burned flesh nauseated him. He could see the dead remains of many animals perished in those fires.

All my life, I helped lives in distress. Today, I was the cause of the distressing and ending of so many lives. Mahadoo was overwhelmed with anguish. While constructing the equipment, he knew the destructive power of his inventions. But seeing the destruction in person caused him great pain. Although they added Fort Panha to Atmaraj, this significant victory was not an occasion for joy and celebration for Mahadoo.

. He and a few senior Mormos went to inspect the new weapon called 'the cannon.' The Zigador had recently purchased it from a Mleccha merchant. The Mleccha who had sold the cannon also instructed the Zigador's men during the battle. He lay dead next to it.

Mahadoo started looking over the cannon, but standing on the ramparts and surveying the vista of death and destruction, he again became overcome with grief. As he started walking back, he wanted to take a vow never to fight again. *I will never pick up or make another weapon.* As he took a deep breath to speak, he abruptly paused. From the corner of his eye, Mahadoo saw a slight motion in the debris of a collapsed building with a high-pitched, crying sound. He sprinted to the spot and cleared the area. Underneath, a crying baby crawled out from the wreckage, having miraculously survived the carnage. It was well-dressed and most likely from the Zigador's family. Mahadoo picked up the baby and hugged it close. *Sadly, sometimes war is the only way to establish prolonged peace,* Mahadoo thought as their tears intermingled.

I must fight for you. I will have to fight so that there will be peace and there will not be any war orphans. You are not an orphan. I am here for you. The baby stopped crying as Mahadoo wiped their tears and started walking towards his camp, holding the baby close to his chest.

After walking for a few hours, as the sun started sinking over the horizon, Mahadoo stopped at a village. He knocked on the door of a house with an adjoining cow shed. A kindly lady opened the door. As she was about to speak, their eyes met. She remained silent and gestured for him to come in, offering him a seat. As the lady retreated to an inner room, Mahadoo gently caressed the baby's forehead. Staring at the fire in the hearth, his mind wandered to the day when he had demonstrated the final working model of the weaponized catapult to Saumitra.

"Today, you have taken up the mantle of a warrior. Many actions you will perform as a warrior will be extremely burdensome on your heart and mind." Saumitra had patted his back. As a shadow of worry crossed Mahadoo's face, Saumitra continued, "Perform your righteous duty in the way that is fit to be an offering to Dramho."

The lady had returned. She placed a plate of foodbefore Mahadoo and picked up the baby.

I have done my righteous duty for Atmaraj.

The lady glanced at the tranquility spreading on Mahadoo's face and smiled as she started feeding the baby.

* * *

Veershri stood on the deck of the fireship, watching the sunset over the simmering waters of the Swamini Sea. She felt fortunate that no ship from Fort Basrud had encountered her fireship and the fake Frangi ships. At nightfall, Veershri ordered the crew to pull up the anchor and start sailing the fireship toward the fort. Basrud had a small lighthouse that provided a guiding beacon as the ship sailed closer.

After the fireship departed, the three other warships hoisted the Frangi flags and sailed toward Fort Basrud. Once they were close enough to be seen, they again dropped their anchors. Aboard the ships amidst the shroud of darkness,the soldiers' hearts were brimming with a blend of emotions. As they fervently prayed for their land-soldier brothers' victory, a sense of unease and restlessness gnawed at them. They yearned to be immersed in the action alongside their comrades rather than waiting in the shadows of uncertainty.

Serendipitously, many of the Zigador's trading ships had joined the warships moored near the Fort that week. The Fort had festivities and celebrations to welcome the sailors and goods. All the sailors from the ships had disembarked to partake in the festivities. The Fort was decorated with bright oil lanterns with colorful designs. There was loud music, and dancing women entertained the sailors. Even the night watchmen in the observation towers on the Fort left their posts unattended.

Nobody noticed the phantom-like fireship gliding near the Basrud Zigador's ships. Once they were close enough, Veershri and the other sailors tossed grappling hooks to tie the fireship to the nearest ship. After lighting the fuses, Veershri and her crew escaped on their rowboats. The fuse length was long enough for them to get to a safe distance.

After rowing for some time, they heard a deafening noise as the fireship exploded. They thanked Dramho and congratulated each other. In the distance, they saw the ablaze Basrud vessels against the pitch-black water and sky, with the conflagration spreading from one ship to another.

On hearing the loud explosion, Daryaveer ordered the soldiers on the land side to attack the front gate with battering rams and climb the ramparts with ladders and grappling ropes. However, the defenders successfully repealed them. After the initial attack, the Zigador and his advisors were confident of defending the fort against the Atmaraj army. They thought that the night blast was an accident. They did not believe that Kolakwa's navy could do much harm.

After the morning dawned, they observed the massive destruction of his fleet by the night fire. When his people informed him that a fleet of Frangis had moored at a distance, they deduced the Frangis had caused the naval destruction.

"My Lord, the moored Frangis most likely are waiting for more Frangi ships to arrive before attacking. They usually invade as fleets of seven to ten ships," the Zigador's advisor informed him.

The Zigador ordered his Mormos. "Attack the coward Kolakwa before the Frangis come. We will get trapped in the fort if Frangis reach us and attack from the seawall. We can break Kolakwa's blockade. Our troops are well rested, while Kolakwa's soldiers must have marched a very long distance to reach here."He led all his four hundred men out of the fort, heading towards Daryaveer's men. While many of the four hundred were skilled land soldiers, most were sea soldiers used to fighting with short swords on the decks of the ships. The others were mere sailors, not fighters, joining the battle because their master had ordered them.

Daryaveer had not expected the Zigador to attack so soon. However, after the initial surprise, Kolakwa's battle-hardened soldiers accompanying Daryaveer rapidly overcame the Zigadors' army because of their overnight rest, superior training, and experience.

After two hours of fighting, the Zigador's temper cooled down, seeing the rout of his men. He and his remaining force retreated into the Fort. Once inside, his advisors told him about the historically inhuman treatment of the enemies by the Frangi army. "When Frangis had attacked the Mlecchas, they had mercilessly slaughtered many Mlecchas and the Ruler's soldiers who had surrendered," the Zigador's advisors cautioned.

Considering his options, the Zigador sent an envoy offering to surrender if Daryaveer granted him and his people a safe passage. Daryaveer accepted the terms and allowed them to take some goods and small weapons. After the Zigador and his men left, Daryaveer honored an old sailor by requesting him to unfurl the Crimson flag on the ramparts. While the victory celebration was going on, Daryaveer visited the site where the perished Atmaraj soldiers were laid. He recognized some of his close friends among them. With a heavy heart, Daryaveer arranged for the bodies of the soldiers to be carried to their homes. His sadness was tempered when he was notified that the fireship crew had safely returned.

Daryaveer sent a messenger to Fort Vitora to report the victory to Kolakwa. On his way to Fort Vitora, he stopped to visit the villages of his martyred friends. On arrival at his hometown, there was jubilant cheering for his success. But Daryaveer became somber as he turned towards the house of a martyred friend with whom he had grown up. He was at a loss for words to comfort the grieving mother and somberly sat beside her. As he shed tears, the mother wiped his tears. “My only son sacrificed himself for Atmaraj today. I only wish I had more sons to offer to Atmaraj.” Hearing these words of the brave mother, Daryaveer touched the ground before her feet to pay respects.

* * *

Soon, the news of capturing the four forts reached the remaining Zigador of Loha. The stories of the battles struck terror in his heart. He sent messengers to Ruler’s court, pleading for immediate help. While doing so, he also sent many gold coins, jewelry, and grains to Fort Vitora as gifts, congratulating Kolakwa on his recent victories. He also offered support, falling just short of joining Atmaraj.

* * *

Kolakwa ordered a special ceremony at Fort Vitora to recognize the bravery of the soldiers and honor the families of those who had perished. He bestowed awards such as money, farmland, and provisions. Kolakwa also announced that every village would create job opportunities for the adult children and widows of the martyred soldiers, ensuring their livelihood and support. He established a dedicated fund to cover the marriage expenses of widows who might wish to remarry.

From afar, Mamalu watched with great satisfaction that her little seed had grown into a mighty zavba tree. He had matured and collected great associates with a common goal. However, her smile vanished as a cold breeze from the north sent a shiver down her spine. It reminded her of the evil waiting in that same direction that had murdered her father and brothers and was biding its time to crush her son.

Chapter–24

Treachery

After the festivities, Kolakwa called the advisory council."We all know what comes next. Gangwo himself," Kolakwa started the meeting on a somber note, stroking his beard.

Krikaneel predicted, "He will come with a grand army to show off the might of the Empire. It will be much larger than he believes is necessary to destroy us. He will want many generations of Mulkans to talk about this army. So that no one will dare to think of ever-rising against the Ruler Dingir or his descendants."

"Our only action against Gangwo would be a war of attrition. If our peripheral forts and the forts of our allies do not fall immediately, we can keep harassing Gangwo's army. He may decide that making a truce may be better than staying in our area for long," Dramhodas added in a half-hearted voice.

Krikaneel tried to remain upbeat. He added, "It might not be safe for Gangwo to be away from the capital for an extended time. Other factions may assassinate Dingir or try to sway him to their side. There are also rumors that a couple of Dingir's brothers or their children escaped the massacre after Gangwo won the throne for Dingir. They are rumored to be hiding in the far north mountains, waiting to be installed on the throne if someone overthrows Dingir. It is also possible that the Zigadors in his Grand Army may desert him if they believe his power in the capital is decreasing."

"I understand that many of these are just wishful thoughts on our part. But we do not have many options," Kolakwa concluded.

Krikaneel unrolled a map on the table. "There are five forts in our north which will face Gangwo. Three of them are our forts, while two are those of Mulkan Zigadors, who have pledged to join Atmaraj. Our forts will form a strong wall against Gangwo. These will also be the launching pads for small units to go on night attacks and harass Gangwo's army."

Mahadoo pointed at the southernmost fort controlled by the Ruler's empire, Fort Devagiri, northeast of Atmaraj. "I have heard through a traveler that the two Daitya brothers of Devagiri do not have a good relationship with each other. The older Zigador brother is advanced in age. The younger one is ambitious. Per the informant, he wants to break free from the Ruler and start an independent Daitya kingdom."

"Maybe we should make friends with him," smiled Dramhodas.

"Let us think about it," Kolakwa said.

Meanwhile, a senior Mormos opened the window and peered outside. "Last month, the dry season started. I do not think Gangwo will move for another three months. In the dry season, the streams will not have water. There will be no grass on the plains. The wells will be at a low level. Finding water and food will be difficult for his men, let alone their horses."

The other senior, Mormo, stepped forward. "Unless Gangwo takes the longer path along the Marima River. Then there will be enough water."

"That will add almost a month for Gangwo to reach us," added the first Mormo.

"I do not believe that Gangwo is in a rush to come here. I believe that his invasion is a grand gesture to project the Ruler's might. He considers us a pesky pest rather than a genuine threat," Krikaneel opined.

"Dramhodas, can you mark out places along both paths where our troops can hide to launch raids on the Grand Army?" Kolakwa remembered the mural from the Gireshwar shrine.*I wish our ants were more numerous. We will have to make do with how many we have.*

* * *

A month passed after the meeting. Krikaneel and Dramhodas came to Kolakwa. "News has come that Gangwo would start any day. When they heard about the invasion, many Mulkan soldiers and Mormos who worked for the Ruler's Zigadorsdefected and approached the border forts to help defend Atmaraj."

"I'm worried that some of these may be spies and betray us," expressed Dramhodas.

"Order these new soldiers to go to the villages along Gangwo's path and hide. When Gangwo soldiers come to forage for food or kidnap women, they can defend the villages," replied Kolakwa.

One morning, Dramhodas came to Kolakwa's chamber. "My Naresh, our sentries found a Daitya yesterday evening at our gate. He claims to be an envoy of the brother of the Zigador of Devagiri. He wants an audience with you and has a proposal for us."

"Bring him over," acceded Kolakwa.

"I have searched him thoroughly," said Dramhodas. As an extra safeguard, Kolakwa's bodyguards searched him again. The man had a horrible-looking scar on his left forearm, which the guards hesitated to touch. The envoy laughed, saying that even his wife did not go near it. "That was from the spilling of liquid fire," the Daitya volunteered.

After the two guards stepped out, the man said, "My master is Bidero, the younger brother of the Zigador of Devagiri. My master was born through a different mother than the Zigador. After their father died, the Zigador took the fertile lands and gave my master the arid ones. The Zigador has always been hateful to Master Bidero. Last week, he sent his soldiers to my master's future bride's village and claimed her as his own. My master believes you are the only one whom he can ask for help." The messenger kneeled, saying, "My master wants me to help you capture Fort Devagiri. I know the hidden tunnels and entrances. Once you capture the Fort, give him his fair share. He will remain forever loyal to you."

The messenger opened a large parchment map on the table. They crowded together to study the map. The man started marking with a quill. "Here is a hidden door used by the spies in our father's times. Even the Zigador do not know of its existence," He spoke softly as he crept closer to Kolakwa. As Kolakwa stooped towards him to hear clearly, the man used the sharp end of the quill to tear open his scar and pull out an 8-inch iron knife, which, in one sweep, he swung towards Kolakwa's neck. That instant, Dramhodas's hand flung up and hit the assassin's elbow, pushing the knife above the neck but towards the face. The point pierced Kolakwa's left eye. Kolakwa elbowed the man, who fell but got up again, pulling Kolakwa's sword. Dramhodas swooped with his sword and slashed the assailant's neck. Bleeding profusely, the assailant stabbed himself in his chest with his knife and died.

There was yelling and running. The medicine men came with bandages. They sowed the gash on his face. However, Kolakwa lost his left eye. Dramhodas and the guards who searched the man were beside themselves with grief.

"He must have done this either for money for his family or hatred towards us. Although the plot was cowardly, it was ingenious, and the man was heroic." Kolakwa said as his medicine man bandaged his face.

* * *

A few days later, a spy brought information that in two weeks, Gangwo would leave Dabrahoor to invade Atmaraj. Most of the preparation for this expedition was near completion. Kolakwa ordered all the available forces and equipment to the northern part of Atmaraj for defensive purposes. He also sent more soldiers and provisions to Sangram, Vishram, Kumbha, and other smaller forts in the north.

Everyone tried to act normal, but the air on Fort Vitora was thick with tension. They had expected this calamity to happen one day. Now, that day had come.

Chapter–25

Might of Gangwo

"Gangwo has left the capital. At least forty thousand men are with him; ten thousand are from the Ruler's army, and thirty thousand are with the twenty or thirty Zigadors joining him. Our spies say more will join him as the army marches towards us." Krikaneel tried to appear calm, but the tremor in his voice was apparent.

"We knew this would happen. The grace of Dramho had delayed this disaster for a long time, but we knew this would happen one day or another. I had hoped that by this time, most Mulkan Zigadors, or at least many of them, would have drawn inspiration from our success and joined us to present a united front against the Ruler. However, such a scenario has not materialized. Instead, every gain for Atmaraj has come at the high cost of extensive bloodshed for Mulkans on both sides. While we have witnessed increasing soldiers and Mormos joining our cause over time, only a few Zigadors have aligned with our side." Kolakwa gave a pensive look at the fluttering Crimson flag in the courtyard.

Dramhodas joined them. "Our entire army is around eight to ten thousand soldiers. Gangwo will annihilate us if we engage him head-on. Newer soldiers might run away at the prospect of facing such an enormous force."

"Our spies have sent information that their weapons include door-busting rods and trained armored elephants that ram on the doors of forts to burst them open. The handlers also intoxicated the elephants and let them loose in the enemy's army or villages to cause havoc and destruction," Krikaneel added.

"Gangwo's army will start breaching many of our peripheral forts to the north soon. Our forts do not stand a chance," Dramhodas worriedly paced the room.

Kolakwa patted Dramhodas on his shoulder and said, "We cannot sacrifice our men by open battle. Let us harass the Gangwo's army by attacking their flanks and rear, using only a few of our men. We attack at lightning speed, cause damage, and rapidly withdraw before they can respond. We can cause enough damage to sow discontent among Gangwo's soldiers but not engage in a head-on fight to risk too many of our men's lives. Remember how a pack of wild dogs attack a lion."

Krikaneel sadly added, "However, in this case, the lion is gigantic, and the wild dogs are too few."

That same day, Dramhodas started focusing on organizing small groups of soldiers to conduct lightning strikes. These groups hid in hills and forests. They built small huts which had provisions to last for a few months.

Fort Vishram was the first major Fort to face Gangwo. The defenders put on a prolonged resistance to the last man.

The Daitya soldiers who had joined Atmaraj and stayed behind after Kolakwa and Krikaneel took over the Fort put up the bravest fight. Many infiltrated the enemy camp at night wearing the uniform of the Ruler's soldiers and mixed with them using their Daitya language skills. They set fire to provisions and killed two Zigadors. Unfortunately, they were discovered. Rather than getting caught and tortured, they killed themselves shouting, "Long live Atmaraj." Their sacrifice profoundly affected Mulkan soldiers who were fighting in Gangwo's army. A few deserted Gangwo's army, ashamed of them selves. Some Daitya Atmaraj soldiers mixed with the Ruler's soldiers and laid low, waiting for an appropriate opportunity to help the Atmaraj cause. They feigned injuries and avoided going to battle against Atmaraj soldiers.

The only way for Gangwo to take Fort Vishram was to breach the massive main door. The last section of the approach path to the main entrance had walls on both sides with slits through which defenders could shoot arrows. Gangwo tried to break open the main door using armored battle elephants and ramming rods. The defenders had spread large star-shaped iron pieces on the ground in front of the entryway, which pierced the elephant's feet, causing them to retreat. Although their armor protected the elephants, the defenders's arrows killed hundreds of attacking soldiers who could not clear the iron stars from the ground.

Gangwo kept sending so many men that the defenders ran out of arrows. Afterward, Gangwo finally managed to break the giant door. Once the outer door was broken, the inner doors gave way with little resistance. No amount of bravery by Atmaraj soldiers could stop the overwhelming number of invaders.

Fort Kumbha was next to fall after a heroic attempt to defend it for one week. It was impossible to stop the war elephants and the massive deluge of soldiers.

The sheer resistance of Kolakwa's forces surprised Gangwo. He had never had this much difficulty defeating such a few people. Even smaller forts put up heavy resistance. Gangwo used separate groups of Zigadors to attack different forts so that the experience of the incredible resistance by each of the forts would not discourage the attacking men of his army.

As weeks passed, Gangwo's army razed and lit on fire many villages, Mulkan shrines, and fields. They committed atrocities on village people and told them they were paying for Kolakwa's crimes. The Daitya preachers accompanying the army forcefully converted thousands of Mulkans to the Daitya way. Thousands more resisted and were tortured and killed.

* * *

"Finally, we have some good news, Naresh. Our lightning strike groups frequently attack Gangwo's army, putting terror in his soldiers. Our soldiers attack when the enemy is the least alert. We attack at midnight, just before dawn, and at dinner time. Last time, they were even successful in burning down Gangwo's tent. Less than one hundred soldiers attack at lightning speed, throw dense smoke causing fireballs, cause property damage, and disappear into the darkness. There is no attempt to engage the enemy soldiers. Sometimes, they attack multiple times with gaps of a few hours. Another tactic is to attack, run, and have another group waiting to ambush the Ruler's soldiers chasing the fleeing attackers," one Mormo shared with Kolakwa.

Another Mormonodded. "On multiple occasions, they set fire to Gangwo's food stores. Sometimes, cattle with firecrackers attached to their tails were driven into Gangwo's camp at night, causing the soldiers to think they were being attacked and thus disturbing their sleep. Our soldiers are also hiding in the villages on the pathway of Gangwo's army. When Gangwo's soldiers attack any village, they expect no resistance from the unarmed, helpless villagers. Imagine their surprise when our soldiers spring out of the houses and attack the attackers. This harassment has demoralized many of Gangwo's men, who cannot sleep at night anymore because of constant fear of surprise attacks."

Many smaller forts north of Fort Vitora fell under Gangwo's onslaught. Sometimes, there were betrayals by insiders either for money, a promise of position, or blackmail against kidnapped loved ones. When soldiers on Fort Salher put heroic resistance in the defense before surrendering, Gangwo murdered the surrendering Atmaraj soldiers after they had laid down their arms.

In Fort Salota, the defenders piled rocks behind the door, delaying its capture. Early during the defense, a traitor guided the enemies to a small hidden tunnel entering the fort. As enemy soldiers crawled in a single file, the brave wife of a guard who was incidentally walking by stopped them by smashing their heads using a nearby heavy pestle. She killed each soldier and dragged his body to the side, waiting for the next. She stopped twenty enemy soldiers. Fortunately, a defending soldier walked by and witnessed her bravery. He raised the alarm, gathering people who poured water and dirt down the tunnel, blocking it. Unfortunately, the fort fell after fifteen days of defense.

Spies revealed that the atrocities Gangwo's Daitya soldiers committed on the defenseless villagers, the needless destruction of the Mulkan shrines, and the murder of the surrendered Atmaraj soldiers were causing discontent in the hearts of the Mulkan soldiers and Mormos fighting in the Gangwo's army. As a result, increasing numbers of Mormos and their soldiers were deserting daily.

* * *

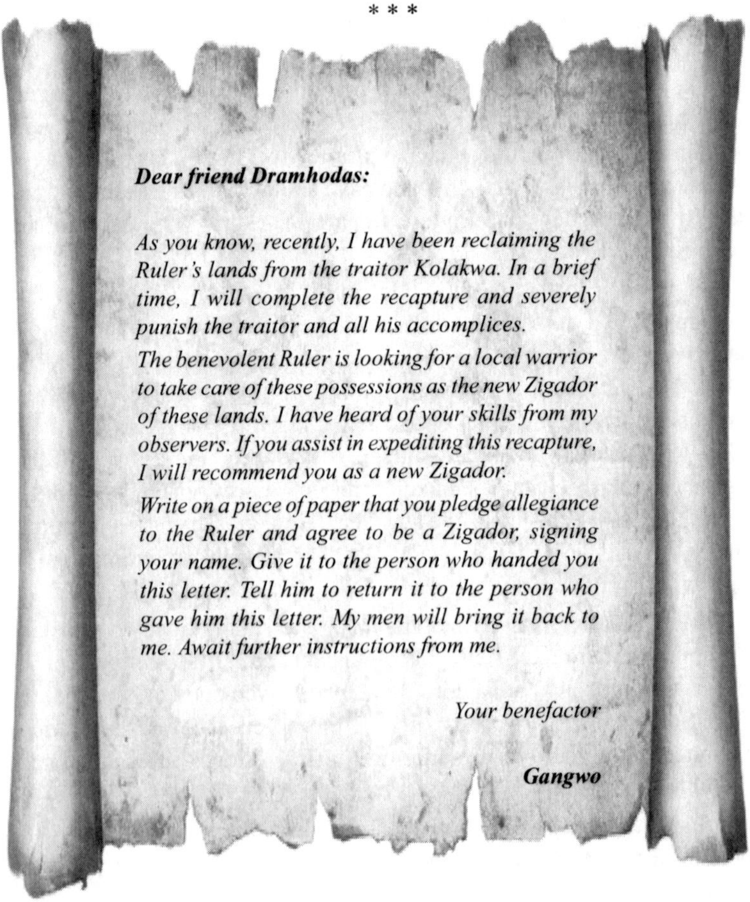

Dear friend Dramhodas:

As you know, recently, I have been reclaiming the Ruler's lands from the traitor Kolakwa. In a brief time, I will complete the recapture and severely punish the traitor and all his accomplices.

The benevolent Ruler is looking for a local warrior to take care of these possessions as the new Zigador of these lands. I have heard of your skills from my observers. If you assist in expediting this recapture, I will recommend you as a new Zigador.

Write on a piece of paper that you pledge allegiance to the Ruler and agree to be a Zigador, signing your name. Give it to the person who handed you this letter. Tell him to return it to the person who gave him this letter. My men will bring it back to me. Await further instructions from me.

Your benefactor

Gangwo

One evening, a soldier approached Dramhodas. "An unknown man approached my brother in the village and gave him some silver coins to deliver this packet to me, which is addressed to you. I will be honest with you, Dramhodas. My brother gave half of the coins to me. I have told no one about this package."

As the soldier walked away, Dramhodas opened the package. Inside was a letter addressed to him, signed by Gangwo.

Dramhodas recollected the Zigadors he had seen, with absolute power over their lands and their people, their troops, a retinue of servants, wealth, respect, everything he did not have. Walking to his room, he overheard one of his soldiers say, "Is Atmaraj just a futile dream? Is a dream worth so much destruction and death? How long will this go on?"

Chapter–26

Is this the End?

"My Naresh, our brave soldiers have defended Fort Salher for the last fifteen days. Faced with this, Gangwo has changed his strategy. He has ordered half his army to encircle the fort and lay a siege, hoping to starve the defenders into submission. The rest he is leading towards Fort Javli," Dramhodas passed the report he had just received from a spy.

Sensing that Dramhodas had more on his mind, Kolakwa asked, "What do you suggest?"

"The road from Fort Salher towards Fort Javli goes through a long, narrow mountain pass with steep sides. As Gangwo's army goes through this pass, it will be stretched into a long, thin column, providing us with a rare opportunity. A group of our men will attack from the front end of the pass, while another group will attack from the rear end.

Since the enemy will be crowded in a narrow space, only a small number will face our soldiers. Even with fewer numbers, we can cause much damage. We will loudly cry 'Hail Atmaraj' every ten minutes. It will signal fresh soldiers from the back to the front while the exhausted front soldiers retreat. Given the new, rested soldiers, facing the same enemy soldiers every ten minutes will place us at a significant advantage. The rested soldiers will replace the fighters in cycles. Their soldiers in the middle of the column will be uselessly trapped, unable to contribute to the fighting. Even if they realize what we are doing, they cannot coordinate this same strategy. Simultaneously, we will attack the center of the column from the side hills with large stones and arrows," Dramhodas said excitedly.

The plan made sense, and Kolakwa agreed to it. Dramhodas started preparing for the mission. He divided the available soldiers into three groups. After consulting with senior Mormos, he drew detailed maps. Dramhodas sent soldiers to collect large boulders on the top of the hills on both sides of the pass, ready to be pushed over onto the Gangwo's army.

As the day of the attack came close, Dramhodas became increasingly worried about the secrecy of his plan. Too many Mormos and their soldiers knew of the preparation because they needed to coordinate multiple groups. The enemy spies could get the details.

As the news came to Dramhodas that Gangwo's army was a day's march from the pass, he gave orders for one group to hide near the entrance of the pass. Once most of the army entered the pass, they were to attack the rear. He ordered the second group to go to the top of the two sides of the pass and rain the boulders and arrows on the army as it passed. The third group was to be led by Dramhodas to attack the army as it exited through the front of the pass. Dramhodas hoped to face Gangwo himself, leading the army.

Hours passed as he waited anxiously at the exit, but no one came through the pass. He sent a soldier to check the pass stealthily, who returned saying that Gangwo's army had stopped at the mouth of the pass instead of entering.

Suddenly, Dramhodas heard Gangwo's soldiers at his rear. A vast number of Gangwo's men attacked from the back of all three Atmaraj groups. Dramhodas's group was the only one with a way out by escaping from the ambush. As his men, some of whom were his older relatives and friends from his village, implored him to get away with them, Dramhodas made his decision. *I will fight on my accord. My decision, my right, my duty. No one is ordering me. I only fight for Dramho, Atmaraj, and my men.*

Dramhodas ordered, "This is my order. All of you will escape to Javli. Live to fight another day. Hail Atmaraj, Hail Dramho." Dramhodas had never directly ordered his elders. He always suggested his orders. Today was different.

Dramhodas turned and rushed toward the other two groups of trapped soldiers. The enemy outnumbered Dramhodas's men by a ratio of five to one.

Dramhodas had leaped into a large group of Daitya soldiers with the flexible five-blade sword Saumitra had given to him. He cut the enemy to pieces, giving the appearance of tall grass being mowed down by a scythe. Every Atmaraj soldier fought bravely, but to no avail. The number of enemies was too overwhelming. Although many of Gangwo's men were killed, barely any Atmaraj soldiers survived. No one surrendered. Gangwo had ordered that if any of his soldiers retreated, they should be summarily killed by his other soldiers. None of Gangwo's men could retreat from Dramhodas's flexible sword onslaught.

Dramhodas was getting exhausted as more soldiers kept attacking him. His shield had broken after fending off many spears thrown at him. He wrapped the cloth of his headgear around his left fist to act as a shield. The sweat mixed with blood from his head wounds was pouring on his face, getting into his eyes, obscuring his vision. He frantically tried wiping his face on his sleeves, which were also soaked in his blood. He was fighting almost blindly. However, since so many Gangwo soldiers surrounded him, he still managed to kill many. He was chanting Dramho's name to keep going.

Dramhodas killed an increasing number of Gangwo's men, causing Gangwo to become mad with anger.

"Join me, you fool. I will spare you and reward you," Gangwo stood on his elephant and hollered at Dramhodas. He ordered his elephant driver to charge the elephant towards Dramhodas from the rear. Without waiting for the elephant to hit Dramhodas, he threw three spears at Dramhodas's back in quick succession, of which two pierced him through his broken armor.

As he fell, Dramhodas murmured, "Dramho, I was a servant only to you and no one else. Take me, Dramho. Take care of Atmaraj." He smiled as he dropped his head in the lap of his beloved Atmaraj.

The elephant driver heard Gangwo order him to prod the elephant and crush the fallen Dramhodas' body, followed by a maniacal scream and demonic laughing. He turned to look at Gangwo, who had pulled off his helmet. Tears were rolling from his eyes. He was clutching his head and shrieking words in the Mulki language. Although battle-hardened, the elephant driver, an old loyal soldier, trembled at the look of pure insanity on Gangwo's face. He prayed. *Ghumu, Dramho, anybody, please save my master*. He turned the elephant and drove him back to Gangwo's camp.

A few of the Atmaraj soldiers escaped and reached Fort Vitora. They narrated the great debacle and the bravery of Dramhodas and the men. Some traitor had betrayed Atmaraj by giving information about the plans to Gangwo.

As they sat in the Dramho shrine, Kolakwa and Krikaneel avoided looking at each other as tears drizzled down their cheeks. Mahadoo just sat staring at the Dramho. *First Rokba, now Dramhodas is gone. I pray I am next. I cannot take more losses.*

They hid the news from Mamalu, who was now ill, almost bedridden.

Savitri invited Krikaneel, Triya, and Mahadoo over for lunch, knowing they would not eat if left alone. She hugged Triya and wiped her swollen eyes with a cold damp cloth.

"We should not lose our way in the fog of grief and anger. We need to keep thinking." Kolakwa after the silent lunch.

"I have asked our spies to watch the Mormos who have survived and try to find out who the traitor was," Krikaneel assured them.

"I knew this day would come. Our people have a long history of betraying each other for small rewards. We will soon catch the traitor. Until then, we must be cautious and watch each other's back," Kolakwa put on a brave face as they agreed to meet the next day. He silently recited a patriotic song Saumitra had taught him, fighting the overwhelming feeling of hopelessness.

The fear that someone was destroying Atmaraj from within cast a dark shadow on everyone in Fort Vitora. Everybody started suspecting each other. Paranoia polluted the usual atmosphere of camaraderie and trust.

Every day, Krikaneel tried to assuage Triya's grief but could not bring out any words. One day, Triyacaught Krikaneel staring at a dent in a wall, which Dramhodas had caused while showing off his strength during childhood play. Holding his arm, she gently said, "Every warrior who chooses his path knows that death is not an 'if' but a definite 'when.' All warriors aspire to a noble death. My brother got his wish. I thank Dramho for that."

* * *

Fort Javli put in a long and heroic effort at defense. A spear thrown at Gangwo just missed him and killed his elephant driver. This close encounter with death, in what was supposed to be a simple expedition to stamp out the rebels, greatly annoyed Gangwo. Soldiers from Javli used the hidden doors on the ramparts to come out at night and raid Gangwo's army on suicide missions. The farmers in the surrounding area set fire to their crops and granaries rather than let Gangwo's men get them. When Fort Javli ultimately fell, Gangwo could not find a single living soldier. Most had perished in suicide raids. A few who were alive hid in secret rooms and, for the next few days, would come out at night and kill the sleeping Gangwo's men. Unfortunately, they were discovered and killed. A handful escaped to Fort Vitora.

Gangwo's army approached Fort Vitora and increased their destruction and atrocities in the surrounding villages. The cruelty of Gangwo knew no bounds. Gangwo himself took part in the brutality, sometimes ordering a soldier to commit torture, then intervening and doing it himself. Gangwo had hoped that Kolakwa would not be able to control himself after hearing the massive destruction and cruelty toward his subjects. In a fit of rage, he would rush to battle with Gangwo's army head-on. Then Gangwo could easily destroy him.

However, with the moral support of Krikaneel and Savitri, Kolakwa maintained self-control. A month passed, but Gangwo made no progress in the siege of Fort Vitora. Ample stores of grains kept the defenders well-fed. The deep wells provided abundant water. Gangwo's blockade of the Fort did not severely affect its dwellers. The defenders repealed multiple direct assaults on the main doors. Krikaneel's spies carefully observed all the gate guards to prevent traitors from opening the doors.

There was a spiraling in the frequency of the warnings of Gangwo's Zigadors and Mormos that their Mulkan soldiers were getting increasingly restless. The long-dormant self-respect and sense of honor were being stirred in the Mulkan soldiers. They openly voiced anger against the needless destruction and inhumane treatment of men, women, and children. The number of desertions increased exponentially. Moreover, the nightly raids on Gangwo's camp sapped the morale of his soldiers.

One day, a spy brought the news that the Shamonda's two sons in the North western Kingdom were leading a revolt against the Ruler. The relatives and the descendants of the original Northwestern Kingdom king, who had fled to take refuge with barbarians from the far west, were supporting the brothers. These descendants were allowed to leave when Shamonda defeated the king of the Northwestern Kingdom. Now that Gangwo and a sizable portion of the army were away, they had joined the two brothers who were attacking the west sideof the Ruler's empire.

"Why would the Northwestern Kingdom King's descendants side with my brothers, who are the children of the man who defeated them?" asked Kolakwa.

"I have heard over the years that our father was very generous to the defeated Northwestern king's relatives and descendants and let them leave with enough wealth to sustain themselves and their families. Our father's second wife, the mother of our brothers, was the niece of the defeated king, whom he treated very well. Therefore, our Northwestern brothers are related by blood to the descendants of the older king," Krikaneel replied.

"Do you think our brothers are trying to help us?" Kolakwa asked, hoping that his deepest wishes were coming true.

"It does not matter whether the brothers are doing this to establish their own kingdom at the time when the Ruler's side is weak, the relatives of the old king are exacting revenge for the defeat of their ancestors, or they are trying to help us. This development will only make Gangwo want to return to the capital urgently," Krikaneel replied hopefully.

* * *

At Gangwo's encampment, some Daitya Zigadors and Mormos warned Gangwo, "We may be unable to keep the Mulkan soldiers under control much longer. There are open talks of mutiny. If a rebellion among the Mulkan soldiers ignited in a small corner, it would spread to destructive proportions. Further, given the far west barbarians attacking the empire, we are worried about our families in the capital."

"I think I can draw the snake Kolakwa out of his burrow tomorrow. He will not tolerate this," Gangwo assured them. Armed with a massive hammer, Gangwo went to the Gireshwar shrine and shattered the Dramho crystal. He was confident that seeing his beloved shrine destroyed, Kolakwa would lose his calm and come out of the fort to attack Gangwo in the open.

On hearing the news of the destruction of Gireshwar Dramho, Kolakwa walked to the Dramho shrine in Fort Vitora. He lit an oil lamp and sat cross-legged on the grass mat, meditating on the brilliance of the Dramho crystal as the light from the lamp refracted through the multiple irregular facets. He prayed, "I am just your instrument. But based on the mother, teachers, friends, and followers you have given me, I believe I am the tip of your sword. The time has come for me to pierce the heart of the evil and destroy it or get destroyed trying. Based on what the spies have told us, now may be the best opportunity to strike at the core of the evil. Please bless me with the clarity of thought, strength of body, and calmness of mind to fulfill my role as the piercing tip of the sword in your hand."

As a gentle breeze flickered the flame of the oil lamp, its refracted light on Dramho made the crystal shimmer and look alive.

The following day, Kolakwa called Krikaneel, Mahadoo, and Savitri to his chamber. He also invited his three senior-most Mormos. Kolakwa said, "I think Gangwo must be getting impatient and desperate. The events in the Northwestern Kingdom must have made him eager to return north. He would grab an opportunity for a quick conclusion of this expedition." I will send this letter to Gangwo. He read a letter he had composed earlier.

"This is extremely perilous. Gangwo will attack you with treachery. Even if he is unarmed, Gangwo is so strong that he can kill you with his bare hands," Krikaneel warned.

"We will work on that. In the last few years, we, too, have learned some tricks from our enemies, my dear Krikaneel," Kolakwa uttered with a slight smile.

After pausing for an instant, he looked at all the assembled people in the room in the eyes, one after another. "If Dramho desires, I will be victorious. If I lose and fail to return due to death or become a prisoner, I

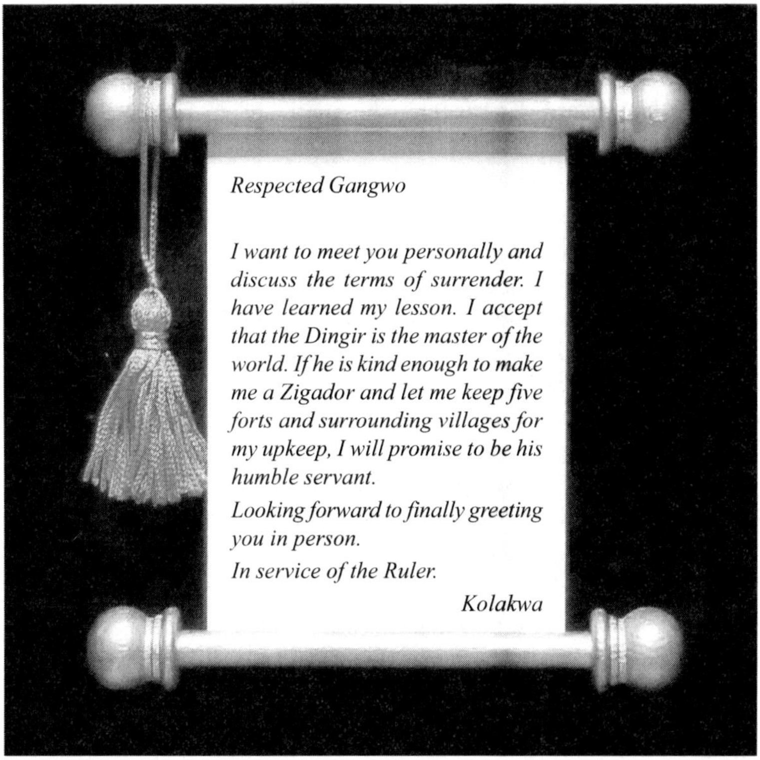

order that you will not pay any ransom or exchange to rescue me. I want you to make Krikaneel the next leader of Atmaraj. After him, he will choose the next leader."

Kolakwa took a few steps towards the other senior Mormos. "Give me your word, witnessed by Dramho, that you will support Krikaneel as you have supported me. Our struggle will continue for multiple generations, and the leader will choose the successor every generation," Kolakwa urged. Some members of the council dabbed their tears from their eyes.

After the meeting, Krikaneel went to Kolakwa's chamber. "My Naresh, who will go with you as your bodyguard? We cannot trust anybody, not even our senior Mormos. So let me come with you," Krikaneel beseeched.

Savitri stepped forward, "Krikaneel, if you die with our Naresh, who will continue the fight? I trust you. You are competent with training and knowledge. Our Mormos and soldiers have known you since birth and will accept you as their leader. I do not think your birth circumstances are an issue anymore. Suppose anything happens to our Naresh. You are our only hope to continue leading this fight. Just because I am married to our Naresh does not qualify me as the leader."

Kolakwa was surprised that Savitri was so brutally forthright."I will go as his bodyguard. Krikaneel," she continued. "You have seen my fighting skills. Nobody wants my Naresh to live more than me. I will make sure he will come back safe."

Kolakwa nodded in acquiescence.

Afterward, a messenger was sent to Gangwo to arrange a preliminary meeting between Krikaneel and Gangwo's secretary on neutral grounds. Krikaneel delivered Kolakwa's letter to the secretary. Krikaneel put forward more stipulations. Gangwo and Kolakwa would meet at an equal distance from Gangwo's encampment and the door to Fort Vitora. Both armies would stay at least one hour's travel distance from the meeting site. Kolakwa and Gangwo would be unarmed and accompanied by one bodyguard carrying one weapon. Krikaneel offered to set up a tent in the neutral territory and suggested that no time be wasted exchanging gifts.

The nextday, a messenger arrived, saying that Gangwo had agreed to the terms. They finalized the time of noon on the day after three days.

On the day before the meeting, Kolakwa went to his mother's chamber. After touching the ground before her feet, he sat next to her. "Mother, I am going to meet Gangwo. Do you have any suggestions for me?" he asked.

Mamalu placed her hand on Kolakwa's head and warned, "Gangwo is very deceitful. He murdered your maternal grandfather and uncles. I pray to Dramho to give you enough deviousness to counter the evil of Gangwo. Take as many precautions as you can. Any tactics you use to protect Atmaraj will be on the side of good and will have Dramho's blessing. Be victorious, my son. Atmaraj needs you. There is more to be done; more of Dramho's wishes are to be fulfilled through your hands."

Afterward, Kolakwa and Savitri retired to their private chamber. Kolakwa hugged her. "Savitri, your father, and brothers warned you about the possibility of a short life for me. Now, you are decreasing your life span on your own accord by coming with me."

Savitri looked into his eyes, "My Naresh, I trust your abilities. My faith in Dramho is firm. My faith says that we will be victorious."

Grasping her hands, Kolakwa replied, "If Dramho has other plans for me, I trust Krikaneel to carry on the struggle. After him, Dramho will take care of Atmaraj. We humans are just fragile instruments through which Dramho's will manifests. His will becomes true regardless of what we try." They hugged each other, wishing they had more time to spend with each other in this life.

Chapter–27

Meeting with Gangwo

Kolakwa's men raised a spacious, simple tent in a forest clearing located one hour's marching distance from the entrance of Fort Vitora. The tent had an entrance on either side. Gangwo's army also retreated the same distance from that site and set up a camp. The top of the tent hoisted the flags of the Ruler and Atmaraj.Under Kolakwa's orders, the servants ensured that the Ruler's flag was more prominent and flew slightly higher than the Atmaraj flag.

On entering the tent, it was easy to see that there were no places to hide weapons. A single table without drawers was kept in the center, with two chairs on opposite sides. A parchment paper with mutually agreed terms was placed with two quills and an ink pot for the signatures. There would be no food or drink.

As Gangwo prepared for the meeting at his camp, he concealed a formidable dagger in the belt around his waist, carefully hidden beneath his tunic."Nobody would dare to search me," he murmured. As he caressed and admired his Daitya facial scars in the mirror, he abruptly paused. "Why not?" he exclaimed. Reaching into a drawer of his desk, he picked up the ring belonging to the founder of the Daitya faith. After twirling it on his gigantic palm, Gangwo removed his necklace and strung the ring through it. Afterward, he wore the necklace again.

Gangwo had ordered his trusted right-hand man and body guard to accompany him. This man was reputed for his incredible strength and mastery in sword fighting. Legends spoke of the time when, with a single stroke, he cleaved an enemy soldier from shoulder to pelvis and even the horse that the enemy rode into two pieces.

Gangwo told his bodyguard, "Once you hear me say 'Long live the Ruler,' you should immediately cut off the head of Kolakwa's bodyguard without waiting for instructions."

The bodyguard hid two throwing knives in his belt and tied one to the side of his leg. He also carried his sword.

As he prepared for the meeting, Kolakwa summoned the man from Fort Devagiri, who had constructed the scar concealing the knife on the forearm of his failed assassin. The man created a similar scar on Kolakwa's forearm to hide the knife gifted by the Mleccha Queen. Kolakwa was certain Gangwo would insist on a body search for concealed weapons.

After the eye injury, Kolakwa started wearing a Crimson-colored patch over his injured eye. For this meeting, he removed the patch to look more menacing. Kolakwa's cap had a metal ring inside to protect his skull. The rising sun symbol on his forehead was deliberately larger than usual to annoy Gangwo.

Kolakwa put on the chain mail with the neck guard gifted to him by the Mleccha queen. Remembering the warning from the Mleccha man about the weakness of the armor against a strong stab attack, Mahadoo added a layer of reptile leather with overlapping scales to make the back portion of the chain-mail armor more resistant to a piercing weapon. He also advised, "My Naresh, I suggest that you hunch down and limp when approaching Gangwo, feigning weakness and disability. This will make Gangwo overconfident and less alert."

Savitri had sharpened Queen Amma's sword, which was gifted by her father. Her long arm sleeves hid sharp knives. A sharpened iron chakram was painted golden to look like an ornament and hidden in her headgear. She also prepared a fake mustache and beard, along with a fake scar on her forehead, in order to conceal her feminine features.

On the meeting day, Kolakwa and Savitri rode from Fort Vitora with fifty soldiers. The soldiers stopped at a ten-minute distance from the tent. Earlier, four trusted observers with sharp eyes had crawled stealthily in pairs within the observing distance of both entrances of the tent. Kolakwa had instructed them to blow conches regardless of whether Kolakwa or Gangwo came out of the tent, indicating that the meeting was over.

The fifty troops had been ordered to slowly advance towards the meeting tent as the meeting was taking place. They were to attack Gangwo and accompanying troops as soon as they heard conches signaling that the meeting was over.

Overa thousand Atmaraj soldiers, reinforced with a few hundred deserters from Gangwo's army, had entered the surrounding forest the night before and waited. The story of treachery and the death of Dramhodas was fresh on everyone's mind. Therefore, everyone was very vigilant.

A large number of soldiers had come from other forts from the south and east over the last few days and had hidden in the villages surrounding Gangwo's army. Savitri's father had joined this group with his Mormos and their soldiers. An hour before the Kolakwa-Gangwo meeting, messengers had reached these soldiers with orders to get ready and stealthily advance toward Gangwo's army. They were to launch an all-out attack on hearing the conches. Kolakwa hoped that the valor of his men and the home turf advantage of the battlefield would be enough to defeat Gangwo's army, which, even after the massive desertion, was at least three times larger than the combined Atmaraj forces.

As the time of the meeting approached, Kolakwa and Savitri advanced to a point within five minutes of walking distance of their side of the tent. Gangwo in his horse-wagon and his body guard, had reached a similar distance on the other side. His accompanying fifty men waited at a ten-minute distance.

The bodyguards raised their arms to signal each other. Both dismounted and approached the tent to examine for hidden weapons or other suspicious findings. Gangwo's bodyguard stared in disbelief at the small stature of Kolakwa's bodyguard.

While the bodyguards were inside the tent, Gangwo stood in his wagon, puffing his chest. He was confident that his vast stature must have struck fear in Kolakwa. But having observed Shamonda for decades and knowing him to be a crafty and brave warrior, Gangwo was uneasy. He patted his dagger as if reassuring it and flexed his arm and chest muscles, reminding himself of his strength.

"Even if his kid is half as crafty as Shamonda, I should be cautious," Gangwo muttered. But observing Kolakwa's stature, his arrogance returned.

The bodyguards palpated the undersurface of the table and the chairs, checking for hidden weapons. After nodding to each other, they retreated out of the tent and stayed where they could closely watch each other. "I will make this quick," Gangwo said to his bodyguard. After I have finished the dog, you can cut off his head and send it to Dingir. Then, send his headless body back to Fort Vitora.

As he stepped into the meeting tent, Kolakwa remembered Saumitra's words. *You are merely an instrument of Dramho to re-establish justice. Maintain equal poise of mind, unaffected by pride or sorrow in victory or loss.* With this in mind, Kolakwa prayed, *Dramho, now everything is in your hands*.

Kolakwa and Gangwo entered the tent from opposite entrances. As his sight fell on Kolakwa, Gangwo could not believe that a person of such a small physical stature could cause so much trouble for him. As his eyes met Kolakwa's good eye, Gangwo expected to see pure hatred and anger on Kolakwa's face, just as it was boiling in his heart and mind. But all he saw was serenity and peace.

The calmness on Kolakwa's face unnerved Gangwo. He no longer felt in total control of the situation. Irritated, he spoke in his booming voice, "Come, dear Kolakwa, son of my departed friend, Shamonda. Give me a hug."

Kolakwa smiled, saying, "Uncle Gangwo, you are like my father's brother. I was told that my father saved your life during the Great War. I trust you. After all, who would harm the son of the man who had saved his life?"

Any average person would have felt a pinprick in their conscience. But Kolakwa knew Gangwo was a fiend. This person had no sense of gratitude.

Kolakwa stepped towards Gangwo. Gangwo rapidly walked towards him and held him in a bear hug. Gangwo then changed his stance and lifted his right arm to grab Kolakwa's head and neck under his armpit and apply severe pressure. Because Kolakwa was stooping as advised by Mahadoo, Gangwo could not grasp his entire neck. With his left hand, he pulled the dagger from his belt and stabbed Kolakwa's back.

Luckily, the Mleccha chain armor protected Kolakwa. However, Gangwo's strength started crushing the neck guard of the armor, and the pressure from Gangwo's arm began to occlude the blood flow to Kolakwa's brain.

Kolakwa felt darkness descending in front of his eyes. With immense effort, he scratched off the fake scar on his forearm and pulled out the sharp blade. He stabbed Gangwo under his breastbone and cut down to his pelvis. Gangwo let out a loud, earth-shattering scream. Gangwo's skin was thick by human standards. Kolakwa inserted both his hands into the incision and tore apart the belly muscles, pulling out Gangwo's guts.

Gangwo's screams astounded his bodyguard, stunned by this unexpected turn of events. In a daze, he struggled to decide whether to attack Kolakwa's bodyguard or rush into the tent to aid his master. Those few seconds gave Savitri time to dash inside. Once inside the tent, she confirmed Kolakwa was okay. She then turned to face Gangwo's bodyguard, who had followed her. On seeing Gangwo lying on the floor, Gangwo's bodyguard raised the sword to strike Kolakwa.

Just at that moment, Savitri thrust her sword to block the blow. The force of the bodyguard's sword strike was so great that Savitri's sword broke. But it deviated the bodyguard's sword away from Kolakwa. The striking blade hit the table and lodged in it. As Gangwo's bodyguard tried to dislodge the sword, Savitri stabbed the bodyguard with the broken sword in the chest.

"Thank you for saving my life, Savitri," Kolakwa barely uttered.

"Queen Amma's sword saved you, me, and the Atmaraj." Savitri touched the broken sword to her forehead.

Both stepped out of the tent. On seeing Kolakwa, the observers blew their conchs, signaling the fifty warriors to advance and attack Gangwo's accompanying troops. The soldiers blew their conchs and yelled, "Long live Atmaraj," as they galloped towards Gangwo's men. As they crossed the meeting tent, the soldiers were overjoyed to see Kolakwa and Savitri getting on their horses and riding towards Vitora.

Gangwo's soldiers were confident that he would kill Kolakwa and were in a celebratory mood, not expecting to fight. On seeing Atmaraj soldiers riding towards them yelling, "Gangwo is dead, Gangwo is dead," they hastily started getting ready to battle. In the meantime, some of Gangwo's soldiers rushed to the meeting tent. Once they confirmed his death, they lost any desire to fight and fled to the main cantonment.

They reached the main camp, screaming, "The devil Kolakwa has killed Gangwo!" Upon hearing the news, panic seized the base. The Daityas could not believe how their invincible leader was dead. Many Zigadors tried to rally their troops, but to no avail. Most Mulkan soldiers in Gangwo's army either ignored their Zigadors and started running away or turned on the Daitya soldiers.

Alerted by the blowing conchs, the Atmaraj soldiers hiding in the forests and the others previously hiding in the villages attacked Gangwo's main camp. Although they were fewer, the shouting of slogans and blowing of conches and trumpets gave an appearance of a much larger Atmaraj force. Kolakwa's men attacked from three sides, leaving one side open for the enemy to escape.

Initially, a few of Gangwo's soldiers started fleeing. Discouraged by Gangwo's demise and tired from the long campaign, the other soldiers also started running, resulting in a complete rout.

* * *

After returning to Fort Vitora, Kolakwa visited Mamalu, who gave him a thick gold bracelet she had hidden for thirty years. "This bracelet belonged to my father, your grandfather. You have avenged his murder."

Chapter–28

Aftermath

A month after Gangwo's defeat, Krikaneel came to Kolakwa one afternoon. He reported, "My Naresh, our spies in Dabrahoor, have brought news about the latest developments. The Ruler's army has stopped the combined forces of our brothers and their allies, although losing lots of land in the northwest. A truce is being negotiated."

"Have any spies reported that the void caused by Gangwo's demise is changing the power structure at the Ruler's court?" Kolakwa asked.

Krikaneel shook his head in a negative.

"Since Gangwo's defeat, our soldiers liberated all the lands and the forts captured by him. Even Fort Devagiri is now in Atmaraj. The Mormos and soldiers at the fort were angry after hearing the assassination attempt on you. After Gangwo's defeat, they became bold and rebelled, taking over the fort. In the resulting fight, both Zigador and his brother Bidero perished. The fort is now part of Atmaraj," Krikaneel continued his report.

"That assassination attempt gave us the idea for hiding the knife," Kolakwa smiled.

"Some Zigadors in the lands outside Atmaraj have also switched sides and have allied with us. We will send an Atmaraj charter of rights guaranteeing the right of protection of life, property, and honor to the Zigadors to sign, witnessed by their village heads. We have posted spies to ensure that the Zigadors rule with the same sense of fairness as the rest of the Atmaraj." Krikaneel bowed and departed.

In Fort Vitora, Kolakwa called an advisory council meeting. A fresh addition was Krikaneel's wife, Triya. Triya provided the perspective of ordinary citizens, particularly women from Atmaraj, because of her experience living with them.

At that moment, Mamalu stepped into the room. "In the last three hundred years, no Mulkan king has been coronated. It is time to rectify that," Mamalu said, looking at Kolakwa. Everybody was pleasantly surprised to see the bedridden Mamalu get up and walk.

"Why do I need to be coronated?" asked Kolakwa.

"My Naresh, coronation will give a sense of beginning to our people. We will no longer be looked upon as a bunch of rebels and upstarts. You will be a proper king, and the subjects of Atmaraj will experience a sense of pride," Krikaneel said enthusiastically, each word echoing a sense of determination and optimism.

Kolakwa retorted, "This feels like too much of a self-glorifying ritual."

Krikaneel was persistent, "My Naresh, you will sit on the throne representing the will of Dramho. Your throne will be called Dramho's throne, and the wisdom of Dramho will flow through you to all of us. We will be instruments of Dramho's will."

Finally, Kolakwa reluctantly agreed.

* * *

The advisory council chose an auspicious date for the coronation based on the advice of the head priest. Around this time, a small group of soldiers arrived, bringing a solid gold jewel-encrusted throne. The leader of the soldiers addressed Kolakwa. "My Naresh, we found this throne in a hidden room in Fort Devagiri. On questioning the treasury keeper for the old Zigador, he informed us that this throne belonged to an ancient Mulkan king whose descendants were defeated by the Daitya Zigador's ancestors. They stole and hid the throne without passing it on to the Ruler."

The throne was in the shape of a chair on the back of a flying eagle, clutching a snake in its claws. Krikaneel explained, "An elephant head design adorning the top of the chair's backrest signifies wisdom. The front ends of the armrests, molded in the shape of alion's head, are gripped by the palms of the person sitting, signifying control over animalistic thoughts like anger, jealousy, arrogance, and attachment." The chair also had an attached umbrella with a large Dramho crystal on its top, symbolizing Dramho's protection. Many jewels were embedded throughout the throne. "With the dawn of a new era, the right to sit on this throne belongs to you, my Naresh. It is an heirloom from our cultural ancestors," said the Mormo who brought the throne.

Kolakwa looked overwhelmed by the prospect of sitting on such a priceless throne. Fearing that Kolakwa would refuse to accept the throne, Krikaneel jumped in and thanked the Mormo. He declared, "We will summon a jeweler to design a matching crown for our Naresh Kolakwa and the future Nareshs, who will grace this throne. We will embed the crown with the crimson Dramho crystal that Rokba had discovered in the puzzle box from Mahadoo's teacher."

Kolakwa closed his eyes. *The crown will be placed on my head. But the coronation is for everybody.*

On the evening before the coronation day, Krikaneel requested an audience with Kolakwa. As he entered the room, Kolakwa noticed he was carrying a flat object covered with a crimson silk cloth.

"This is your coronation gift from Saumitra. He charged me to safeguard it till the appropriate time."

Kolakwa bent forward and touched the object with his forehead. He lifted the cover, exposing a copper plate with an engraved message.

"You must be the unwavering lighthouse of Atmaraj. Life's unpredictable events will sway many around you, just as driftwood is tossed about by the sea waves, elated during favorable times, and downcast during the challenging ones. But you shall remain grounded in your steadfast devotion to Atmarajand stand resilient. You will be a lighthouse, unyielding against the fleeting waves of joy and sorrow that ebb and flow at your base. Let your enduring spirit be the beacon that guides others, motivating them to come together and elevate to their highest potential.

May Dramho always make you victorious

Saumitra

Tears flowed through Kolakwa's eyes, dropping onto the glistening plate.

On the day of the coronation, pitchers from the land's rivers were brought in and ceremonially showered on Kolakwa. An enormous number of flowers were showered on the guests. Holy chants from ancient scriptures resonated from the tent of coronation. All the attendees blessed Kolakwa. Grains, cows, and money were distributed among the poor. Flowers, various nuts, and scented wood were offered into the sacrificial fire. Kolakwa was showered with gold coins, which were then distributed to the families of all the soldiers who had perished in the wars to expand Atmaraj. The security was well maintained, and many spies loyal to Kolakwa intermingled with the guests.

An old man who was a representative from Kolakwa's brothers in the Northwestern Kingdom presented himself with many gifts and conveyed apologies from the brothers for not being able to attend the coronation due to minor insurgencies in their area. He then requested a private audience with Kolakwa.

During a break in the ceremonies, after necessary security precautions, the man was invited to the Kolakwa's audience room. Hehanded Kolakwa a small wooden box. On opening the box, Kolakwa was surprised to see a pair of copper earrings with small crimson Dramho suspended from them. "This is your inheritance from your father. These earrings have been passed for generations along the lineage of holy men. Your grandfather Raiba's teacher bequeathed them to him.. Your grandfather deemed your father Shamonda a rightful heir based on his achievements. On his deathbed, your father instructed your brothers to pass them on to you. In the future, you will decide the next bearer of this honor and responsibility," the man said with tears in his eyes.

Kolakwa was too stunned to wipe the profuse tears running down his cheeks. The man stepped ahead and asked, "Can I adorn you with these earrings? I removed them from your father after he left his body. No other hands have touched them since then."

After Kolakwa nodded, the man replaced Kolakwa's jewels-encrusted earrings with Shamonda's.

Later, as he sat on his throne, Kolakwa inspected the happy guests in the massive tent and envisioned Rokba and Dramhodas smiling at him from the front row. A curtain of sadness descended over him. This sadness then changed into anger. W*hich one of these people had betrayed Atmaraj, causing us to lose Dramhodas?*

Chapter–29

New Beginnings

"We vow to dedicate our lives to overthrowing the yoke of foreign rule and establish Atmaraj where no one will be oppressed, and everybody's land, body, and mind will be protected as holy. Here is my blood to sanctify my vow."

Kolakwa, Krikaneel, Mahadoo, Savitri, Triya, Bhumi, and little Rokba kneeled in a circle. Unknown to everybody, two little lives were also present in their mother's wombs, who jumped when their mothers shed their blood drops. Kolakwa ran his thumb on the sharp edge of his sword and ran a stream of blood into a small pit where the Gireshwar Dramho crystal used to stand. Others followed the age-old ritual. Even little Rokba participated with his mother, making a pinprick on his tiny finger.

As they silently prayed, Kolak wagazed around the circle. His eyes paused at the spot where Rokba and Dramhodas had stood before and became heavy with sadness. He inhaled slowly. *Dramho, please keep this circle expanding.*

Kolakwa stood up and pointed at the Giresh war crystal pit. "Let the pit be a reminder for the coming ages that everyone should be constantly vigilant, united, strong, and willing to sacrifice their lives to prevent this from happening again."

This concludes the story of the birth and early years of Atmaraj.

Notes

I did not include a few interactions in the book. However, as an afterthought, I believe that you, my readers, should be privy to these:

"Remember, my little Naresh, neither a horse, elephant, nor a tiger, but only the weak lamb is sacrificed in a ritual. Never be weak in strength, number, or wealth."

–Saumitra.

* * *

"Am I not too young to dream of challenging the Ruler? Why are the adults not doing anything?"

–Kolakwa, at age eight, asked Saumitra.

"Last week, a bear handler visited Fort Vitora with the performing bear who danced and begged for money. The performing bear was most likely an orphan found by the handler, who put a metal ring through its snout to tie a rope through it. The cub was most likely castrated to become docile. When these captured cubs are little, the handler forces them to stand in a heated pan sitting on the fire to hurt them into submission. The next time they see a pan, they remember the pain in their paws and become subservient to the handler, never fighting back."

"Do you remember the black bear we encountered three years ago while visiting the southern parts of our land? The bear mauled our soldiers, and he escaped after fighting for more than half an hour. Its mother trained the wild bear cub with love and safety yet gradually exposed it to danger to develop its strength and confidence. The two bears we saw were similar in size and age. But you can see the difference in the temperament of those two animals based on their upbringing. My dear little Naresh, unfortunately, the adults who should fight for Atmaraj have grown accustomed to the slave mentality. Occasionally, few people have rebelled and fought back, but they fought as a reaction to a specific insult and fought alone. As a result, they were crushed, and seeing their fate, others extinguished any spark of self-respect in themselves or their children."

Then, straightening up, he said, "I believe that your upbringing will make the difference in whether you become a free wild bear or a dancing bear."

–Saumitra's reply to Kolakwa.

* * *

People will kill each other for small pieces of shiny metal but will gladly sacrifice their lives when inspired by a few words of a beloved leader.

–Saumitra, on the eve of the attack on Fort Sangram.

* * *

Always remember that no stone is useless. Just as every stone can be made functional by the person with the right idea, every man, woman, and child is useful for Atmaraj. You must find their best use.

–Saumitra to Kolakwa, just before they met Rokba.

* * *

Glossary

Advisory Council: Senior advisors to Kolakwa.

Atmaraj: Land of freedom, self-governance. Dream of the heroes of this book.

Bhumi: Rokba's lover and mother of his child, whom Mahadoo marries to shelter her from society's scorn.

Bidero: Younger brother of the Zigador of Devagiri, who sent the assassin to murder Kolakwa.

Brago: Title of the head of guards on a fort.

Braznee: The family name of Kolakwa, Shamonda and Raiba.

Frangi: A foreign race that competes with Mlecchas for trade-based imperialism.

Bunei: The region in which Fort Vitora was located.

Chain mail: A type of flexible armor made with interlocking metal rings.

Chetaki: A female monitor lizard native to Asia. They are the most intelligent lizards and maybe all reptiles. Mahadoo reared her since hatching.

Dabrahoor: Capital city of the Ruler, who heads the Daityas.

Daitya: Foreign invaders of a race with physical features like the Mulkans but following a different way of worship. They conquered the lands a few centuries ago and subjugated the Mulkan subjects. Overall, very intolerant of other faiths.

Damru: Kolakwa's first and favorite falcon.

Daryaveer: A fisher who became the admiral of the Atmaraj navy.

Dingir: The current Ruler and head of the Daityas.

Dramho: A crystal formed by the crystallized sap of the zavba tree, which represented the divine. The term was also commonly used to address the masculine aspect of divinity.

Dramhodas: Son of Ordora, chief of guards on Fort Vitora. Childhood playmate of Kolakwa and commander of the Atmaraj army in adulthood.

Falconer: The caretaker and trainer of Falcons.

Fireship: A ship built to be filled with explosives and combustibles sailed and steered among the enemy fleet. After being lit on fire, it ignites its neighboring ships.

Fort Vishram: A fort attacked by Kolakwa's army in preventive action.

Fort Basrud: A sea fort attacked by Kolakwa's army in preventive action.

Fort Kumbha: A fort attacked by Kolakwa's army in preventive action.

Fort Devagiri: The farthest fort to the north captured by Kolakwa in this book.

Fort Panha: A star-shaped fort attacked by Kolakwa's army in preventive action.

Fort Salher: Fort of Zigador Jaichand.

Fort Sangram: A fort captured from the Mleccha, later renamed Fort Rokba.

Fort Javli: The first fort captured by Kolakwa's army to punish the atrocities committed by neighboring Zigador.

Fort Rokba: Fort Sangram was renamed Fort Rokba

Fort Vishal: A fort south of Fort Vitora, captured during expansion.

Fort Salota: Fort next to Fort Salher.

Fort Vitora: Kolakwa's capital in Bunei province.

Gangwo: The man wielding the true power behind Dingir's throne.

Ghumu: Daitya's name for the Divine.

Gireshwar: An ancient Dramho shrine, the site of the oath of Atmaraj.

Great war: A large-scale war referred to in this book that occurred more than a decade before the birth of Kolakwa. Details will be described in a future book.

Jaichand: Zigador of Fort Salher. He tries to assassinate Kolakwa with poisoning.

King Maharana Pratap Singh Sisodia: Popularly known as Maharana Pratap. An inspiration to the author. A Rajput King of Mewar, India, who resisted Mogul emperor Akbar's conquests when other Rajput Kings capitulated.

Kolakwa: Leader of the Atmaraj.

Kwekwe: Mleccha festival.

Lodestones: Naturally occurring stones with magnetic properties.

Mahadoo: Orphan who became Kolakwa's friend and confidant. He was a builder of devices and had an exquisite love for animals. In addition, he had an unexpressed love interest in Rokba.

Mamalu: Kolakwa's mother. Great stateswoman.

Maru: Native land of Mlecchas.

Krikaneel: Kolakwa's advisor and illegitimate step-elder brother.

Mleccha: Seafaring alien race of imperialist traders, locally ruled by a Queen.

Mormo: A group leader under a Zigador who commands 10-50 men.

Mulkan: Native people of the lands on which this novel is based.

Naresh: Mulkan word for a King.

Ordora: A senior Mormo, the head of guards of Fort Vitora, the capital of Kolakwa's lands. Father of Dramhodas and Triya.

Port Surat: Mleccha capital on the west coast of the Shantiprastha plateau

Queen Amma: Historic Mulkan Queen who fought against the Daitya invaders. Her stories inspired Savitri.

Raiba: First known ancestor of Kolakwa who transitioned from farmer to warrior. Kolakwa's paternal grandfather.

Rokba: A goat herder who became a warrior.

Savitri: Name of Kolakwa's wife.

Shaisto: Mleccha general, cousin of the Queen with tremendous strength, who oversaw Fort Sangram.

Shamonda: Kolakwa's father and Raiba's son.

Shivaji Bhosle: A King in western India, popularly known as Chhatrapati Shivaji Maharaj, was a gallant warrior and morally upright ideal to people on the Indian subcontinent who started the liberation of the Hindu people of India from foreign Islamic rulers in the 17th century.

Shreeti: A deity representing the feminine aspect of the Divinity.

Swamini: Sea to the west of Kolakwa's lands.

Swaminidurg: The first sea fort constructed on the coast by Kolakwa.

Tipki: 'Spot.' Pet female Cheetah, which belongs to Savitri.

Triya: Krikaneel's wife, Dramhodas's younger sister, Ordora's daughter.

Veershri: Daryaveer's love interest. Member of the crew on fireship during the attack on Fort Basrud.

Saumitra: Kolakwa's teacher, whose background is not revealed in this book.

Zavba: Tree whose shape represents the flag of Atmaraj, whose crystallized sap forms the Dramho crystal.

Zigador: A warrior chieftain who controls a large piece of land and is aligned with an overlord Ruler.

About the Author

Originally hailing from Mumbai, India, Mandar Pattekar has called thc USA his home for over three decades. Since childhood, the stories of Chhatrapati Shivaji Maharaj, who initiated the liberation of his homeland from the Adilshahi and Mughal invaders, have been intricately woven into the fabric of his being. His childhood pastimes, such as constructing play-forts with rocks and mud, and fighting mock battles with sticks, evolved into an adult passion for history. This passion manifests as a penchant for story-telling and writing on historical, Hindu philosophical, and cultural themes.

Now retired from his medical profession, Mandar resides in Peoria, IL, with his wife and three grown children. Actively engaged in volunteering for educational and social initiatives within an underprivileged area in Peoria, he also serves as a mentor to the youth. His diverse collection of articles can be found at www.pattekar.org.

Footnotes

1. A Zigador was a warlord who had a thousand to five thousand horsemen under his command. Few had more than ten thousand. They administered large swaths of land in the empire, paid annual taxes to the Ruler, and swore allegiance to him. They supplied men and resources to the Ruler, in case of war.
2. A Mormo was a warrior who had twenty-five to one hundred men under his command. Some or all may be horsemen. A Mormo administered two to five villages of his Zigador's realm. All Mormos swore allegiance to a particular Zigador, and through him to the Ruler.
3. Equivalent happenings in our dimension are the Spanish Inquisitions in Southern Europe, South America, and Goa – India. Also, during the Islamic invasions in the Indian sub-continent.
4. Lotus stands for regeneration. This hints at an apology gift to Mamalu towards the regeneration of their relationship.
5. Arsenic disulfide, which reacts with silver to form black silver sulfide.